Shadow Walk: The Gathering

by

Erin Collins

Artistic Endeavors

First Edition

Edited by
Nancy C. Lepri
Shawn Guideau

Formatted by:
Laurie Christopherson

Front cover design:
Sean Dickey

ISBN-13: 978-0-9800733-7-9

ISBN-10: 0-9800733-7-5

PUBLISHED BY

Artistic Endeavors Publishing, LLC

www.artisticendeavorspublishing.com

For my family . . .

Husband Larry; children Chrystal and Sean;

my mother, Margie; my brothers and sisters, Sam and Jeff,

Tina and Tammy;

my granddaughters, Brittany and Ashley.

And in precious memory of my grandmother,

Elizabeth Swain Huckabee,

my father, Samuel W. Haley, Sr.,

and my brother, Chauncey Wayne Haley.

F irst, I thank God. To God be the glory.

I thank my husband, Larry, for your patience and for taking on responsibilities that are mine; my daughter Chrystal, my son Sean, and my mother, Margie, my brothers Sam and Jeff, and my sisters, Tina and Tammy, for all your encouragement with my dream, and believing that I could do it. Thank you for your support and love through this adventure. I love you all.

I also want to give a special thanks to the following friends, but let me say this before I continue: For all the time you have given me, sacrificed your own writing time, your talents, your input, your love; thank you, thank you, thank you. None of this would be possible without your help, support, and encouragement.

Shay Wells, for sitting up nights with me; helping me through the rough spots; threatening to kick my butt if I gave up, and being a wonderful friend and encourager. Shay, I thank you for assisting with editing; brainstorming with me, and just being there; thank you most of all for your friendship and love. I love you, Sis.

Edna Cline, for also sitting up nights with me; researching for me; helping me through rough spots as well; helping me to get timelines right; picking my brain, (it's a wonder I have any brains left); and being a wonderful friend. Edna, I thank you most of all for your friendship and love. I love you! ((((Hugs)))))

Tony Wilson, for taking me in hand when I wanted to give up; for making me laugh when I wanted to cry; for being a sounding board when I needed one. Tony, I thank you most of all for your friendship and love. I love you bunches!

Pam Reese, Nadine Laman, Pat Guthrie, Sheila Behr, Linda Vernon, and so many others, I thank you all for your encouragement, suggestions--sigh--there is so much I want to say, but do not have room for it. Thank you all for being there for me.

Thank you, Barbara M. Hodges, for believing in my talent, for rooting for me with your own publisher, for mentoring and helping me, even after that deal fell through. Thank you for all the time you have taken out of your own busy schedule to assist me with editing. Thank you for teaching me to pull it together.

A special thanks goes out to Joe, owner of CompuDoc in Wills Point, for keeping my computer up and running. Thank you, Joe!

Last but not least, all the staff at Light Sword Publishing, for helping me to polish this book and making it zing; the art department for creating a cover that intrigues the reader; the marketing staff for your wise advice, your hard work, your input, and your zeal. Thank you all for everything you have done to make this book what it is.

I love you all!

Genesis 6: 1-5

Now it came to pass, when men began to multiply on the face of the earth, and daughters were born to them, that the sons of God saw the daughters of men, that they *were* beautiful; and they took wives for themselves of all whom they chose.

And the Lord said, "My Spirit shall not strive with man forever, for he *is* indeed flesh; yet his days shall be one hundred and twenty years."

There were giants on the earth in those days, and also afterward, when the sons of God came in to the daughters of men and they bore *children* to them. Those *were* the mighty men who *were* of old, men of renown.

Then the Lord saw that the wickedness of man *was* great in the earth, and *that* every intent of the thoughts of his heart *was* only evil continually. (NKJV©)

Matthew 24: 36-37

But of that day and hour no one knows, not even the angels of heaven, but My Father only. But as the days of Noah *were*, so also will the coming of the Son of Man be. (NKJV©)

Chapter 1

On the corner of East and Main, Cassandra Withers paced back and forth. She paused, scanning the area again, but she could not see much beyond the streetlight's wan glow.

Why did I offer to stay late at the pizza parlor tonight? I should have taken the ride my boss offered when he left. "Still no answer." Cassandra stomped her foot.

Cassie stood five-feet, six-inches tall. Even in her uniform, her lithe figure showed through. Her ebony hair fell just past her hips. Tonight, she wore it in a loose French braid. Cassie's eyes, blue as sapphires, now held a mixture of concern and a little bit of fear. Unlike most teens, Cassie followed all the rules, obeyed, and was more sheltered than most teenagers were.

Years before, her father, who had stopped for a few items at the store, was killed during a robbery. Monica Withers became overprotective after that. Cassie was only three at the time.

Cassie noticed a dark panel van turning the near corner. As it came closer, she saw a driver and a passenger. Knowing she was alone in a deserted area of town, her heart pounded in her ears and her knees shook. *If my mother had shown up when she should have, I wouldn't be alone,* Cassie thought.

The driver pulled the van up in front of where she stood, and stopped. For a long moment, the driver just looked at her. She grew more nervous and jumped when he spoke.

"Hello there."

Cassie looked around in vain hope that she still was not alone and did not answer him. It was just her, the van, and the two men. *Should I run? I could never outrun that van, and they might even run me over.* Cassie knew she was trapped.

"Cat got your tongue?"

Cassie shifted from one foot to the other, not sure what to say.

"Do you need a ride?" he asked.

Beads of sweat popped out on her forehead. Finding her voice, she stammered, "N-no, thank you, Sir. I d . . . don't need a ride. I . . . I'm waiting on my mom to pick me up. She'll be here any minute now."

She saw him looking around. *Where is Mother? Please, God. Let my mother show up.*

The driver flashed his badge out the window. "FBI--don't be scared."

Cassie approached, but remained an arm's length from the van. Although his ID looked official, she stayed cautious, the echoes of her mother's oft-repeated "be wary of strangers" running through her head.

"You know, it's dangerous for you to be standing out here all alone. I can wait here until your mother arrives."

He stepped out of the van and lit a cigarette. Standing by the open door, he explained, "My partner hates cigarettes."

Cassie attempted to use her cell again to call home; still no answer. The man unnerved her for some reason.

Cassie looked up when she heard sizzling, followed by a pop. The streetlights went out and the entire city fell into darkness, the full summer moon the only illumination.

"That's what happens when air conditioners overload the power grid," he said, a slight smile on his face.

Cassie stood frozen in fear, arms crossed over her chest, staring as he crushed the cigarette out. The air grew thick, the tension crackled. She struggled to draw in a deep breath.

He sprang toward her and wrapped one arm around her neck. The combination of sweat, tobacco, and Brut cologne, combined with her fear, threatened to unleash the pizza she'd had for dinner. She swallowed the bile rising in her throat, and wet herself.

His voice came close to her ear. "Stay still or I'll break your neck."

In horror, she watched as he pulled out a syringe from his pocket and removed the protective cap with his teeth.

"No, no!" Suddenly finding energy, she kicked him, cracking his shin with the heel of her ankle boot. His hold loosened and he cursed as she jerked away, but not before he jabbed the syringe into her leg. She sprinted for a nearby alley.

From his touch, it started--again. The familiar sting spread across her forehead. Even as she ran, she could not stop the psychic episode. Cassie's present location diminished from sight, her eyes filled with a gray haze. The stalker's voice faded into the background, as the familiar buzz grew louder. She forgot her peril.

Cassie's senses reassembled, and she found herself home. As she surveyed the shambled apartment, her mouth dropped open. Shattered fragments of bric-a-brac glistened across the floor. Guts from the sofa and chair cushions covered the living room, stuffing and foam lay everywhere, the covers left' ragged and torn. In a daze, Cassie moved through the debris. Discarded drawers from her bedroom dresser lay on the carpet--the contents littering the worn shag. She ventured further into the apartment.

In her mother's bedroom, Monica Withers lay sprawled nude upon the bed, her body unnaturally positioned, legs splayed; her head hung off the mattress at an odd angle. Blood dripped into the crimson pool beneath her.

Cassie let out a vaporous scream before her actual surroundings reappeared.

"Momma, Momma!"

"Your mama isn't coming to get you," she heard his voice behind her.

Immediately, she knew; the man pursuing her--the one on her heels-- had killed her mother.

Cassie gasped as she found herself back in the alley. Dizziness swept over her, causing her to stumble and fall into a pile of garbage, the sting of glass cutting into her knees making her cry out. She tried to stand, fell again, and crawled a few feet forward. Behind her, she heard laughter. *Get up. Run,* her mind cried, but her legs would not cooperate. She rolled over onto her back; saw him as he stood over her.

A strange numbness flowed through her. Unable to move, she felt the sting as he injected her with the remainder of whatever was in the syringe. Everything went black.

~

Agent Scott searched the area to make sure it was still deserted. He went back to his prey, lifted her effortlessly, and headed toward the van. His accomplice, Patterson, waited in the back, holding the door open. Scott tossed her in. The two men slammed the back door shut, got in the front, and headed east out of town.

Patterson glanced in the rearview mirror as he heard the girl moan. "Why is she waking up? She shouldn't be waking up."

"You moron, you didn't put enough stuff in the syringe."

Scott went over the passenger's seat into the back. Patterson grimaced, but kept looking straight ahead. He knew Agent Scott all too well and the man made him sick. He hated what would come next. Scott was notorious for abusing young girls.

Patterson resolved to keep his eyes on the road. He might have to hear it, but did not want to *see* what Scott would do. He heard the struggle. The thuds and grunts from the back told him the girl was fighting for her life.

"Please, don't," he heard her cry. "I want t . . . to g . . . go home."

Patterson nearly lost control of the van as her primeval screams echoed through it, as Scott kept hitting the girl. Through the noise of the struggle, he heard Scott curse. Patterson glanced back in time to receive warm blood splatter across his cheek.

"Did you have to sling blood all over me?" Patterson grabbed a rag and wiped his face.

"The little bitch bit me. I couldn't help it." Breathing heavily, Scott asked, "Did you bother to bring another syringe?"

"In the duffle bag."

"Well, pull over and help me." He hit the girl again.

Patterson jerked the wheel, sending the van into a skid through the rough gravel along the edge of the road. In one motion, he jerked the transmission into park and rolled over the seat into the back.

The girl remained frigid with terror, her face streaked with blood. Scott stared down at her and smiled as he drew his fist back again.

Rotten-egg bile almost gagged Patterson as it rose in his throat. He swallowed it back down. He grabbed Scott's upraised fist, just to hold him back, knowing better than to get into a physical confrontation with him. Patterson tried to reason with him.

"Dammit, Scott, if you kill her, you'll make us both lose more than our finder's fee. Our lives won't be worth flea spit."

Scott looked up, blinked, and grunted as he injected her with the new syringe. He smiled again as he ripped her uniform top open.

"Hey, not this time. They've warned you."

Scott pulled a gun from a holster inside his jacket--cocked it and pointed it in Patterson's face. "We've played this game before. You know you can't stop me, partner. We're in this together and you know it. Now just get your ass back into the front and drive before I decide to collect the fee solo."

Patterson knew better than to argue with Scott. Scott would not hesitate to use the gun on him. As if to remind him, the scar in his right side where Scott had shot him before, began to throb violently.

~

The sickly sweet odor of blood and urine assaulted Patterson's nostrils as he scrubbed the red stains at a local carwash. He hated being Scott's clean up guy.

Scott, holed up in the local safe house, had told him to go to hell when he asked for his help. Patterson refused to allow himself to think about what Scott was probably doing to the girl right now.

He shook his head. Scott would not escape--not this time. Moreover, he was not going down with him. Scott had become unstable, dangerous, and a threat to Tanas Global's security.

~

They traveled along the deserted New Mexico highway. The passengers in the van, along with the landscape, sweltered under the undulating heat waves.

Patterson turned to look at their acquisition. The subject in the back of the van groaned, but did little else.

"How is our specimen doing?" Scott asked.

"Not good, Scott--thanks to you."

"That's not my fault. It shouldn't have fought back."

From behind a copse of stunted trees, a non-descript, white jeep Cherokee barreled toward them. Scott slowed and finally stopped as it blocked their path. An armed guard in drab-green fatigues carrying an M16 got out and walked to the driver's side window. Providing the correct password to the guard, Scott continued on to a side road, heading toward New Mexico's southwestern Tanas labs.

~

The New Mexico desert lay desolate and still beneath a waxing moon. Secret experiments conducted, caused desert life to respond in strange ways. A rattlesnake waited on the desert floor for its next victim. A desert rat scurried on its way to its burrow. The snake coiled, ready to strike. Instead, the diamondback lashed out, striking itself repeatedly until at last, it gave one last quiver, and lay still. Moments later, nothing remained but an indentation in the sand.

On the edge of a cliff, a coyote, camouflaged by its mottled tan and black coat, devoured a still thrashing jackrabbit, confident within the night's black veil. The coyote froze in mid-bite. A moment later, in utter silence, it flung itself from the cliff onto the rocky terrain below. The bloody, dying rabbit yielded mute testimony to what took place, as it bled out into the sand. Of the coyote, however, nothing remained.

Jim Cantrell, an avid prospector, tossed another stick into the fire, whispering to his old pack mule, Boss, who munched on oats in an old tin bucket. The mule seemed content enough, but just in case, Jim tied the rope from Boss's halter to a pillar-shaped rock to make sure the wily escape artist stayed put.

With a smile and a warning shake of his head, he turned back to the fire. "The only part about desert camping I really don't care for is carrying my gun." He threw more wood on the fire. "Never know what you might find in a woodpile, eh, Boss? Got some nasty critters last year, remember? I hate scorpions."

Jim treated the mule more like his partner. He and Boss had been a team for more years than Jim cared to recall. He walked over, checking the tether again before turning in for the night.

"You aren't much for conversation, but you're good company." Jim patted the old mule's neck.

Pulling his harmonica from his shirt pocket, he breathed life into the antique. The notes flew, soft and long, floating toward the stars, soothing him, feeding his soul. He gazed upward at the moon as he played, relaxed in the peaceful solitude.

Heavily bearded, with bits of gray among dark brown whiskers, flannel shirt, jeans, and worn-out boots, he looked as though he came from another time, another era. Yet, his rough exterior belied his keen intelligence.

A wealthy man with a wife and two kids, he lived in a posh suburb of Santa Fe and needed this time away to relax. Still, he had responsibilities, so his cell phone shared space in his saddle pack, along with his antique prospecting tools. The only modern equipment housed in the pack was his surveyor's tools, including a portable GPS tracker, a 20X Econo Line Level and Transit Level, and a laptop with mapping software. He took the cell phone from the pack, knowing that his wife Amanda would call soon. Yawning, he spread out his bedroll. The lull of the desert silence called to him and he gave up the fight to stay awake. The phone would awaken him. Just as his eyes closed, Boss brayed, panic in the sounds.

Jim leapt up, looking for a snake or a scorpion, anything to explain the mule's behavior, but found nothing. Jim tried to calm him. "Quiet down, Boss. Quiet down. I can't help you if you don't."

The more the mule struggled, the tighter the tether became. His heart pounding, Jim watched in frustration.

Jumping back from the mule's flailing hooves, Jim helplessly stared at the frenzied animal. His panicked movements had tightened his halter around his neck. At last with his sides heaving, the mule dropped first onto his knees and then onto the desert sand. Jim leapt forward, but by the time he got the tether loose, it was too late. Boss was dead. He stared down at the old mule. What had happened? Words like embolism and aneurism whirled in his head. There had to be a reason; and he considered himself a reasonable man, but--it hit him--he had to run, he did not know why, but he had to. Even as he tried to make sense of the need, his feet acted, and he ran into the night leaving everything behind.

A quarter of a mile from camp, he froze--but not by choice. Something stopped him, held him. In the black of night, he could neither see nor hear anything, yet no matter how much he struggled, he could not escape.

Light fell from the sky and he raised his eyes, blinded by its brightness.

"Don't fight me. It won't do you any good."

The voice was young and female. He tried to scream, but his mouth seemed glued shut. His breathing quickened, his heart beating so fast he was sure it would jump out of his chest.

"Take him."

The wind kicked up around him. Sand bit into his skin and made his mouth gritty.

"You're going to sleep for a bit now."

For a brief moment, he saw it hovering above him and then all went black.

Silently, the stealth craft slipped away heading back to Tanas.

The sudden ringing of the cell phone echoed off   the canyon walls, and finally, fell silent.

All became still once more.

Chapter 2

Gold Hill, New Mexico, like many ghost towns in the California, Arizona, and Nevada deserts, hosted spirits of slain miners--and those who tried to jump a claim. Icy gusts whispered laments of unfulfilled dreams and broken hearts. Yet, this shadowy area held secrets and innuendos darker than any tabloid could invent.

Tanas Global's Labs guarded those secrets--many of them decades old. There, in the ancient caverns of Tanas, special research demanded certain flexibility in conduct. Answers to questions required procedures that might have made the cruelest terrorist scream. For Tanas, the cost seemed quite reasonable. The answers were all that mattered.

The surface part of the building, camouflaged, blended in with the rugged terrain. Most of the structure, buried deep within the foothills of the Little Hatchet Mountains, remained well hidden. A mile beneath the ground, an aggressive scientific institute practiced its craft; working toward its ultimate goal.

The compound's interior was large with plain, institutional gray walls, relieved only by the occasional note board for posting shift schedules or inter-department memos. The front lobby, which typically housed a reception area, remained empty. A small door in the center stood between immoveable walls. These walls arched into a circular fortress, as though in defense of the compound. It offered the only relief from the emptiness.

The soundproof citadel housed a futuristic command post complete with monitors, computers, GPS tracking system, one television, and three small teams of round-the-clock guards. Other armed guards kept their various strategic posts throughout the complex. All areas, including living quarters, offices, and bathrooms came equipped with surveillance cameras, though the bathroom cameras were discreetly positioned to afford the user some illusion of privacy.

A blip on the GPS tracker alerted the guard at the monitor that an employee had arrived. The guard already knew the white-coated scientist's identity before he entered the lobby.

Dr. Franklin Barnett walked over to the hallway door on the right. Placing his micro-chipped right hand on the Identi-pad, he simultaneously submitted to the Retina Scan with no more thought than unlocking a door with a key.

After hearing the heavy door's distinctive click, he went into the inner sanctum, paying little attention to the same gray that adorned the lobby walls. The only relief from the monotony along the hallway was the occasional office door.

As Barnett entered one such door, Dr. Adam Hanson, commander-in-chief and head scientist, glared at him.

"Dr. Barnett, glad you finally decided to join us," Dr. Hanson said flatly, as he turned from the group standing in front of a wall. A huge corkboard dominated it. Numbered Polaroid photos of young women covered half the board; the other half, numbered Polaroids of young men.

A large conference table eclipsed the room. High-backed charcoal-gray office chairs with comfortable cushions surrounded the table. Stacks of dossiers waited on top. Each file boasted tabs with a corresponding number to a photo on the wall. Within each one, information on the designated subject included blood and tissue type, test results from extensive physical, psychological, and other various testing--especially paranormal studies.

For the moment, the group studied two photos. Subject 1335709 had the blood type and physical features they sought. Its psychic potential was impressive. However, Hanson did not like the way they acquired it, as reported in the file. As he read the acquisition report, his face turned red and the veins popped out on his forehead. "We paid to have the female brought here without strong-arm tactics," he yelled. "How did this happen?

"The specimen could have been acquired better. There is no excuse as to why it suffered such serious injuries and trauma. I just hope they didn't damage it beyond use. I hate to waste good subject material. Moreover, this one showed promise. We'll have to wait for it to recover, if it recovers, that is," Hanson bellowed. He continued as he read further into the report.

Dr. Hanson, known for impatience, seemed hollow--soulless--without a conscience. He only became animated and cordial when piqued into talking about any successes in his various projects; and he was particular with whom he chose to share his successes.

A small, balding scientist, with a nametag reading "Michaels" on his lapel, approached hesitantly with a prognosis report in his hands. Adam's apple bobbing in his nervousness, he choked out the words, "Sir, the specimen is expected to recover fro . . . " His voice faded under Dr. Hanson's icy stare.

Having received many of Dr. Hanson's outbursts of temper, Dr. Michaels cringed, hoping the head of Tanas would not go further.

"I ordered the specimen to be acquired undamaged. How could one of our acquisitions be so difficult? It's not as if the subjects are so powerful that they would be able to resist this much. These acquisitions must be treated as valuable," he shouted, as he looked at the pictures of the badly beaten girl.

"Scott Finley was the operative who procured this one, right?" he shouted again.

"Yes, sir. Operative Scott, along with his partner, Patterson, acquired this one," Dr. Michaels offered, his knees shaking.

"I realize he couldn't just allow it to get away, but there was no excuse for his further action. He is finished." He addressed an agent who stood by, waiting for orders. "Have him brought back to Tanas--now. I'll not have any more subjects damaged like this one by incompetents like him." He followed his statement with an assortment of expletives. "By the way, make an example of Scott for anyone else who might resort to similar tactics."

Hands trembling, the agent dialed his secure cell phone and whispered into it. "Sir," he said in a trembling voice, "It's taken care of. The question mark will be deleted."

All the men in the room seemed to be glad they were not Scott. With Doctor Hanson, in a situation such as this, there were no second chances.

"The other acquisition has come to us by much better methods," Hanson stated. He absent-mindedly nodded his approval. *Finally, someone who knows how to obtain good subjects*, he thought. He made a mental note to use the hospital orderly that did so good a job. The orderly should be good for a few more acquisitions, but no more. It was too much risk for more than a few.

"Use this orderly for another five subjects. After that, he will be of no further use. It's a shame when a good man gets a bad case of e-coli and dies of it. You never know when you can eat a bad burger or burrito," he added almost as an afterthought. It came out cold and deliberate which was how he meant it.

He smiled as he read the other file in his hand. Subject number 1335799 proved very cooperative during the tests, even the most painful ones. Tissue samples, blood work, and DNA were outstanding. Its psychic profile proved even stronger than the other subjects' did. 1335799 was strong, only sixteen, and had very active ovaries. The female had a uterus and pelvis perfectly structured for giving birth. The biggest bonus was that the specimen was still untouched, which optimized the potential to be an excellent breeder for many years to come.

"I believe subject number 1335799, will be the most optimal for our breeding program, gentlemen." Hanson decided.

The scientists agreed. They always agreed.

The group moved to the other half of the board to choose one of the male specimens. These were much easier to choose from, for they all volunteered for blind studies at various universities--universities innocently connected to Project EVAH: En Vitro Advancement for Humanity. They agreed to participate in Tanas's various studies on human reproduction. Some sperm donors were medical students doing theses or finals in fertility studies; others were those who needed money in a hurry. There were extensive screening processes for participation. Intelligence was one of the main requirements to enter the donor program.

Dr. Hansen selected the male subjects with the highest sperm counts to donate. There were a lot to choose from, since all of them were virile, healthy young subjects.

It did not take long to make the choice of who would sire the next child; at least once their sperm had a few changes made to it.

~

Kathleen Miller had been in a drug-induced coma for quite some time. She still could not remember anything about her former life. The doctors told her she would have to re-learn everything. They told her she had been in a terrible accident that had killed her parents. She was alone now, since she had no other family. Although she retained no cognitive memory of her parents, she still grieved their deaths. She mourned over her loss of recollection and the fact that she could not attend their funerals.

The doctor was straightforward about her condition. "Miss Miller, in all probability, you may never remember your past," Doctor Hanson had told her. He assured her, however, that she could still lead a full, productive life upon release.

Kathleen occupied her time when she was not undergoing tests or therapy by watching videos and DVD's and reading. Overall, she accepted her condition.

~

Another plea to find Cassandra Withers, age sixteen, blared from a television within the guardroom in Tanas's lobby. America's Most Wanted Host, John Walsh, described Cassandra's alleged abductor. "His name is William Allen Kingston, a known child pornographer. Cassandra, abducted six weeks ago from right outside the pizza parlor where she worked, needs your help. During authorities' investigation, they found her mother, Monica Withers, dead in their small apartment. Authorities believe her murder may be connected to this case. If anyone has any information, please contact America's Most Wanted."

Cassandra's photo, superimposed to the right of the screen near John Walsh's head, lent drama to the plea.

John Walsh continued. "Another young girl who went missing around the same time as Cassandra is Kathleen Miller, also age sixteen. She disappeared after completing her shift as a volunteer at a local hospital. Kathleen is a vivacious girl, an honor student, well-behaved, and had no reason to run away. At the moment, we have no viable suspects in Kathleen's abduction. Again, if you have any information on either of these two abductions, contact us here, at *AMW* . . . I'm John Walsh."

One of the guards snickered after hearing John Walsh's plea. "They'll have a helluva time finding either one of them," he joked.

"Yep," the other one agreed.

~

Nine months later, a comatose Cassandra gave birth to a baby boy by C-section. The child, severely deformed, subsequently died. Fifteen months after she was reported missing, they found her skull and part of her skeleton. Her remains required forensic authorities to identify her through dental records.

Kathleen Miller was never found.

~

Jim Cantrell screamed. "The Grays, the Grays. Keep them away from me," as another probe violated his rectum.

Jim's wails echoed through the lab--his eyes wildly searching in vain for relief.

At every arterial pulse, the Grays inserted hair-thin tubes, microscopic cameras attached to each one. The intense burning as they traveled throughout his blood system flamed like hot coals searing into the walls of each artery. They did not bother to sedate him anymore. He had already gone insane, although he had lasted longer than the others had.

One of the small figures peered into the man's ravaged face. A hand with long, spindly fingers came from the wide arm of a gray robe. It tapped a second thin tube leading from the man's kidneys. Jim Cantrell screamed again.

The "Grays" was as good a name as any, and they had taken to calling themselves that. Gray-One, Gray-Two . . . .

Gray-Nine prepared for the next experiment. Getting out the instrument tray, he began his work. He added the metal frames to the man's eyelids to keep them open and placed a paralyzing fluid in his eyes to keep them still. Gray-twelve came into the room. She carried the needles for the eye probing. As Gray-Nine began, he wondered if the man could see the needle coming closer, just before the stabbing pain pierced his brain.

Just how long would this one last? He hoped it would be a little longer. His date for the betting pool was still twenty-one days away. There was always one betting pool or another. Some very elaborate. It was something they had picked up from the humans, finding it amusing.

Gray-Nine lucked out. Just twenty days later, Jim Cantrell died, and no one had picked day thirty-three. Gray-Nine discovered the body in the early morning hours. Jim Cantrell had chewed his tongue in half--his face frozen in a grimace of terror.

~

The local sheriff 's office found his body just ten miles from his campsite. It bore all the earmarks of death by wild animals. The medical examiner attributed his exsanguinated body to dehydration and exposure to the desert heat.

Chapter 3

Sirius Tanas, leader of the Recondites, stood in his domain deep underground in Tanas's belly, below the offices, labs, and living quarters the humans occupied. The dampness of the rocky interior served his nature well. It was late in the day and his mind cried out for freedom from his body's earthly confines. Shedding his mortal shell was painful, but worth it.

He inhaled deeply and willed it to begin. His pale, fragile skin cracked; silver and black scales became visible, glistening like obsidian, beneath a thin cloak of blood. Expanding his leathery wings, he stretched them, fanning them to dry off. His round pupils elongated into slits, replacing former pale blue eyes, the green glow of new irises now shining in the darkness.

Humankind, stupid and so primitive, would never know until it was too late.

Her existence touched him again. He felt her presence--just beyond his reach. It was like an itch between his wings he could not scratch. He bellowed his frustration, releasing a hair-raising screech. He did not know who she was, but he knew she was a successful hybrid; the female breeder that Tanas Global had still failed to produce.

His clawed fingers clenched into fists. It would be years before he could really communicate with her. Wasted years. Without the ability to make contact, he would not be able to teach her. Yet, he had to try. He did not want her to come to maturity without proper guidance--discipline. She would be a force to reckon with by then. She might actually become his equal.

Where was she? How did this happen? Answers *would* come--at a great price to some of the humans. He narrowed his eyes and ordered Dr. Hanson to come to him *immediately*.

Chapter 4

Scott Finley had writhed and screamed for three days under his captors' attention. They started by leaving him strung up by his wrists, teasingly close to food and water but not close enough to touch either. On the second day, they soaked his body with a fire hose, his nerves screaming in agony at the icy blasts. Attaching electrodes to his exposed armpits, stomach, and inner thighs, they watched as they shocked him with low voltage. Eyes glowed in silent contempt for him as his body arched, screams tearing from his throat. Another blast of the cold water revived him repeatedly, refreshing his pain.

Ah, but the best they saved for last. They released him from his manacles, strapped him into a chair, and belted his hands to a butcher-block. With surgical precision, they amputated each finger, cutting through flesh and bone a layer at a time, ignoring again his screams of agony. After removing each digit, they went back to the first nub, now a bloody stump and began the agonizing process of cauterizing each one with a white-hot iron poker.

Scott passed out before they finished his first little pinky. They brought him back to consciousness with strong smelling salts. They had just turned their interest to Scott's testicles when Sir's orders reached them.

~

The guards dumped Scott's barely recognizable form into a chair. Sir strolled around the seat, knowing silence can be its own torture. When his muteness finally produced a defeated whimper from the form, Sir spoke softly, continuing to circle the chair. "Tell me--as I have no idea--what did it feel like when that electrical current surged though your body? Did your teeth break? Did your muscles cramp? Did you scream?"

Silence.

"They say you were hung from the ceiling by your wrists; that you haven't eaten since we arrested you, and weren't allowed to drink either. I'm told the human body can survive for a long time without food, but without water, internal organs begin to fail after three days."

Again, silence.

"I am really disappointed in you, Scott. How does it feel to have no fingers? Is it painful, still? Do they still burn from the hot irons? Tell me and perhaps I will ease your pain."

What was left of a pitiful excuse for a man refused to look at him.

Sir walked around the chair again. He ran a finger along one of the gaping wounds on Scott's body, causing the man to scream. He allowed himself a moment of satisfaction.

With casual contempt and the precise control any neurosurgeon would envy, he invaded the protected vaults of Scott's mind.

Scott's head shot back as though someone had punched him in the face. His eyes bulged, coming out of their sockets. He screamed and grabbed the sides of his head. Pale, thick liquid oozed from his ears through the still bleeding stubs that had been his fingers. Blood trickled from the corners of his mouth. He went still, his arms dropping to his sides, his head falling forward.

Sir glared at the men still in the room. "As you all know, I'm not a cruel man. However, loyalty is tantamount to Project EVAH's success. I recompense loyalty. I will spare Patterson Finley's life. He had enough loyalty to turn in his own brother. Let this one," he pointed to the body, "be a lesson to you; insubordination carries a heavy penalty."

Sir dismissed them with a wave of his hand.

Chapter 5

Patterson Finley typed in the name he had discovered; Sirius, which meant, "the name of a bright star in the constellation Canis Major--the dog star--derived via Latin from Greek meaning "burning." Not only that, but the site referenced an ancient biblical prophecy naming him as the catalyst for the coming of the Antichrist.

Patterson and Scott grew up pounded with religion--literally. His mother especially, would take her large family Bible and beat him and Scott with it every time she thought they needed punishment. She preached for hours after she beat them, telling them how evil the world had become, how evil they were. Then she would place them both in a special "cell" she had built in the basement of their home. Sometimes, they stayed in there for days, and were only allowed bread and water.

Their father was no better. He and Scott knew he was spineless. He gave in to the witch--as they called her--on everything.

Patterson was fifteen and Scott was eighteen when they burned down the house with their parents trapped inside. They had so ingeniously devised the plan that they had gotten away with it. Now, his mother's sermons echoed through his head. What he discovered about Sir made his blood run cold.

At last, he had an ace to protect himself, to become one of the inner-circle. He could not believe his luck, but it put the fear of God in him, too. He needed to figure out how to use this knowledge to his advantage--and to ensure his life. He was always methodical in his endeavors. This was one area where he and his brother differed. Scott sealed his fate by his uncontrollable impulses. Patterson decided to make sure he controlled his.

Who can I turn to? he thought. *No one,* was the answer.

Was he brave enough to confront Sirius? He had never known him as anything other than Sir. What could he do now? He spent considerable time planning his strategy. Within three weeks, he had it all laid out. He requested an appointment with Sir.

~

Though reluctant to acknowledge minions like Patterson, Sir decided to grant him an audience. He wondered why Patterson became so bold. The man was up to something. As he drummed his long fingers against his teakwood desk, Sir concentrated on Patterson's mind. He could see what his plans were. *Stupid mortals--they are so easy to manipulate, so easy to read. He thinks he's smart enough to blackmail me.* There would be no surprises when Patterson showed up. Other men--better men than Patterson--had tried the same thing with him throughout the ages; all had failed. Their names ran though his mind and Sir toyed with his 'mice' again: Caesar, Alexander, Napoleon, Hitler, Fidel Castro, and more recently, Jim Jones. He especially liked toying with Jones.

Sir smiled. He snapped his ice blue cell phone from the desktop and punched Dr. Hanson's number in on the redial. He was ready for Patterson.

~

Patterson stood outside the inner sanctum. He had never been this deep under Tanas before. His ears even popped on the way down in an elevator that Tanas made sure remained hidden. He made a mental note of its location. He also made a note on how to manipulate the mechanism to reveal it.

Patterson, in spite of his bravado, shook uncontrollably. He had heard of the 'alien' being who controlled Tanas, but now he knew who--*what*--he was about to confront.

As the heavy titanium doors to Sir's domain slid open, they exposed a waiting area. Huge, oversized sofas and chairs dominated the room. Plush cushions insured comfort for those who waited. The walls, sparkled with opals and ice blue sapphires, made Patterson shiver with cold, while at the same time, his greedy side wondered how much all those gems could fetch.

On one wall, a cappuccino machine gurgled, promising cups of whipped coffee. The Gray who had accompanied him offered him a cup. Patterson was very much aware of the Grays. He had worked with them many times before, whenever he delivered acquisitions. His hands shook as he sipped the frothy liquid.

Gray-Four entered into what first looked like just another wall. She--at least he thought Gray-Four was female--touched the wall and another door opened. She disappeared.

He calmed his nerves with a second cup of cappuccino. When the wall opened again, Gray-Four motioned for him to follow. As he stepped through the portal, he swore he smelled a sulfur-based stench, along with decaying flesh--which he knew all too well.

~

What--who, he saw, shocked him. Patterson did not know what to expect, but he did not expect a human-like form. He was rather good looking, in a shyster-lawyer kind of way. He reminded Patterson of a young Don Corlione from *The Godfather*.

"Sit down, Patterson, and tell me why you're here." Although he spoke in a soft voice, Patterson knew it was a command, not a request.

"I . . . I mean . . . Sir, I know what your real name is, and--and I know . . . wh . . . what it means," Patterson choked out.

Patterson watched as Sir sat behind his desk. He leaned back in his chair, softly rocking. His hands near his chin, he tapped his fingertips. He waited long moments before Sir spoke again. As he waited, Sir looked at him, staring through to his soul. Patterson struggled to keep from shivering. He did not want to appear the coward--like Scott.

"So, Patterson, what would you have me to do? I am not used to dealing with such resourcefulness," he said.

Patterson's ego level rose. He knew a boldness he did not have before. "Sir--or shall I call you Sirius? I want in. I mean, I want in on the secret workings of Tanas. I believe I could be a real asset to you, and to Tanas. As you know, I have been loyal to the point of snitching on my own flesh and blood. There's nothing I would not do for you, Sirius."

Sir narrowed his eyes into slits at the insultingly familiar usage of his name. His jaw muscles flexed. "First of all, never call me that name again. You are quite lucky you are not a pile of ashes right now--and never forget that I do have the power to do just that. But, you do present a good argument. I believe you are correct. I think you *would* be a valuable asset to Tanas."

Patterson swelled his chest out, feeling as if he finally made it into the inner sanctum. "Sir, I will never make that mistake again. I am only too happy to handle any assignments you may have for me, Sir. I will never reveal your full name, or your origins to anyone."

"Oh, I know you won't, Patterson. Welcome aboard." Sir offered his hand to seal the offer.

Patterson stood up to shake Sir's hand. As he grasped it, he felt a hot sensation and instantly, he remembered nothing more until his mind screamed.

~

Patterson knew he was in liquid. His eyes burned as he struggled to open them, but he could still see. He could also breathe. Still groggy, he examined his surroundings.

His arms floated freely in the syrupy liquid. He could not move his head, so he felt his body. He was nude. His throat hurt. He placed his hand on the indentation at the base of his throat and felt a breathing tube.

He knew there was a face mask on his head. *That must be there to keep me from drowning,* he thought.

He felt tubes in each arm, and felt a catheter coming out of his penis.

Within his line of vision, he noticed bubbles bouncing upward to some place beyond his sight. It reminded him of an aquarium. Then he knew; he had become one of the specimens he had collected over the years for Tanas.

He panicked, thrashing around in the fluid in a vain attempt to escape.

He watched one of the Grays approach his container. On the outside, he noticed an IV pole with a bag of fluid. It injected something into it. Immediately, he felt a familiar sensation and the acrid taste of ether-- heroin--it had been so long since he had any. He soon stopped panicking.

In a drug-induced stupor, he watched through the blur of the very warm fluid as the Grays worked on other specimens. *What happened?* he wondered.

Patterson jerked awake. *Hey!* He knew no one could hear him, still his mind yelled out for someone to help.

~

One day, he saw Hanson approach.

He began taking notes, reading the data that tickered out of the various machines. Patterson could not tell what was on the thin ribbons of paper, but he knew Hanson could.

Hanson walked up to a microphone on the outside of the container and Patterson heard a click in his ears as Hanson turned it on. He watched Patterson's eyes as he pinched the oxygen tubing, cutting off his only air. Patterson once again panicked.

Hanson released the tube, allowing the air to flow once more, waiting for Patterson to calm down. "I know you can hear me, Patterson," Hanson spoke into headphones attached to Patterson's ears. "What you're floating in is not just a simple saline solution. Thanks to our alien technology, we've come up with a solution that will sustain you indefinitely. Did you know that without this chemical," Hanson pointed at the bag of pink fluid, "your skin would already have sloughed off, and your internal organs would have shut down?

"The chemical solution for normal saline is NaCl. That is sodium (Na), mixed with chloride (Cl). If I were to pinch, or stop the flow of the precious fluid to your body, you would die. We want you alive. We have many wonderful experiments planned for you."

When Patterson thrashed around in a vain attempt to fight his predicament, Hanson said, "Calm down, Patterson. You *did* say you wanted to help in any way you could. Now . . . you are."

Hanson left.

Days, weeks, months could have passed and Patterson would not know the difference.

The day finally came when they let him out of his container. The Grays washed his eyes, removed the protective contacts, and showered him. Although he had suffered mild burns all over his body from the saline, his pain was mild.

His real pain had just begun.

Chapter 6

Sirius, once again reluctantly reverted to his humanoid persona. He walked to a mirror and looked into it. Ice-blue eyes stared back at him. He chose a dark suit and slicked his black hair. He used to be so beautiful; the most beautiful creature ever created. Now, he would always be hideous--unless he was in human form.

In time, he would reveal his true identity, but not just yet.

He paced. The more he thought about the girl, the angrier he became. He forced himself to settle behind his desk and wait.

Dr. Hanson arrived in a hurry; he always did when Sirius commanded his presence.

Sir stood, leaning across his desk. "Hanson, I want answers, and I want them now."

"Sir, I'm not sure what you mean. The one subject is doing well, she--"

"You are clueless, aren't you, Hanson? You have no idea?"

"No--no, Sir."

"There is a successful hybrid in existence, Hanson. I have felt her existence for weeks now."

He allowed the news to sink in. Sir saw Hanson's face pale under his dime store tan. Sir narrowed his eyes.

"She's around three years of age. That is usually the age of initial empathic contact. I cannot make a full connection with her until she comes to maturity. Bottom line is, somebody screwed up. You know the consequences of such flagrant incompetence. The only reason you are not dead right now, Hanson, is that you are the best in the world at genetic research. That's the only thing that saves your ass.

"Hanson, I want as many men on this as possible. Find her or heads will roll. You get my meaning?"

"Sir, you know I am always at your command. Just tell me what I must do and it shall be done."

"I want to know how she got here, how she slipped away without detection."

"Sir, if I may suggest? I can put a team on this. They will ferret out old records. It could take some time, however. There's over a million subject files in our records, as you well know."

"Hanson, do I have to think for you, or can you manage that? Considering the child is around three, figure it out. Her incubator could be anywhere from fifteen to thirty years of age, by my calculations."

"Sir, I know on my watch, not one subject has ever escaped this lab. As you know, I have faithfully served you for twelve years now. It has to be from Dr. Wendellson. It must have been during his tenure."

"See to it, then."

After Hansen left, Sir touched a button on his desk, which lifted a small trap door in the top. A miniature elevator rose, bringing him a cup of chamomile tea. He began to drink the boiling fluid. In his mind's eye, he saw Hansen walk down the hall, whispering a prayer.

Chapter 7

Baltimore, Maryland 1985

Leah happily colored while *Sesame Street* filled the television screen. She was not paying attention to Bert and Ernie playing the numbers game.

Her mother, Maggie, was busy baking.

Attracted by the smell of homemade chocolate chip cookies, she toddled into the kitchen. "Mommy, I want a cookie, please. Mommy, cookie is 'C'."

Distracted, Maggie asked, "What did you say, Sweetie?"

"Cookie is C. It's a letter, Mommy. C is for cookie."

"Leah, that's right. Mommy is proud of you for learning that. Here's your cookie. Now go play while I finish this batch, okay?"

"Mommy, cookie is c-o-o-k-i-e."

Shaking her head, marveled at the intelligence of her daughter, all Maggie could do was say, "That's right. Where did you learn that?"

"*Sesame Street*, Mommy," she said, laughing.

"Oh, I see. You just learned that, huh?"

"Oh no, Mommy, I seen that the other day. Today is all about numbers. Uno, Dos, Tres, Cuatro, Cinco, Seis, Siete, Ocho, Nueve, Diez. That's Spanish. In English: one-two-three-four-five-six-seven-eight-nine-ten."

"Leah, honey, that's very good. What else did you learn?"

Leah bowed her head, and a single tear fell from her eyes.

"Leah, why are you crying?"

"Mommy, I don't want the bad man to talk to me anymore. Can you make him stop?"

Maggie kneeled down and took Leah by her shoulders trying her best to remain calm. "Leah. Sweetie, who wants to talk to you? Did a man approach you when you were outside playing?"

"No, Mommy. He wants me to talk to him in my head. I don't want to. He's not nice."

"Leah, sweetheart, tell Mommy what you mean."

"I know he knows I'm here."

"Sweetie, who knows you're here?" Maggie asked.

"Him; the one who wants to talk to me inside my head, Mommy. You can't see him. He's in my head."

"Is he perhaps a pretend friend?"

"Mommy, I think he is a real pretend, but he's not my friend. He scares me."

"Well, then. Just pretend he isn't there, okay?"

"Mommy, he won't go away when I try to pretend he's not there. Can you make him stop?"

"Leah, let me call Daddy and he'll make the bad man go away, okay?"

"Okay, Mommy."

Maggie watched as her daughter returned to her coloring books. Something felt wrong. It was not the first time she had felt this vague apprehension since Leah was born; but now it squeezed like fingers around her heart. She grabbed the phone and dialed Joshua at the base.

"Honey, I just had an interesting conversation with our daughter." She told him about it and concluded with, "Honey, I'm worried. What should we do?"

"Mags, I think you need to downplay it. If you just treat it lightly, she may forget about it. It's probably just from a nightmare. Just keep it low. You have to stop being so overprotective, honey. It's not good for you or her. When I get home, I'll make the bad man go away. Tell her that. After all, it's not the end of the world."

"Mommy, he told me something," Leah interrupted.

"Just a second, baby, I'm talking to Daddy."

"But Mommy . . ." Leah covered her ears, not wanting to listen anymore. "C is for cookie . . ." she sang, drowning out his last whisper.

"You are my destiny, child."

~

Where was she? Sir used all the will power he had in his arsenal to control the rage that threatened to take over. He could ill afford to allow his "true" nature to be unleashed at this point. *My patience will pay off soon enough, he thought.*

He had to find her; she was already powerful enough to elude his messages. He paced the room. How had this happened? Years of research and they had not produced one successful hybrid. Just what path had been taken to bring this child to the here and now?

Chapter 8

The Beginning of the End: Bridgeport, PA, Circa WW II

Danielle lightly tapped her feet to the Andrews Sisters' *Boogie Woogie Bugle Boy*, as it blasted from the old, borrowed Victrola.

The USO dance swung into full speed. Some couples jitterbugged to the music. Others whispered intimately, heads so close they touched, hands entwined. Even with the cold, a few couples slid outside and into the garden behind the hall.

Danielle smiled as she studied the room. Buffet tables groaned under the weight of turkeys, huge bowls of mashed potatoes, tureens with giblet gravy, platters of cranberry sauce, and an array of vegetables. Pies and cakes, guaranteed to please any sweet tooth, finished the feast. Crocks of Wassail, apples bobbing in the hot liquid, warmed the revelers.

Cardboard scarecrows, pilgrims, and Horns of Plenty concealed once stark walls. Crepe-paper ribbons webbed the ceiling, while suspended paper turkeys danced on strings. The tables, covered with bright orange, gold, and red cloths, softened from the glow of candlelight. A huge cast iron stove at the end of the hall provided the only warmth. Windows etched in a lacework of frost greeted the falling snow.

Dannie had at last found a free moment to settle into a chair when she saw him coming toward her. The polite refusal on her lips remained unspoken as he murmured his request.

"May I have this dance?"

"Thank you, I would love to," she said after he finally choked it out.

"I . . . I'm Private Samuel Browne, with an 'e'."

"It's nice to meet you, Samuel."

"Call me Sam. Everyone does."

They both stepped forward at the same time, and his foot came down on her toes. His face blossomed with scarlet. "I'm sorry. We don't get to dance much."

"That's fine. I'm rusty myself." As she smiled at him, she noticed he still barely needed to shave, and even suffered from the angst of pubescent acne.

Dear, Lord. How young are they being sent over? Protect them, Lord, she prayed.

The music ended and he led her back to her chair.

"Thank you."

Danielle sat down again in her chair. Her stomach growled and her eyes turned to the buffet tables. She returned her gaze to her hands in her lap. *Maybe if I don't make eye contact for a few minutes. My feet are killing me. Was Samuel the seventh or eighth soldier I've danced with in the last twenty minutes?*

Aching feet or not, she was glad Wanda suggested they come to the dance. The good Lord knew these soldiers needed this reprieve from the war and she felt privileged to be part of it.

Dannie slipped off her shoes. *Stomped toes and ankles aching from too long in my high heels, but it's worth it.* She settled her feet back into her heels. *I need something to eat.*

A gust of cold air drew her attention and she glanced toward the door. She felt her breath catch. The soldier squared his broad shoulders and glanced around the room. He seemed more dignified in his dress uniform, more confident, more . . . everything . . . than the other soldiers she'd danced with earlier. Danielle averted her eyes then looked again--an unseen magnet polarizing their gazes into one.

With exaggerated effort, she concentrated on the buffet table. While she was deciding between turkey and ham, a strong hand reached past hers and took a plate. She glanced up into the new arrival's warm green eyes. His eyes, even more dramatic up close, pulled her once again.

"My name is Lieutenant . . . I mean, Ethan Anderson."

"Danielle. Danielle Hodges, how do you do?"

She tried to concentrate on the array of food.

The man in line behind them cleared his throat loudly. The intent stares focused on them reminded her they were holding up the food line. She moved down to the selection of vegetables with Ethan at her side.

"It's nice to meet you, Danielle. Would you care to dine with me?" he said with exaggerated formality, bowing as he asked the question.

How could she resist such charm? "Thank you, sir," she said, giving a shy curtsey. She took his offered arm and he escorted her to a small table near the warmth of the stove.

She slipped her napkin over her lap, protecting her only party dress--a soft blue taffeta, which complimented her rich chestnut hair and blue eyes.

"So, Ethan, what brought you here to Bridgeport, Pennsylvania?" Danielle asked.

"My job did. I work for--or worked for--Goodwin Medical Equipment and Supply."

Ethan then told her about his childhood. "The sisters at the Catholic orphanage where I was raised were kind to me, but because of The Great Depression I was not adopted. Couples wanting to adopt, wanted strong, strapping boys, able to help with chores and relieve the burden from the men and their wives. Since I leaned toward frailness as a boy, prospective parents considered me un-adoptable."

Danielle looked at him. *He sure grew out of the scrawny phase nicely.* She blushed at her train of thought.

"I took some night courses to earn a business degree and just finished it about six months ago. That's when I went to work at Goodwin; at least I did until my draft number came up. I just finished basic training. I have a twenty-one day furlough. My college education enabled me to enlist as an officer, rather than a private, so I'll be attending officer's training. I'm not sure what they'll send me over for, but I don't care. I'm just honored to serve my country." He smiled, revealing hidden dimples on each cheek, matching the Kirk Douglas cleft in his chin. Danielle's heart skipped a beat as she smiled back.

"Enough about me, tell me about you."

"My parents died in a flu epidemic in 1925. I was five at the time. Charles and Hilda Sykes, my godparents, raised me. Uncle Charles is the town sheriff."

"Do you remember much about your parents?" Ethan asked.

"Vaguely. I remember my mother standing at the kitchen door, calling for me to come in for dinner--the smell of homemade bread baking in the oven. My father always smelled like tobacco. He smoked a pipe which stuck out from under a very red handlebar mustache." She smiled. "I always feel a strong sense of love when I think about them. The rest of it is fill-in from my aunt and uncle. From what they told me, my parents had a wonderful marriage.

"My godparents saved a lot of things for me from my mother and father. Aunt Hilda used to tell me she was saving them for me until I married, but I don't think I want to try that until this war is over."

"Yeah, a lot of my buddies have married women they hardly know. I think it's the uncertainty of the future this damn war has brought to all of us."

Her eyes widened slightly at his use of profanity.

"Pardon my language, Danielle. It's just there seems to be such anxiety. No matter where you go, the tension cuts like a knife."

"I know what you mean," she said. "We seem to eat, think, and sleep this war. Before Pearl Harbor, World War I was something I only read about in a history book, but now that I'm *living* the Second World War, it's *too* real," she finished.

"I lost three friends I grew up with to Pearl Harbor. They perished on the U.S.S. Arizona. I was still here working at a gas station while finishing school. I can't imagine what they went through. I would be on that ship with them, if I hadn't broken my leg a year and a half ago. They had to do surgery on it to fix it." He looked into her eyes. "I just wish this war would be over so I could be back at my old job. Goodwin is a great company to work for. And I loved my work."

She sighed. "I just wish I *had* a job. My roommate is *not* going to be happy if I can't pay rent next month. I can't believe the competition for secretarial positions in Bridgeport. You'd think with all the river industry, I could manage to find a job in the field I trained for."

He snapped his fingers. "Say. Why don't you apply at Goodwin Medical Equipment and Supply? I spoke to Mr. Donnelly, who supervises the order requisition department, a few days ago. He was looking for another requisition clerk to replace someone who recently married. It may not pay as much as a secretarial position, but it would get your foot in the door."

"Why, thank you, Ethan. I want it understood that I get the job on my abilities. I *do* have references."

"Fine. I'll call him to see if that position is still open, okay?"

"Okay."

"If you'll give me a phone number where I can reach you, I'd be happy to let you know."

She gave him the community phone number to the apartment house she and Wanda shared.

"Danielle?"

She looked up to see her roommate coming toward them. Wanda stopped beside her and looked from one face to the other, her short blonde curls bobbing, her gray eyes flashing. Danielle felt her cheeks heat as she hurriedly said, "Ethan, this is my roommate, Wanda Hilliard. Wanda, this is Lieutenant Ethan Anderson."

They shook hands.

"Can you get home on your own? I'm going for a drive with Blake," Wanda said. Danielle hesitated. Blake was a soldier they had met earlier in the evening. Did her friend *really* know what she was doing? Nevertheless, she could not refuse the sparkle in Wanda's eyes.

"Sure. I'll take a taxi."

"That won't be necessary. I'd be honored to drive you home," Ethan volunteered.

Seeing the eager expression on Ethan's face, she said, "Thank you, Ethan. I would love that."

The rest of the evening passed in a blur of dancing, conversation, laughter, and fun. She had never experienced so much emotion with any of the other dates she had gone on. Ethan was just so different, and she felt herself slipping from her resolve not to get involved too heavily with anyone while the war was on.

They arrived at the brownstone where Danielle lived. As she started to get out of the car, Ethan jumped out, ran around to her side, and opened her door for her. He insisted on walking her to her apartment, just to make sure she arrived home safely.

She blushed when Ethan did not leave immediately. They stood there in awkward silence for a moment. Finally, Ethan spoke up. "Danielle, would you like to have dinner with me tomorrow night?"

"I . . . sure, I'd love to. G'night, Ethan." She quickly unlocked the door and went inside.

Wanda was waiting up for her as she walked in--her face glowing.

"I couldn't wait until you got home. Blake is the most wonderful man in the world." She hugged herself. "Danielle, he's asked me to marry him. I couldn't believe it. Of course, I told him I would have to think it over," she paused, taking a breath.

She knew Wanda well enough to let her go on until she ran out of wind. Listening to her talk when she was excited was like watching a balloon when the air is let out, spinning around until it collapsed.

"Blake has at least three weeks before he leaves. Do you think that's enough time to know if I love him and want to marry him or not?" she finished.

"Wanda, you have to make those choices on your own, Honey. I'm in a bit of a dilemma myself over a similar situation."

"Okay, my friend, give."

"Well, Ethan is so different, Wanda. I don't know what it is, but . . . I think I could fall in love with that man. There's just something about him. He's polite, a perfect gentleman. He's *very* good looking . . . and those green eyes. I could get lost those eyes," Danielle said dreamily. Looking up, she noticed the smirk on Wanda's face. "What?"

"Dannie, Dannie, Dannie. What happened to your resolve to not get involved so soon?"

She laughed and squeezed Wanda's hand. Her heart sang a song she had not heard before. One she knew would be her lullaby tonight. "He's worth thinking about."

~

Ethan and Danielle spent as much of the next twenty-one days together as possible. On their seventh date, he took her to a movie. She gazed at Ethan through the flickering light of the huge movie screen, the skepticism on his face as he watched the newsreel.

"I noticed you weren't very impressed with the newsreel, Ethan. Why?"

"Dannie, I know this isn't very popular, but I think a lot of what's shown is propaganda. I don't share that opinion with just anybody. It's not a widely accepted viewpoint."

"I know, Ethan. I feel the same way, but never voiced it, until now. From what I read about World War I, they have to be just giving us the more positive aspects of this war."

"I'm so glad to hear someone else with the same opinion."

~

They strolled along the square. Danielle loved the shops decorated for Christmas. The snow-covered window displays housed cheerful elves, rotund cherry-cheeked Santas; faces in perpetual smiles. Miniature Lionel trains lumbered along tiny tracks and through small tunnels, the smoke popping out in little puffs. Brightly wrapped gifts drew the wide-eyed wonder of children.

They passed posters of Uncle Sam, donned in the patriotic tuxedo and top hat, pointing his finger and saying, "I want you!"

Danielle put her hand in the crook of Ethan's elbow, and they strolled some more.

Time rushed by for Danielle. When the day arrived for Ethan to ship out, Danielle clung to him, wishing with all her heart that he did not have to leave. As they stood on the platform near the train, the hissing steam from the engine cloaked them against the world.

"Ethan, I'll miss you."

"I'll miss you too. I'll write to you. Don't forget me. Dannie, I "

She put her hand over his mouth. "Ethan, don't. Just get on that train, okay? I hate long goodbyes. I'll be here when you get back."

She stood there, her smiling lips trembled as she watched the departing train and her heart broke in two.

Chapter 9

Danielle tried to concentrate on her work, but clock watching slowed down her days. Time, her enemy, refused to budge. She lived for Ethan's letters. Every time she received one, she read it over and over, savoring the poetic words he often penned. With each letter, the faint smell of his now-familiar *Aqua Velva* drifted to her. She drank in the woodsy aroma.

She had lucked out in finding an apartment. Although the dwelling was small, it was affordable. Danielle felt blessed to have it at all since they were so hard to come by. Sometimes she stood in the doorway just looking, imagining coming home to Ethan, fixing him dinner, giving him the paper. She dared not allow her thoughts to wander into the bedroom. That part of married life was still mysterious, frightening.

Wanda, now married, had little time for Danielle. She was happy for her friend, but sorely missed their late-night talks, the giggles over Blake and Ethan, as they shared details of their dates.

On a Saturday afternoon in August, trying to cool off in a pair of shorts, her shirt tied at her midriff, Danielle sipped on iced tea. She paused from Ethan's latest letter, cooling her sweaty brow with the chilled glass. "I'll be so glad when winter comes." She sighed.

She adjusted the small oscillating fan so it would blow on her. Going back to Ethan's letter, she hung on every word. Her small fan ruffled the paper. Danielle grumbled as a knock on the door interrupted her.

Mrs. Heathrow, her landlady, got to the point. "Danielle, there's a call for you on the hall phone."

She ran to the phone, hoping it might be him.

"Hello?"

"Ethan," she squealed upon hearing his voice, hugging the phone. Six months had passed since she had last spoken with him. "Where are you calling from?" Her heart pounded.

"I'm on an evening pass in town and had to call you. How are you, Dannie Girl?"

She thrilled to the nickname he used. "I'm fine, busy working. We've even had to work some overtime to process requisitions for our military sales."

"Sounds like you've got your work cut out for you, Dannie."

"I do."

"Dannie, I re-injured my leg in Officer's Training. The doc wants me to rest for the next twelve weeks. I'm coming home 'til I'm cleared for combat."

"Oh no, Ethan. Are you okay? Did you break it again?"

"No, and I'm fine. It's just soft tissue strain. I have to use a cane for a while, but doc said it should mend. Listen, Dannie, I wanted to do this in person, but I can't wait," he said.

"What is it, Ethan?" Her heart sank. She worried her lips with her teeth.

"Look. I know we haven't spent much time together, and I know you didn't want to do this until the war is over, but, will . . . will you marry me?"

She was speechless for a moment.

"Dannie? Dannie, are you there?"

"Y . . . yes, I'm here."

"Do you need time to think about it? Listen, I'm in love with you, but if you . . . if you don't feel the same way, I'll understand."

"Ethan, I love you, too. But I meant what I said about waiting until the war is over."

"I understand, Dannie, but like I said, I can't wait. I want to spend the rest of my life with you. You're my stability in this crazy world. I want to--need to--know that you're going to be there when I come home. Grow old with me, Sweetheart."

The operator cut in, asking for more money. She heard Ethan tell her to wait a minute so he could find more coins. Danielle heard the chink, chink; the operator saying he only had three more minutes.

"Dannie," Ethan said after being reconnected, "I want to spend the rest of my life with you. Please, marry me."

Her heart quickly won the battle over her voice of reason. "Yes, Ethan. Yes. I'll marry you."

"Dannie, you pick the date. I'm coming home on September first. That's in three days. By the way, I wrote Charlie a few weeks ago to ask for your hand. He said yes, with his blessings."

"Well. Now I know how well Uncle Charlie keeps secrets."

"I love you, Dannie Girl."

"I love you, too, Ethan."

~

Danielle stood on the stool Hilda had told her to fetch. She fidgeted with the tiny beads on the bodice of her mother's wedding gown. "Dannie, I won't ever get this altered before September sixth if you don't stop fussing so," Hilda scolded.

Danielle lifted her head in frustration and noticed Uncle Charlie looking at her. He wiped his eyes, muttering something about dust.

Danielle looked at her aunt and smiled.

"Aunt Hillie, does the dress look okay? I mean, how do I look in it?"

"Honey, you look like a princess. Your mama would be so proud. There. Finished. Go look in the mirror, Sweetie."

Danielle gazed into the full-length mirror. Taking the corners of the skirt, she whirled around, turning first one way, then another. The white silk, covered in layers of chiffon, had conformed to her body under Hilda's expert handiwork.

Grabbing the small veil hanging on one side of the gilded full-length mirror, she smoothed out the netting and tried it on. As she stood there, she thought of her mother's wedding pictures displayed on the wall of her living room.

"I look like her, don't I, Aunt Hillie?"

"Yes, you do. And you're just as lovely as she was, if not lovelier."

~

Ethan and Danielle took their vows at the small Methodist church they attended, Charlie strutting as he walked her down the aisle. Pastor Nichols officiated. Danielle's tears matched the shiny gleam in Ethan's eyes as she approached him and took his arm. She was in a dream.

"Do you, Ethan Winthrop Anderson, take Danielle Angelica Hodges, to be your lawfully wedded wife? To have and to hold. "

The preacher's voice faded into the background as Danielle watched Ethan's face as he said, "I do."

Danielle breathlessly responded in kind, as the preacher repeated the vows to her.

"I do."

The ceremony was over before she knew it. The reception was modest, with grape juice replacing wine or champagne. The food offered amounted to finger sandwiches, some cheese and crackers and an assortment of fresh homegrown vegetables. Danielle thanked Wanda's mother Marianne for baking the wedding cake. She outdid herself--three tiered, with tiny rosebuds formed from pale pink icing.

Danielle tried paying attention to all the well-wishers, but could not concentrate. She could only stare at her new husband and the small matching gold bands on her and Ethan's fingers.

They did not travel anywhere for their honeymoon due to gas rations, but Charles and Hilda offered their home to them for two weeks, giving them more privacy. The proud parents stayed at Danielle's during that time.

Their wedding night, Danielle took a long time in the bathroom. She stared at her small breasts, wondering how Ethan would feel. *Will he like my body? Will I be the sort of lover he will be happy with? How badly will it hurt?* All the thoughts raced around in her head, vying for answers.

She felt sick to her stomach as she pulled on the flimsy negligee Wanda had given her as a gift. She tried to remember the talk Hilda had with her, first explaining the pain, then the enjoyment of sex, even orgasms. Blushing at that thought, she hoped she was right. She wanted to enjoy their lovemaking. Steeling herself, she came out of the bathroom, her whole body shaking.

She stood there in the middle of the bedroom, waiting. *Say something,* she willed him.

"Dannie, you take my breath away. You look like an angel."

Shyly, she went into Ethan's arms, her fear melting away as he held her.

Ethan proved to be a very patient and understanding lover. A passion stirred in her that she'd never known existed. As they made love, she went to the edge of eternity then gently came back to earth, wrapped in her husband's embrace.

~

She woke up before him in the mornings, fixed him breakfast, and served it to him in bed in spite of his protests. "Listen, with only three months before you ship out, I'm spoiling you, Ethan Winthrop Anderson. If I spoil you now, maybe you'll be extra careful and be sure you come home for more of it."

Ethan took her in his arms. "Oh, baby. You don't have to do one thing to spoil me. You did that the first night we met."

They moved his things into Danielle's tiny apartment. Danielle worked each day, coming home to find Ethan preparing dinner, or trying to find places to store their now doubled belongings.

One night when she came home, Ethan, surrounded by boxes, some half empty with the contents scattered over the living room, poured over the classified section of the paper. "Dannie Girl, we're simply going to have to move," he said without looking up. "I can't find another nook or cranny to put anything in."

"What? No kiss or 'hello, Honey'?"

She watched him get up, almost tripping over the items and kicking them in frustration. She put her hand to her mouth, trying to hide a grin.

Grabbing her by the shoulders, he kissed her long and hard. "Hello, Honey."

It was some time later before they perused the few rentals listed. They found one they could afford. It was a nice large one-bedroom in a converted brownstone. Ethan moved them while Danielle worked. He agreed to paint the apartment for the deposit, and they settled in a week later.

~

Danielle invited Wanda and Blake to dinner, once they were settled. Ethan and Blake liked each other, which delighted the two wives. The couples went to the farmer's market, to the movies, and before the cold set in, picnicked in the country. Ethan and Blake enjoyed sports and attended the local football games. The two men spoke of the talents of women who had taken over major league baseball during the war.

Ethan, Danielle, Wanda and Blake, spent snow-filled evenings, playing games, listening to the radio, and eating together

Thanksgiving, the four, including Wanda's parents, gathered at the Sykes's home. The festive dinner reminded Danielle of the USO dance just one year before, when she met Ethan.

Their first Christmas, they spent with Charles and Hilda. Hilda asked Dannie how she found married life as they were preparing the holiday feast.

Danielle's face turned beet red. "Aunt Hillie, what you and I talked about . . . before my marriage, I mean. You were right. Thank you for being honest with me."

"That's what I'm here for, Honey. You know, we can talk about intimate things such as this, but it is not for everyone's ears. I wanted you to have the best marriage possible--both in the bedroom, and out of it."

~

On December 28, 1943, Ethan received his orders to ship out. He would report to his base in four days.

The next three days, they did not venture out of the apartment, clinging to each other, loving as much as they could against the war that would separate them.

On Ethan's last evening home, Charles and Hilda invited them to a going away dinner. Wanda and her family attended, also. The dinner consisted of Hilda's famous pot roast, a rarity at the time. The meal was finished off with fresh potatoes, carrots, and home-baked yeast rolls. A homemade apple cobbler left nothing more undone.

Wanda stood up during the meal. "Guess what, everyone? I am expecting!" There were hearty back slaps among the men, hugs, and happy tears between the women, and all around good cheer.

The next two years were to bring mixtures of celebration of new life, grief over death, and one long nightmare for the two friends.

~

Wanda prepared lunch and she and Danielle chatted. After lunch, they washed dishes together. Wanda rinsed the plate and set it on the sideboard.

"It has been so nice having you around these last couple of months." She glanced at Danielle and chuckled. "Makes the dishes go a lot faster too."

With a tiny gasp, she rubbed her slightly rounded tummy, then grinned and took Danielle's hand. "Quick, you've got to feel this."

The baby stirred within her womb and Danielle felt the flutter of life, the ripple of movement across Wanda's abdomen. "Oh wow," she whispered in amazement. "That is so sweet. What does it feel like?"

"Oh god, Danielle, it is so . . . There's a baby in there. I can't believe it and then he moves--like this--and I know. It's another life, a brand new little person." A bright smile lit her face. "It's just the best feeling in the world."

She and Ethan wanted children, but had decided to wait until the war was over. Since she was an only child and Ethan an orphan, they both wanted to have many kids. Danielle had no idea just how significant the life of her own child would be--how much it would change history--forever.

~

Since Blake was unable to come home when Blake Jr. arrived, Danielle, along with Wanda's parents, waited. Then, finally, the announcement, 'It's a boy--a lively one,' sent tears of happiness flowing all around. Danielle hurriedly phoned Blake's parents with the good news since they could not travel. She cried for joy with them.

Danielle and Wanda's mother took turns taking care of Wanda and Little Blake once they went home. Eight months later, they took care of Wanda and Little Blake again, when his father was killed in action. No matter how much Dannie tried to comfort Wanda, it did not help. All she could do for her friend was to be there and pray for her. It took the military a number of weeks to ship his body home so they could bury him. When the soldier handed Wanda the folded flag, Danielle felt a strong sense of foreboding. She knew Ethan was fine. She had just received a letter from him the day before.

Still, she could not shake the deepening fear that something was not right.

Chapter 10

Danielle held the phone on her shoulder as she processed another order of medical supplies to the war department. She completed the monotonous routine, and stretched. She sighed, wondering if so much gauze, bandages, sutures among other critical items, meant the soldiers were losing. This had been the fifth order for this week alone.

The ceiling fans did little to alleviate the summer swelter. As Danielle wiped the sweat from her brow, Mary, a coworker, spoke up.

"Want to have lunch with us today, Danielle? Some of us are venturing outside to escape this heat."

"That sounds heavenly. I'd love to. It's almost lunchtime now. What I really want is an ice cold bottle of cola."

"You and me both."

As the lunch hour approached, the women became more animated. The phones usually slowed down about now, and it gave the workers a reprieve from the never-ending orders they processed. Danielle, her back turned from the main door leading into the requisition department, had been laughing at the story Janice told her. Suddenly, the laughter stopped. Typewriters fell silent.

She looked across at Mary, whose face seemed to have changed to stone. "Mary, what's wrong, don't you feel we. . . .." Danielle turned to the direction Mary looked.

She grew pale, as she saw the Western Union messenger slowly walk to Mr. Donnelly's office door. It seemed the messenger looked right at Danielle, sympathy in his eyes. Attempting to shake the sudden frigid cold that froze her in mid-sentence, she shivered violently.

In the months since Ethan had shipped out, a number of the somber young boys brought news to Goodwin, delivering the message that someone's son, husband, or brother would not be coming home.

Since Blake's funeral, Danielle's anxiety over Ethan had grown. She jumped every time someone knocked on her door, or the phone rang; but especially when the messengers came.

Now, she had such a knot of dread in her stomach she thought she might get sick; there was something so ominous about this day, this hour, that she could not shake it.

Mr. Donnelly's personal secretary came out of the office and stepped into the room. Danielle watched as she walked toward her. She stopped breathing, hoping it was not her turn, yet wishing none of them had to go through it.

Pam Towers stopped at her desk.

"Danielle, please come with me."

Danielle rose, but her heavy legs refused to budge. She stood for a moment by her desk before Pam took her elbow. She turned to look back as Pam ushered her to Mr. Donnelly's door. The looks in her coworkers' eyes were unmistakable--sympathy battling with relief.

She sat down where Mr. Donnelly indicated.

"Are you Mrs. Ethan Winthrop Anderson?" the messenger asked.

"Ye--yes, I am." She was so nervous she could barely speak.

The young man handed her the yellow envelope after she signed his tablet.

Her fingers shook as she read it.

> *We regret to inform you that your husband, Lieutenant Ethan Winthrop Anderson, was reclassified POW, on May 25, 1944.* Stop.
>
> *Location unknown at this time. Stop.*
>
> *Have contacted Geneva committee on his condition and location.* Stop.
>
> *Please contact your nearest Army office for further information.* Stop

As Mr. Donnelly guided the messenger out of his office, she heard him say to Pam, "Give her a moment."

Danielle sat in the chair, the telegram gripped in one hand, a damp handkerchief in the other. She looked up as Mr. Donnelly re-entered his office. "Is there anything I can do for you, Danielle?"

"Pray for him, Mr. Donnelly. Pray that he comes home to me." Her hands shook; tears cascaded down her face.

"Danielle, since it's Thursday, why don't you take the rest of today and tomorrow off ? Maybe you can find out a little more information in the morning."

"Thank you."

"Danielle?"

She finally looked at Mr. Donnelly.

"I'm fine," she sniffed. "Thank you for your kind offer, Mr. Donnelly. I . . . I'll be here on Monday."

With great effort, she pulled her shoulders back, strode purposefully down the hall and into the elevator. Once she was safely inside, her knees collapsed and she fell to the elevator floor sobbing. She felt little comfort knowing he was still alive; knowing people experienced things worse than death. She had heard of some of the atrocities that happened to POWs.

~

Danielle's hands shook as she dialed the phone. "Aunt Hillie," she cried. She could not say more.

"What is it, Sweetie? What's happened?"

Finding her voice, Danielle responded. "I . . . I got news about Ethan. Can . . . can you come over right away?"

"Oh good Lord. I'll be right over."

"Aunt Hillie? Can you let Wanda know?"

"Don't worry about that. I'll take care of it. Everything will be just fine, Sweetheart."

~

In no time they were all there encircling her as she explained the telegram. Until Aunt Hilda took the crumpled telegram from Danielle's hand, she had not noticed she still held it.

Once they read the message, Danielle said, "I won't stop hounding the military until I know *how* Ethan is, at least. They may never tell me where he is, but before I'm through they'll tell me exactly what condition he's in!" She stuck her chin out, her brave front evident.

~

Hilda furrowed her brow at Dannie's hollow cheeks and the dark circles around her eyes. "You've got to get more rest, child. The good Lord has His reasons. Just remember that. I'm going to run you a bath. When did you eat last?"

Danielle shook her head. The thought of food made her stomach dip. "The bath sounds great."

Hilda's usually pleasant face grew stern. "The bath first, then you will eat a little soup " She held up a hand in warning as Danielle started to protest. "You *will* eat."

Danielle meekly nodded.

"Did you call Pastor Nichols?"

"No. I will, but. "

Hilda walked to Danielle and pulled her in for a long hug. "You just never mind. I'll do it. We'll ask him to add Ethan's name to the prayer list."

Tears welled up in her eyes as she watched Danielle walk away. She was the child she was never able to have and was proud of the way they had raised her. She knew her Dannie could handle just about any situation, but she could not keep from worrying about her.

As Danielle soaked in the clubfooted tub, Hilda called Charles at the sheriff 's office.

"Charlie," Hilda spoke when he answered the phone. "I'm worried about our daughter. I know you have an old friend in the war department. Can you do something about this?"

"Hillie, I can make some well-placed calls. I might be able to get some information from Buck," Charles said, thoughtfully. "He's a Colonel at Fort Mead."

"That would be good, Honey," Hilda replied. "I'll stay with Danielle tonight and you see what you can find out from him as soon as you can."

"All righty. I'll call him right away. Maybe he can find out somethin' before supper tomorrow night. Then our Dannie won't be so worried."

Hilda agreed. "You let me know something as soon as you find out."

"You know I will, Honey Bunch."

"Don't you Honey Bunch me, you Old Fossil."

Comforted by her husband's promise, Hilda set about making herself a bed on the couch.

~

Danielle held the phone to her ear, once again on hold. She thrummed her fingers on the end table, trying to will someone to speak to her. Waiting for this official or that department and generally getting the run around, threatened her sanity.

They finally put her through to a Captain Burrows.

"Mrs. Anderson, Ethan was on patrol behind enemy lines in Europe. They ambushed his company and took them prisoners. Ethan is in one of the POW camps. He sustained injuries, but not serious ones. We should hear something within the next few months. I apologize for the length of time it may take to get further information, but we're dealing with enemies, and they don't always cooperate in these matters."

"Matters? *Matters*? Captain Burrows, my husband is not a 'matter'. He is my husband, an American, and one of *your* soldiers." Danielle raised her voice with each word. "I expect to have some answers soon, do you understand?"

"Mrs. Anderson, I . . . I'll try my best to find your husband, I promise." He hung up before she could say anything more. It was the last time she ever spoke to him.

~

Days drifted slowly into weeks and then months. Every week or so found Danielle on the phone on hold, or waiting for a return call, only to receive the same information.

Everything and everyone being war-oriented enhanced her grief and worry. The movies were about war; military romances with heart-breaking songs of longing.

I'll be home for Christmas, played on the radio endlessly. She could not escape the loneliness, the helpless feeling of not being able to change anything. She tried to take her mind off her circumstances by staying active. Friends and of course, Charles and Hilda came by, took her places, invited her to some of the socials occurring frequently.

In 1945, the war was finally over. Troops came home, but not her Ethan.

In New York State, the country's heroes marched in precision down Madison Avenue. Men and women kissed, not knowing each other, frenzied by the victory for freedom. Wives ran into the arms of husbands too long gone from home. Fathers looked in awe at their children, some seeing them for the first time. Tears of happiness, radiant faces in rapt joy, appeared everywhere. The entire country celebrated together.

Danielle caught it all on a pre-movie newsreel. She had gone to see a comedy with Wanda, who was trying her best to cheer her up. She ran out of the theater in tears, Wanda in pursuit.

When Wanda finally caught up with her, she was almost in tears herself. "Oh, Dannie, I'm so sorry. I wasn't thinking. I didn't mean to make you cry."

"Wanda, it isn't you," she said through her tears. "It's just that . . . I want Ethan, dammit!"

~

It happened two weeks after the victory celebrations. She was at home when officers paid her a visit. There was no telegram this time.

"Mrs. Anderson, we're here to inform you that Ethan has not been found. We don't know if he is still alive or not, so he has been officially declared missing in action."

Dannie shook her head, denying their words. "But . . . but you said he was a prisoner of war . . . all this time . . . all the phone calls. You never really knew?"

"His name was given to us. We only just discovered through the Red Cross that he wasn't among the prisoners. We're doing all we can to locate him. We'll keep you informed as often as we can. We're so sorry."

She sat on the couch looking from one officer's face to the other, trying to allow the new news to sink in.

"Is there anything we can do for you, anyone we can contact before we leave, Mrs. Anderson?" one officer asked.

She turned to the officers. "No, thank you. I'll be fine. I will be calling at least twice a week until I get some sort of answer. I want my husband back in whatever kind of condition he may be in. I could accept his death. I could accept it if he came home maimed. I cannot, and *will not*, accept this."

"We understand your need, Mrs. Anderson. Please feel free to call as often as you wish."

"I promise you, we will do everything to find him," the other officer assured her.

Their statement gave her little comfort, knowing what she had already been through with the bureaucracy of the military. The worst was over; or so she thought.

Chapter 11

Ethan finally came home the summer of 1947.

Danielle paced, waiting at the train station for him. She thought about his homecoming. There would be no hero banners, no ticker tape parade--just one man on a train. But it was enough. Oh God, it was enough.

As the train pulled in to the station, she strained to try to spot him. Many soldiers departed the train cars, but none of them appeared to be Ethan.

She was about to give up when an older man approached her. The man, thin and drawn, seemed ancient. When Danielle looked into those deep green eyes, she knew: Ethan *had* made it home.

"Ethan? Ethan, is that you?"

"Dannie Girl."

How can this be? This man isn't the man that I married. What do I do now? Danielle's awkwardness showed. In strained silence, she led Ethan to the car. They placed his bags inside the trunk and headed home.

It would be months before everything seemed more normal.

~

Ethan remembered nothing about his ordeal while missing in action, and now it was if Danielle lived with a stranger. Gone was the man who used to tease her, hug her, and hold her close at night. Gone were the long talks, the closeness. They rarely made love, and when they did, it was not the same.

Gone also was the man who had pledged his undying patriotism for his country. In his place was a man haunted by ghostly phantoms.

Once an open, communicative person, he was now given to mood swings, often not speaking to her for days at a time, bouts of anger marring their relationship.

After one particularly bad fight, Danielle considered leaving. She called Wanda.

"I don't know what I'm going to do. His anger--no, rage--scares me sometimes, Wanda."

"Has he hit you?"

"No, I don't think he would ever do that. I'm more concerned that he may hurt himself. He is so different from the man I married, I just don't know if I can live with him."

"Dannie, let me ask you something; do you love him?"

"Wanda, you know I do."

"Then stand by him. You *did* take the vow, 'for better or worse'. He's wounded, Dannie; not in his body, but his soul. Something horrible happened. The best thing you could do for him is pray."

"You're right. It's just so hard. Thanks for listening."

"Anytime, Sweetie, anytime."

~

She hated the long walks he started taking; she was never invited. He became more secretive. The mood swings worsened. He began having nightmares, horrible screams filling the apartment. All too often, he woke drenched in sweat.

Unable to stand it any longer, she begged him to get some help.

"Ethan, honey. You have to see someone, *please*. You can't go on like this."

"Danielle, *nothing--no one*--can help me. If I can't remember, who the hell can?"

"Ethan, look at me." She turned him to face her.

"If you don't get help, I will have no choice but to leave."

His shocked expression told her she'd hit home.

"This is how it is. You get some help. You have to remember, or at least come to terms with whatever happened to you. I know it won't be easy, but please try--for our sake."

He sought help through the VA, seeing a psychiatrist who specialized in assisting traumatized soldiers. Although he still could not remember much of his ordeal, the counseling helped him through the worst.

Eventually, they both reconfirmed their faith and life began to change for the better.

~

Gradually, Ethan became more the man she had married, though there remained a haunting within him.

Ethan got his job back with Goodwin Medical Supply. Danielle continued as office manager for the requisitions department. Ethan became the representative for medical supplies for all VA hospitals in the northeastern U.S. He often went away on business.

They saved money to buy a home. By 1949, they had saved enough to start house shopping. None suited Danielle. She would say, "It's a nice house, but it just doesn't feel quite right." And the search continued.

They had almost given up when they found the five-acre farm during one of their picnic trips into the country in the late summer. Danielle urged Ethan to stop, excited when she spotted the place.

When they stopped, Danielle jumped from the car and ran into the yard.

"Ethan, this is the home I want," she said hugging her chest.

"Dannie Girl, this place is awful. Look at all the work that needs to be done."

Weeds infested the yard; the house needed a fresh coat of paint; some of the shutters hung by one hinge. The front screen door was torn. It looked hopeless.

"Oh, please, Honey! I can see so much potential," she pleaded. "At least check on it for me," she finished.

The sparkle in her eyes, the hopeful expression on her face; he could not refuse.

Ethan found out the property was one of many small farms that fell victim to the crash of '29. Foreclosed upon, then abandoned after the bank went under, the house and land had deteriorated a great deal over the years. Ethan and Danielle bought the place for the back taxes owed to the county. They were able to pay cash for it, with money to spare.

When they walked through it the first time, Ethan realized it was structurally sound, which greatly relieved his initial trepidation.

The house, a stately turn-of-the-century Victorian, had twin gables at each end. Using their leftover money, they completed the renovations, some they did themselves. Ethan painted the outside a soft white and accented it with colonial blue shutters and trim. The Andersons hired a contractor to install a new, wooden-shake roof. Danielle and Ethan both painted and papered the interior.

The floors of the home were all hardwood and refinished with a rich mahogany stain, creating a beautiful sheen, which held soft reflections of the Early American furniture. The muted light from chiffon-covered windows and the huge area rugs scattered about provided an understated elegance to the interior.

One day, as they were painting an upstairs bedroom, Ethan snuck up on Danielle and swiped paint across her face.

"Ethan," she squealed, "just look at my nose!" She arched her eyebrow and looked at him with an evil gleam in her eye.

"Oh no, you don't, Dannie Girl," Ethan said. "You wouldn't dare."

Danielle already wielded her loaded paintbrush, ready to strike.

They chased each other around the room. She finally caught Ethan on the head with oyster pink paint.

Exhausted, they fell to the floor, laughing.

"Ethan," Danielle said dreamily after catching her breath, "won't this be a lovely room for a little girl someday?"

"Mmm-hmmm." Ethan looked down at her, his head propped on his hand. A fire that she had not seen in forever burned in his eyes. He leaned in and passionately kissed her. "Dannie, what say we christen this room?"

Much later, after they showered together, they talked about their desires regarding children.

"Ethan, I'm happier now than I have been in a long time, but I want a baby--your baby. I just don't understand why I'm not getting pregnant," she lamented.

"Dannie, honey, the doctor said it would just take time. Besides, we might have just succeeded. You were a holy handful, lady," he said, adding a wolfish grin and sexy wink.

Danielle felt warm blood flood her cheeks.

"I love it that I can still make you blush after six years of marriage." He pulled her close and kissed her. "Oh, Dannie girl, I'm blessed to have you as my wife."

"Not as blessed as I am," she said and then smiled. "Let's go watch the sunset from the veranda."

Danielle loved the huge six-foot wide veranda surrounding the house. The large clapboard floor of the porch glowed with a soft patina from the light oak stain that coated it. Cozy sitting areas created with wicker chairs and rockers held splashes of bright, multicolored cushions. Glider sofas and wooden porch swings, suspended from the tall ceiling, painted colonial blue to match the shutters. Wicker tables, various potted and hanging plants, completed the look. Ceiling fans hung in uniform distances, cooling the veranda from the cross breeze created by the oversized fan blades.

Danielle and Ethan spent many hours on their veranda reading or simply enjoying the evening breeze after a long day's work. Sometimes they had dinner outside.

They particularly enjoyed watching it rain that first spring. They even made love on the hammock in the back, the spring rain as their only music, each moving in rhythm with nature and each other, passionate in their ardor. The love they felt was deep and abiding. They were not only married, they were lovers and best friends.

The first winter snows created a private wonderland for them. They thoroughly enjoyed decorating for Christmas that first year. Even though the home was in the country, they made that Christmas one to remember. They hung lights inside and out with twinkling white strands of round bulbs. A huge tree stood in the living room near the fireplace, stockings hanging cozily nearby. Garland adorned the mantle and stairway banister. They transformed it into a gingerbread house, giving the illusion of a Norman Rockwell painting. They even built a large snowman in the front yard. An exhilarating snowball fight assured them of mugs of hot chocolate to warm them up.

In the spring, Danielle put her green thumb to work and changed the weed-infested yard into an elegantly landscaped garden. She set flowerbeds along a large stone path, which led to the front porch. She planted rose bushes, trees, and multicolored perennials in a glorious pattern, which created a beautiful framework for the now lush, green lawn.

During the war, the government encouraged people to plant victory gardens, allowing the large farms to supply as much food to the fighting men as possible. In those years, one could travel the country and spot these gardens everywhere. There were small gardens in the side yards of stately homes, in window boxes in the large cities as well as community gardens in some of the smaller towns. Danielle planted a vegetable garden in a large square at one corner of the voluminous back yard in keeping with that tradition. She planted tomatoes, peas, and corn, among other vegetables. In addition, she grew root types such as, carrots, potatoes, sweet potatoes, and beets.

Ethan and Danielle continued trying for the family they both longed for, with no results. Danielle had some false alarms and they were both disappointed each time.

One day, after another false alarm, Dannie lamented, "Honey, I don't understand why we keep failing."

"I know, Dannie. We just have to keep trying, okay?"

Dannie could not trust herself to speak, afraid of more tears, so she just nodded.

For another year, there were no more false alarms.

~

It was late April. Danielle experienced some signs but decided against telling Ethan about it. She did not want to get his hopes up. Trying to conceive for the last year with nothing to show for their efforts except a number of false alarms, was just too painful. She and Ethan were disappointed too many times. The crushed expectations hit Ethan especially hard. He ached to have his own large family.

Danielle scheduled her doctor's appointment on the first day of her two-week vacation. It coincided with the week Ethan went away on business. She was impatient, wanting to hear the news from the doctor, and had to wait several days for the test results. Three days before Ethan was due home, the doctor called her into his office.

"Well, Mrs. Anderson, I have *good* news this time."

Danielle floated out to the car. From that day until Ethan came home, she busied herself sprucing up the house, while periods of daydreaming of how Ethan would react broke the monotony of chores.

Danielle expected the baby sometime in December. Christmas. The thought gave her an idea. Before she had returned home, Danielle bought a baby rattle from the variety store.

She smiled as she rummaged through the Christmas items in the attic. At last, she found a perfect size box and enfolded the rattle in delicate tissue paper before placing it inside. She found some silvery wrapping paper--smiling little drummer boys and teddy bears sitting in little red wagons looking festive with the holiday-green Christmas ribbons around their necks. Danielle selected some ribbon and completed her task. She looked at the finished work and satisfied with the results, took the wrapped box downstairs.

Danielle looked at the clock and, seeing the time, went upstairs to bathe and get ready for Ethan's return. She removed her clothes and paused at the full-length mirror on the wall of their bedroom. Still in her slip, she took a small pillow off the bed and stuffed it under. As she gazed at herself, she could imagine Ethan rubbing her swollen belly, speaking to their yet-to-be-born baby, crooning his favorite songs. She smiled at the thought.

As she lingered in her bath, she thought of how much life a child would bring into the too-long neglected farm. She imagined children running up and down the stairs playing tag, her, good-naturedly admonishing them about running in the house.

She envisioned days of hunting for clover in the acreage behind the house. She imagined happy, cherubic faces at the dinner table--reflections of Ethan--prattling on about the school day, all of them talking at once. Finally, all her and Ethan's dreams were coming true.

After getting out of the tub, she sprinkled baby powder on her stomach, chest, and back. She drank in the smell of it. She could not wait to hold her baby in her arms, smelling that sweet scent on her child.

Danielle wore her best cobalt dress. It enhanced her blue eyes. She fixed her hair; wearing it loose around her shoulders, the way Ethan liked it, and then completed her look with lipstick and powder.

As she stared at her reflection in the mirror, she noticed a certain glow about her face that was not there before. She heard about the 'glow' of impending motherhood, but dismissed it as an old wives tale. Now she knew it was true.

She put on her best apron; a soft white chiffon and lace waist-tie, a gift from Aunt Hilda during her bridal shower, then busied herself with the time she had left. She completed the final touches on the meal of pot roast, carrots, and new potatoes. Home canned green beans and sliced tomatoes completed the meal.

She baked a fresh loaf of bread that morning and kept it in the warmer oven located on one side of the stove. She also baked an apple pie, one of Ethan's favorite desserts, with fresh apples she purchased from the farmer's market the morning before.

Upon hearing the familiar beep of the postal carrier's horn, Danielle went outside to retrieve the mail. The doors and windows were open to the cool breeze that gently blew. As she approached the porch, Danielle could smell the enticing aroma of the pot roast, which made her stomach growl.

As she returned to the kitchen, she took one final look at her efforts. The table had never looked nicer.

The pièce de résistance was the small gift placed by Ethan's plate, along with a hand written note that said, *How would you like what comes with this for Christmas? Love, Me.*

She had a hard time keeping the news about the baby a secret from her friend, Wanda. When they were having lunch on that Friday, Wanda had said, "Dannie, there's something different about you today. I've tried to tell you several times about Blake's Little League game. You never heard a word. I want to know what's going on. Now, give."

"Wanda, I don't know what you mean," Danielle said, unable to keep a slight smile off her face.

"Okay, Dannie. If you don't want to share with your very best friend, then fine. You're not having an affair, are you?"

Danielle gave her a mock frown knowing what her friend was attempting. Wanda knew this would pique her friend. She knew how devoted Danielle was to Ethan. The bait did not work. Wanda left the lunch date in frustration.

She and Wanda were friends from the day they met. They fought, played, and grew up as adopted sisters. Although of different backgrounds, they found they liked the same things.

Danielle was tall with a slender build. She kept her shining, deep-chestnut hair styled in the sharp, sophisticated look of the forties. High cheekbones and full lips softened her angular face. Her eyes were the first thing people noticed. Almond-shaped, blue, framed by thick lashes, they exuded keen intelligence.

Wanda, on the other hand, was short and full figured, with a round face that bloomed in perpetual smiles. She kept her hair short, partly due to manageability, and partly because it complimented her looks. Her stubborn ginger-blonde hair remained in perpetual tight ringlets, no matter what.

Danielle and Wanda were opposites, yet closer than most sisters. Always there for each other, they shared a strong spiritual connection, walking in deep faith. The girls prayed for each other, one inexplicably knowing when the other was in need. This kept them both from many temptations over the years. Their strong beliefs brought them through the angst of puberty.

They complimented each other. Where Wanda was sassy and vivacious, Danielle tended to be more introverted, yet there was an underlying strength within both women.

They spent time with Aunt Hillie, baking, learning to sew, and other crafts. They also spent time fishing, or helping at the sheriff's office with Uncle Charles. They loved the intrigue there. Of course, with such a small town, most of the intrigue was borne out of their own imaginations. The three musketeers, Dannie, Wanda, and UncleCharles.

Danielle's much-loved Uncle Charles took his job as sheriff seriously. He often twisted his hat in his hands when he told a family bad news. Danielle came to recognize the habit over the years.

The day he sat in her living room, his hat turning in his hands, she knew something was terribly wrong.

Chapter 12

Danielle had just completed the final touches on the exquisite table setting she prepared for their special dinner.

"Thank You, Lord, that the worst is behind us," Danielle said.

With one final look, she answered a knock on the front door.

As she reached the front foyer, she could see through the paned glass door that it was her Uncle Charles. He had his hat in his hands, turning it around by the brim.

She felt such a sense of foreboding, a sense of panic so strong, she had to fight an overwhelming desire to run. Instead, she gushed as she opened the door.

"Uncle Charles, what a nice surprise! Come in, come in. I have a fresh pot of coffee ready. Sit down. I'll make you a cup."

Before he had a chance to protest, she dashed back into the kitchen, fixing his coffee while her shaking hands somehow managed the task. She was just bringing the coffee into the living room, when she had to get the door a second time. There stood Wanda, her face in a concentrated smile.

"Hello, Danielle," she said as she came in.

Danielle stood in the ensuing silence looking from one of her unwelcome visitors to the other. She began to prattle at a hysterical pace, knowing instinctively all this had to do with Ethan.

"I have some homemade apple pie," she offered in a shotgun style.

"I'd offer you a piece, but I'm saving it for Ethan. We have a special dinner planned. I'm going to give him some good news. Guess what? I'm pregnant. Now I need you two to go home, while I wait for Ethan. I want to tell him in private."

She did not hear Wanda repeating her name, until she practically shouted.

"Danielle!"

Danielle stood there staring at Wanda, then in a subconscious need to be close to Ethan, sat in his favorite chair. The kitchen towel once draped over her shoulder, now wrung in her hands.

"Dannie," Charles began. "I'm afraid I have some bad news for you."

Wanda walked over to Danielle and put her arm around her shoulder as she propped herself up on the arm of the chair.

He continued, finding it difficult not to cry.

"Danielle, Ethan was about thirty minutes out of Bridgeport when his car careened out of control on a patch of oil that spilled from a truck."

As Charlie spoke, Danielle began shaking her head back and forth, futilely trying to block out the unwanted information.

Charles cleared his throat. "He was coming home early. It happened last night. Danielle, I'm sorry. He didn't make it."

At the close of his report, Danielle stood and then promptly fainted. She did not remember Charles gently carrying her to the sheriff's car, being taken to the hospital, leaving Wanda to phone the doctor. She did not remember waking up, screaming Ethan's name, repeatedly. Nor did she remember the sedative given to her to calm her down. Overall, she slept for two days.

When she finally woke up, she began sobbing uncontrollably. Eventually, the sobs subsided into soft weeping. The news became stark reality, and she began to accept the fact that Ethan was dead.

She found out later that Ethan had been burned beyond recognition. According to the coroner, he died almost instantly.

~

The funeral was private. Danielle did not choose interment at the famed Arlington Cemetery. She chose the small town cemetery, honoring Ethan's request to keep him close. The military gave him full honors at the funeral, however. A twenty-one-gun salute made Danielle jump with each crack of the rifles, bringing home the finality of his death. Tears began streaming down her face as the bugler played *Taps*. As the soldier placed the now folded flag ceremoniously in her hands, she buried her tears in the red, white, and blue material.

Standing by his graveside, she wondered how she would survive without him. She placed her hand over her abdomen, knowing that at least she had part of Ethan with her.

~

Wanda pulled up in front of the house. The neglect she saw in Dannie's beloved yard worried her. Dannie was a stickler about her yard.

It never looked ramshackle. The front veranda had summer debris all over it. Dead leaves and dry grass had blown all over the porch. Some of the potted plants drooped miserably as though they had not seen water in days.

Wanda closed her car door then listened. Silence. This just was not right. Danielle always had some sort of music playing when she was home. Hurried steps took Wanda to the door. No answer. She tried the handle. Locked. Wanda headed to the back, hoping the back door would give her access. She needed to get inside. Something was wrong.

She found Danielle standing on the veranda, just staring off into space.

"Dannie, we've been worried about you."

"Wanda, you scared me. What do you want?" she asked flatly.

"Dannie, you've got to stop this. I know you--"

"Stop what," Danielle interrupted, "the fact that my life is over? Or is it that the love of my life is never coming home? Is it something else? Have I done something else?"

The lack of pain and emotion in Dannie's voice, the tight lines on her face, the dark circles under her eyes, wrenched Wanda's heart. She knew she was going to have to do something drastic to snap Dannie out of this. She said a silent prayer then continued.

"Dannie, we all loved Ethan. Do you think we aren't grieving too? You've abandoned everyone. You've stopped answering your phone. I can tell you're not eating. Dannie, how do you think Ethan would feel if he could see you like this?"

Danielle exploded. "Wanda, I don't want to hear it! Do you understand? I . . . just leave me alone. I want to die."

Trying not to cry, Wanda took a deep breath. She knew this was going to hurt.

"Okay, Dannie; fine. Go ahead and die. Just don't forget that when you die, you take Ethan's dream for a family with you. I'm leaving now. I won't stand by and watch this, do you hear me?"

Wanda started walking to the front of the house then she heard what sounded like an animal screaming. She ran back to where she'd left Danielle. There on the porch, Danielle lay in a heap, moaning in such a way that it was almost primal. Her grief had finally surfaced.

Wanda knelt beside the sobbing woman, gathered her into her arms, and held her. She stroked strands of hair from Dannie's tear-streaked face and rocked her gently in her embrace.

"It's okay, Sweetie. It's okay to cry." Wanda felt her own tears welling up in her eyes. She tried to quell them. "I know how much it hurts. Remember how you stayed with me during the worst when Blake died? I'm going to stay with *you* through the worst."

"W . . . what about Blake Jr.?" was all Danielle could manage.

"Don't worry. Mom will take Blake for a while. I'll be right here for as long as you need me." The air burned past the lump in her throat as she caught a deep breath. "We'll get through this, Dannie. I'll be right here."

Wanda lost it when Dannie sobbed into her shoulder, clinging to her.

"It . . . it's so unfair! Wh . . . why did Ethan have to die? I loved him so. Wanda, I don't know how I can go on. I miss him so much. I try to concentrate on other things, but I can't. I just can't. I . . . I don't kn . . . know if this pain will ever go aw . . . away."

Tears streaming down her own face, Wanda repeated soothingly, "It's okay. It will be okay. I'm here. I'm here." She continued rocking Dannie as she sobbed out her anger and grief.

Wanda arranged for her parents to take Little Blake for a few days and stayed with Danielle, caring for her, helping her through the roughest part of the grief. It brought back some of her grief over her own beloved Blake. Talking long into the night that first evening, Danielle shared memories, bittersweet, and cried some more.

"Wanda, we went through so much when he was a prisoner of war and then missing. I wish I could make sense of it all. Why? I pray to God and ask Him. I still have no answers."

"Dannie, I know. I went through the same thing over Blake. You have to give yourself some time to grieve. It *will* get better. I promise."

Wanda remained with Danielle until she began fighting back. She watched as a tiny spark of life came back into her best friend's eyes. Satisfied that Dannie was on the mend, she felt safe to leave, but not until she extracted a solemn promise from her to call if she needed her.

~

Danielle continued working at the medical manufacturer as long as allowed. At least she would not be alone so much in the big, empty house. She briefly thought of selling her beloved home.

She received a modest life insurance settlement after Ethan died, since the accident occurred during business and in a company car. She used enough of the settlement to pay off their loan on the car. That was the only debt they ever incurred. She put the rest into a trust fund for their baby's education.

Her boss, Mr. Donnelly, told her to take all the time she needed before coming back to work. She had an excellent rapport with him. He was a fair man, liberal in his viewpoint regarding women in the work force. She spoke to her boss at length about her need to keep working as long as possible, after she mentioned her pregnancy. He was very understanding.

"Mrs. Anderson. I'm so sorry about Ethan, especially after you went through so much during his military service. He was a very kind man and a reliable employee. If there's anything this company can do for you, please let us know. By the way, I'm glad you decided to return to work. I count on you a lot," he finished. He blushed then winced. "Maybe you don't know that. But, it's true."

It was what she needed to hear at that moment.

"Thank you, Mr. Donnelly. I won't let you down. I *will* want to return to work as soon as I am able, after the baby is born. In the meantime, you can count on me."

"Danielle, your job is here as long as you want it."

With her boss's understanding, Uncle Charles and Aunt Hilda's support, and Wanda's shoulder, she got through the next five months.

Chapter 13

Bridgeport, PA, 1950

The tree-lined rolling hills blazed with vivid fall colors as Danielle Anderson drove toward town. She normally took her time along this route, relishing the beauty of the season. The crisp air, the aroma of firewood, and the general feel of harvest; the grand finale of scarlet, bright yellows, burgundies, and fiery oranges, always lifted her spirits. Nature bristled with life, belying the fact it was preparing for a long winter's sleep.

Frustrated, Danielle paid little attention to the painted hills this morning, angry that she'd overslept again. She glanced at her watch. "Darnit. Twenty minutes late for my appointment."

Normally a light sleeper, she failed to hear her alarm this morning. This had happened several times lately. The doctor told her it was understandable since she had been under so much stress the first four months of her pregnancy. Her body was just trying to catch up.

The day began with cold rain accompanied by northerly breezes. Chills ripped through to Danielle's bones in spite of her heavy coat and warm sweater. Dark clouds promised snow soon would follow. She shivered and turned up the heater.

Danielle was so tired she drove her two-year-old Packard as if it were on automatic pilot. Looking around, she discovered she was on Main Street, near the doctor's office. She parked in front of the office located on the town square, fished a nickel out of her pocketbook and fed the nearby parking meter.

Danielle sat on the examination table, while Dr. Bowers wrote up his orders.

"Is there anything I need to stop doing, or eating?" Danielle asked.

The doctor turned his wheeled stool around. "Mrs. Anderson, you and the baby are fine. Just keep doing what I prescribed. Normal activity is fine. It's a good thing you already took a leave from work. You're going to need the rest."

"Thank you, Doctor."

After getting dressed, she handed the checkout slip to the nurse in the front office. "Doctor said one month."

The nurse looked at her schedule books. "How about November 15 at two o'clock?"

"That's fine." Danielle smiled. Turning on her heel, she left.

~

The nurse picked up the phone and dialed a number. A strange, soft voice answered with, "Identify and state your need."

"This is Operative four. The subject in question just left."

She listened to the voice on the other end. The chart was in front of her and she leafed through the pages. "Yes. She is *very* healthy." She listened for another moment. "Anything else you want me to find out?" A single monotone came through the wire. "All right. Operative Four out." She hung up.

~

Danielle headed back toward the farm.

The small life within her kicked. "Okay, Junior," she responded, caressing her swollen belly, "we'll stop and get a snack on the way home."

She wanted to give Ethan a son more than anything so she began using the moniker 'Junior' from the time she found out she was pregnant. Now it was her pet name for the child she longed for--her connection to Ethan.

She stopped at Latham's General Store nestled on the outskirts of town and purchased a small bag of homemade chocolate chip cookies and a pint of milk. These cravings were getting to be an everyday occurrence and Danielle could not resist the still-warm cookies. Mrs. Latham smiled indulgently, asked her about how she felt, when the baby was due and just general chitchat. Each time Danielle went into the store, it was the same conversation.

Danielle answered the older woman's questions as though answering for the first time. She liked the woman and did not want to hurt her feelings. Besides, she knew Mrs. Latham was dealing with her own loss over Ethan.

Danielle protested when Mrs. Latham refused to take any money for the cookies and milk, but the kind storeowner would not hear of it.

"Mrs. Anderson, I wouldn't feel right if I charged you after all Ethan did to help us after Mr. Latham had his stroke."

Danielle glanced at the reinforced grocery shelves that Ethan had fixed only weeks before his death. He had always volunteered for those who could not do minor repairs. She gave in and prepared to leave.

"Mrs. Latham, thank you for the milk and cookies. I'll talk to you soon. Have a nice day."

"You too, dear. Stay warm now and take care of yourself."

"I will and you do the same."

Danielle stepped outside the store, noticing a drop in temperature. She rubbed her stomach and commented, "Looks like we'll need a nice warm fire for tonight, Junior. It's getting colder."

~

The man appeared ordinary. Dressed in bib overalls, he blended in with the farmers. He watched her from the cab of his old Ford. In the truck bed, a tarp covered what appeared to be hay. When he saw her drive out of the parking lot, he walked to the pay phone and dialed a local number.

His boss answered on the first ring.

"I saw her," the man at the store said.

"Is she alone?" the disembodied male voice inquired.

"Yes."

"Does everything appear normal?"

"Yes, sir."

"We do it now. We do not have much time. Is everything in place?" he finished.

"Everything is ready," the farmer confirmed.

The farmer got into the truck and took off in the same direction as his quarry.

~

Danielle ate her cookies on the way home. She took her time now during the short drive, drinking in the beauty of her surroundings. She rolled her window down and breathed in the scent of burning leaves and the rich smell of freshly turned earth. The cookies accentuated the scents coming through her window. She gazed at rolling hills and farmland. In the spring and right before harvest, the fields resembled a huge patchwork quilt; stitched rows of rich-brown furrowed earth, intermingled with flaming reds, autumn-wheat, and gold. Now, the fields were merely an echo of their former glory.

Danielle slowed down to watch several farmers far out in the center of one of the fields. They loaded hay bales onto a wagon to take to the barns in preparation for the long, hard winter.

She continued on her way home. She came upon a sharp curve, slowing to make the turn, when her tire blew out. A skilled driver, she pulled over to the shoulder of the road without incident. She sat there for a while, pondering her options.

She definitely could not change the tire herself, and this road seldom had traffic during this time of day. She could not walk the three miles to where she saw the farmers gathering the hay. Even if she did walk back there, they were so far out in the field they would not hear her calling, and most likely would not see her.

Danielle resolved to wait it out, hoping and praying someone might happen along.

~

Someone knocked on her door, but no, they were knocking on a window and they would not stop.

"Go away and let me sleep," her dazed mind pleaded. The knocking persisted, along with a man's voice, urging her to wake up. As the last vestiges of sleep faded away, she remembered she was in her car, realizing why she felt cold; she had turned the motor off automatically when she pulled onto the shoulder and had fallen asleep.

Once her mind cleared, she found herself staring into the bluest eyes she'd ever seen. They complimented his salt-and-pepper hair, smooth face, and olive, sun-darkened complexion. At the moment, he wore a concerned expression. When he spoke, he showed a set of even, white teeth.

"Madame, are you all right?"

He spoke with a vague, British accent.

"Yes, yes, I--I'm fine. I just got a little cold sitting here. I must have dozed off."

She opened the car door, getting out with difficulty. She was a little stiff from sitting in the same position for so long. He solicitously took her arm and helped her, holding on to her until she felt steady.

Outside the car, she realized it was much colder than when she left Latham's store. She wrapped her coat tighter around her.

"I am Doctor Stephan Fieldgreave."

He pronounced it Steff-'an.

"I am a veterinarian and was on my way to the Sanduski farm to administer some antibiotic shots to a few sick cattle."

"My name is Danielle Anderson, Dr. Fieldgreave. Thank you for stopping."

"You are most welcome, Mrs. Anderson. You are very fortunate that I traveled this way, or you might have had a very long wait. Especially on this road. I will be most willing to change your flat. I am not adept at it, but I can complete the task."

"Thank you again," Danielle said gratefully. "And I hope I don't make you late to the Sanduski farm. I know them and hate to think I might make them wait for you," Danielle added.

"No problem at all, dear lady. I am sure when I inform them that I was assisting you, they will completely understand. Allow me to assist you to my car. I have left the motor running with the heater on. I also have a thermos of hot chocolate. Please, warm up a bit, and help yourself to the thermos bottle." His voice was very deep, authoritative, yet quite soothing.

"Thank you. I don't know what I would have done if you hadn't come along."

She felt warm air circle out to clutch her as he opened his door.

Through the windshield, she saw a light flurry of snowflakes spin earthward. As she drank her hot chocolate, she watched him struggle to get the tire off the wheel. Her rescuer was right. He had little experience with such matters. So unlike Ethan, who was adept with everything he did, she thought. She stopped and willed her mind to concentrate on her immediate surroundings.

She studied the car's interior. The rich cherry steering wheel glistened with clear finish. The matching dashboard, the luxuriant smell of the leather seats made stronger by mink oil, all spoke of opulence and wealth. It was not something a typical country vet would own.

Danielle emitted a deep aching yawn. At first, she attributed her sleepiness to the combination of the warm car and the hot chocolate. She kept looking at the man changing her tire. He began to blur.

As the empty cup slipped out of her right hand, her other hand instinctively covered her belly in an effort to somehow protect her unborn child, realizing the hot chocolate contained drugs.

"Please, God! Don't let my baby die," Danielle murmured before sinking into blackness.

Chapter 14

An old farm truck drove up behind the doctor's car. The man who had been watching Danielle at Latham's, walked toward the doctor's car and looked inside. She was out like a light. He continued to Danielle's car, watching the doctor deftly finish tightening the lugs.

"Is she out?" the doctor asked without looking up.

"Yep."

When Fieldgreave finished, he rose up and looked into the eyes of the farmer in the bib overalls.

"You know what you are to do, yes?"

"Yes. Her house will burn down nicely."

"You brought the cadaver, then?" the doctor inquired, frowning.

"It's in the back, under the tarp. She's still real frozen, too."

"That won't matter in a while. Is she the same height?"

"Yes."

"She has the same hair color, the same stage of pregnancy?"

"Yes, sir."

"I did not see the farmers working in the field as I drove through. I trust they will not be returning any time soon?"

"No, sir, they won't. Don't worry. They're busy trying to save a burning barn. Hay caught on fire from a lantern left lit."

Doctor Fieldgreave marveled at the English slang Americans used, yet it amused him. He learned the King's English in a school run by British missionaries. Israel was still a British colony then.

His mother made sure he learned his lessons well. Growing up in Jerusalem with a strict father who became Messianic when Stephan was ten, made Stephan's life interesting, as his father often assisted the missionaries.

He was by nature and rearing, a patient and compassionate man. Yet, when it came to tasks like this, he became very brusque. It was really a way of protecting himself from some of the things he had to do.

"Very well, then. Let us proceed," he ordered. "Just make sure the victim is burned beyond recognition," he reminded him.

They transferred Danielle to the backseat of Fieldgreave's sleek Mercury and covered her with a travel blanket.

The man in the overalls got into Danielle's car and proceeded to the Anderson farm.

Fieldgreave followed him. They reached Danielle's home in a short time. They were there for no more than half an hour.

Danielle's home, being in such a rural area would prove to work well for the two men. The volunteer fire department was quite far from the farming community. Without another exchange of words, they parted ways. Doctor Fieldgreave turned his car around and then headed back toward the highway--away from Bridgeport.

Chapter 15

He watched her sleep, resisting the urge to caress her face. Wondering if she would accept him, he went over what he decided to tell her. *Everything.* Would she believe him?

~

Danielle woke, disoriented; a vague, groggy headache dulled her senses. As her eyes focused in the shadowy corner, she found herself staring at a wall. Both hands flew to her swollen belly. The life within her stirred, and relief streamed down her face. She and Junior were safe--at least for the moment. She felt the soft wool blanket over her. Someone wanted her comfortable. Still, that act of compassion did not ease her mind.

She was not sure if she was alone, where she was, or why the man wanted her. She imagined all kinds of horrible scenarios, and with difficulty, reined her thoughts under control. *I have to think clearly,* she thought to herself. I *have to protect my baby at all costs.*

She continued to lie still, listening for any movement or stirring. Other than the unmistakable sounds of logs crackling in a fireplace, she heard nothing. After about five minutes, she cautiously turned over and discovered she was lying on a comfortable chaise lounge situated near the fireplace.

She got up gingerly, finding it difficult from the combination of the drug and her disorientation. She found herself alone in what appeared to be a modern, private hunting lodge.

The lodge's enormous great room possessed huge support beams fashioned with logs; stripped of their bark and stained, they ran the length of the middle. A sizeable marble hearth accentuated the immense fireplace at a shorter wall. Several closed doors lined the longer wall. She assumed those were bedrooms.

"All right, Dannie Girl. Think." She knew she was alone, at least for now. She had no idea when or even if the man would come back. As she noticed the skins and various stuffed animals that adorned the other shorter wall, another surge of panic made her queasy.

What if he has left me here and isn't going to come back?

"Okay, get a grip!"

On sheer willpower, Danielle managed to calm herself down enough to explore the lodge. With all due caution, she opened each of the three doors. The first door opened up into a large bedroom with a sitting area. The room sported muted brown, tan, and burgundy. The interior held an aura of masculine virility.

The second door led to a very spacious bathroom, complete with a dressing table. There was a small stool, upholstered in rich burgundy velour in front of it. A luxurious tub took up the entire length of the bathroom's back wall.

The third door led into a duplicate floor plan of the first bedroom. The powerful wood panels softened under the pale blues, mauves, and white decorations. A faint, lingering aroma of lilac permeated the interior. It was definitely a woman's room.

She explored the kitchen, separated from the rest of the great room by a huge bar. The kitchen housed generous cabinets, a large stove, and a modern Frigidaire. The table was large, with comfortable chairs. She discovered an ample food supply, both in the cabinets, and the icebox.

Danielle knew one thing for sure. Someone planned a lengthy stay in this lodge. This made her even more nervous.

"Well, I won't starve to death; at least for now," she spoke aloud, her voice sounding strange and hollow to her ears.

She discovered no telephones, which added salt to her already raw nerves. She went to the front door, discovering it unlocked. She then checked all the windows. They opened easily.

Whoever kidnapped me must be confident I won't try to leave, she thought to herself.

Danielle went back to the kitchen. On the stove, she found a percolator on the back burner. She felt the pot and it was cold. Danielle took the lid off and peered into it. It was clean and empty. She filled it, and after finding a container of Maxwell House grounds in the cupboard, started some coffee, making it a little stronger than normal. She avoided coffee during her pregnancy because it gave her indigestion, but she needed it now to stave off the grogginess from the drug, and to relieve the headache that threatened to come on full force. Besides, she felt the need to do something routine to try to restore the sanity that threatened to flee.

She made a trip to the bathroom while the coffee perked. She used the bathroom, washed her hands, and then splashed her face in cold water. Once she finished, she felt a little better. When she got back to the kitchen, the coffee was beginning to boil. She fixed her coffee then turned the burner down to simmer the coffee. She sipped on the warm liquid, allowing it to clear her head. Venturing over to the big picture window in the living area, she gazed once again at her surroundings. She thought perhaps she could recognize where she was.

She, Uncle Charles, and Aunt Hilda used to go exploring in the mountains surrounding Bridgeport almost every weekend. They were avid fans of the outdoors. The Sykes's taught her how to recognize different mountain peaks, natural landmarks and how to remain oriented to compass directions by following the sun. Even in the dead of winter, she could find her way out.

Danielle spent many summers exploring the areas alone, so she knew the mountains well. She even worked during the summers in one of the church-run camps. She never took in money due to the depression, but the barter system worked very well for the Sykes family. It afforded them some of the necessities they might otherwise go without. The camp catered to some of the children of well-to-do families that escaped the hardships of the Depression, so it always housed ample supplies.

As she looked out onto the snow-covered plateau, she knew she must be far from home. She did not recognize anything. The clouds, gray and heavy with snow, obscured the sun. Compass points would be difficult to establish under the circumstances.

She went back into the kitchen. As she sat there sipping the strong brew, she tried to formulate some kind of plan to save herself and Junior. By this time, her sharp common sense, coupled with the primitive instinct to protect her baby, gave her amazing clarity, and allowed her to think.

Should I try to reason with this man? She thought. *Should I scream? Even if I did scream, no one would hear me. How could I get out of here? What if he comes in and makes me take more drugs? Even if he didn't force more drugs on me, there's no way I could walk down these mountains and survive in my condition if I did get out the door. Still,* she thought, *I couldn't find my way out of here even if I could. If he comes back in a car, could I conceivably knock him out with something?*

She looked at the poker near the fireplace wondering if he would miss it. She decided she could not take a chance on that, knowing that as long as kept her wits about her, she held a better chance of coming out alive. The last thing she wanted was to provoke him.

She had to face facts--she was stuck with no way out, subject to whatever he planned. She could not allow her thoughts to go there again.

"Oh, God, please help me!" she prayed aloud.

Here Danielle sat, no one knowing where she was, not even missing her yet. How long would it be before they missed her? She had not yet given notice to Mr. Donnelly that she was taking a leave of absence in two weeks. This gave her some comfort.

Still, she knew she was in trouble, even though Uncle Charles would be combing the countryside, looking for her. The thought of Uncle Charles looking for her gave her some added strength. She knew once he found out she was missing, he would leave no stone unturned until he found her.

She walked back over to the window, looking out at the white snow, pure, clean. She felt dirty, scared, and still somewhat lethargic. This last condition, she attributed to the drug Fieldgreave gave her. Not knowing what the man gave her worried her for her baby. It was the only thing she had left of Ethan.

"Oh, Ethan! Why did you have to leave me so soon?" She buried her face in her hands, grieving anew for her late husband. She missed him so much. Her bed felt so big, so empty without him beside her.

"I had no choice, Dannie Girl."

Chapter 16

She heard no one come in, she was so lost in her own thoughts.

At the sound of the familiar voice, she whirled around and there, very much alive and breathing, stood Ethan Winthrop Anderson, a load of firewood in his arms.

She startled when he dropped the load of wood.

For a time, she stood riveted to the spot. Thoughts whirled in her head so fast that she could not sort through them. That, mingled with a dizzy spell, threatened to make her faint.

She gave in to her first instinct and threw herself in his arms, drinking in the smell of him that, until now, she'd only dreamed. His scent, the faint smell of his aftershave, mingled with the smell of winter that lingered on him, was real once again. Her tears of joy soaked his jacket as she held on tightly to him.

Ethan eased back just a little, looking at the woman he'd fallen in love with. He touched her silky hair, now grown out a bit, stroked her soft skin.

They stood embraced in each other's arms for what seemed a long time. Suddenly, the impact his living presence hit her like a punch in the stomach.

She wrenched herself free from his embrace, putting a little distance between them.

"Ethan, do you have *any* idea what you put me through these last five months? How could you just pretend to die on me? To think of what we went through during the war . . . what you went through . . . all that happened. What, *what*? Do you want the settlement the company awarded me? Is there some problem you didn't tell me about? How could you do this to us, to our *baby*?"

She paused, waiting to see if he would give her excuses. He remained silent.

She continued.

"You had me drugged. Did you not care? Our baby may be damaged from whatever it was your partner thought might be okay to slip me," she accused scathingly.

"Ethan, this is the most unforgivable thing you could have done to me. How *could* you do this?"

She finally stopped, expending all the energy that gathered in her body, replaced by such a deep sense of hurt, betrayal and sadness; she did not think she would ever feel anything again. She fought an overwhelming urge to hit him. She balled her hands into fists to keep from following through.

~

Ethan cleared his throat. As she looked at him, the deep hurt he saw there tore at his very soul. He loathed himself right at that moment for having to do this to her. Maybe she would understand when he explained everything that had happened. Would she believe him when he hardly believed it himself?

Believe me! Oh God! I don't even believe it, and it happened to me! He thought dejectedly. Yet he knew he would have to make her believe him, somehow. It was for her protection and their baby's protection as well. It made him physically ill to think of what Tanas could or would do to their precious baby if they got their hands on it. When he learned of her pregnancy, he'd hoped she would miscarry. Even now, he had no idea what effects his ordeal would have on the child.

He slammed his fist into his other hand, feeling the sharp sting.

Her reaction to him slamming his fist made Ethan wince even more, as she stepped back from him, perhaps afraid he would strike her next. He saw the fear in her face as she looked at his hands. He dropped them to his side, wondering if they would ever--could ever--go back to the way things were before.

In a soft, gentle tone, Ethan asked her to sit down at the table with him.

Reluctantly, she sat.

"Danielle," Ethan began as he sat opposite her. "I would like for you to hear me out, please. If, after I tell you my story, you want to leave, you'll be free to go. I won't stop you. However, please, hear me out. Please!"

~

Danielle looked at him, her love for him battling with the fresh hurt that wanted to blot him out of her life forever. She thought it over. Knowing she was a captive audience for the moment, she might as well listen to what he had to say, then she and her baby would be out of his life. He would stay dead to her and Junior, she decided.

"All right, Ethan. I'll listen to you," she said flatly, folding her arms defensively across her chest. "But first, I need assurance from you that whatever that *quack* of a doctor gave me won't hurt the baby."

She sat waiting, contempt prominent in her eyes.

"I promise, Danielle. There is no way I would ever hurt you or our baby. What I'm trying to do now, is save you both."

Chapter 17

"Danielle, I did go to Europe. I was a prisoner of war in an awful place. I had been there for about six months. I was suffering from malnutrition, dysentery, and body and head lice. I was so sick. One day, a group of men from our side came to trade prisoners. They chose me and five other POW's. I was so relieved at the time I couldn't stop crying.

"They took me to an Allied base in France, where I recovered from all of the repercussions of being a prisoner of war. I felt like I was in heaven, but I just couldn't understand why I was picked when there were men with wives and children who needed them at home. I had you, but no children and no other family to speak of. I found out later that was exactly why they *did* pick me."

Ethan began to tell her a story that was so unbelievable, it was only fit for a science fiction novel.

~

Occupied Europe--Luft (Stalag) 1

The permeating chill emitting from the compound as his armed escorts shoved he and the others across the camp nearly froze Ethan's blood. After arrival, the German 'hosts' hauled the men to a mass shower room, forced them to strip, then line up against the wall. The shower with a high-pressure fire hose and subsequent delousing proved more humiliating than nudity. By the time they finished with him, muscular bruises, which did not reach the skin, striped his body like underground whip marks. He tried to obey the guards, but their jabbered English came across as grunts and barks; dog-like sounds. But he was the dog.

"Auchtung! Schnell!"

He understood the tone clear enough. "Pay attention. Haul your ass!"

Ethan fought heartsickness for three days before caving in emotionally to a zombie-like state of existence. Looking at the long-term prisoners proved to be another downfall in the beginning. Their vacant stares, bruises, contusions, leaking sores, and emaciated conditions haunted Ethan. Some of the POW's just gave up. Others were bitter. Some gave up the will to live. As a result, many of them died.

Every six months, the captors ordered small beds, flowers, and pastries brought in. The POW's knew not to touch the pastries, however. This was the signal that the Geneva inspectors would be there soon.

The Geneva people soon left. Their curiosity all seemed innocent then. Ethan was to find out years later that Tanas employed several 'Geneva' as scouts to find appropriate subjects. When the Geneva committee left, so did the small comforts. The visits at least afforded him hot showers and allowed him to shave.

Ethan learned his lessons at the end of a Nazi riding crop. Neither he--nor anyone else--said anything negative about the camp no matter how bad it was. As a result, he learned to dance a bizarre minuet of *Wills and Wiles* with his taskmasters.

He remembered another POW. Michael Barringer, Private First Class, arrived three months after Ethan. The camps prohibited any religious material, despite the Geneva Convention authorization. Regardless, PFC Barringer prayed and quoted scripture from memory.

Ethan had attended church his entire life, yet did not sense in himself the intimate relationship with the Lord that Michael seemed to possess. Most of the time, the young man broke the silence by his emotion-filled voice as he spoke of the promises of God out of Psalms or Hebrews. Throughout the long nights as Ethan listened, he developed a better commitment to God because of Michael. An odd sense of comfort began to prevail that God knew some great plan for him that he did not understand.

Ethan continued. "I started praying to God, inspired by Michael Barringer. I began to feel an unusual peace in spite of the circumstances. I will never forget him. Dannie, Michael was turned in by someone in our camp, for his beliefs, but we never found out who the traitor was. He was tortured for three days before he died. They kept after him to deny God. He died, calling for Jesus to take him home.

"We were all forced to watch every day. It was a living Hell before *our* side rescued me. After I recovered from my illnesses, they sent me to another base. At first I thought I was going to come home. I was filling out all the paperwork, being de-briefed, and talking to the Army psychiatrist. I found out later they had told you I was a POW; that you thought that was where I was until two weeks after D-Day."

Ethan watched Danielle's eyes widen.

"Yes, Dannie," he said, "I was recently informed of a lot of things by some very important contacts. These people infiltrated the place where they sent me, though I wasn't aware of it yet. Dannie, do you remember Hitler's ultimate goal?"

He continued without expecting a response.

"It was to produce a super human race; a race of men, specifically, as the most powerful army in the world. He wanted to conquer the world. Well, our side wanted to beat him, or for that matter, beat *anyone* who tried.

"You remember when I finally came home there was a blank spot in my memory? I couldn't remember my time 'Missing in Action'. No matter how hard we tried, I never could reach it."

Ethan could see the growing skepticism on her face.

"Danielle."

He said her name in such a way that for the first time since her tirade of anger, she really looked up into his eyes. Ethan knew she would be shocked.

"Oh my God, Ethan, your eyes! Is this some sort of trick?"

"No, Danielle. It isn't. They did this to me--to us."

As she stared at him, he willed his eyes back to normal.

"I used to not be able to control it, Dannie. It came mostly when I experienced emotional stress. I've learned since to control it very well."

At her speechlessness, Ethan continued.

"I was a big part of an experiment! This experiment is bigger than anyone knows, Dannie. Bigger than Hitler, bigger than anything this world has ever seen. Don't you understand?" he pleaded as he saw the look on her face. "You saw my eyes, Dannie. It's part of the reason they set up plans to kidnap you. They found out you were carrying my child."

He ran his hand through his hair then rubbed his hands over his face in exhaustion. He grew quiet.

~

Danielle fought a no-win battle of emotions, ranging from disbelief to sheer terror as the ramifications of his last statement pierced her already overwhelmed brain.

She finally found her voice.

"What are you saying, Ethan? That they . . . that our baby . . . that they want our child?" she asked incredulously. She jumped up from her chair and began pacing.

"What did they do to you, Ethan? How did they manage to do that to your eyes? Ethan, did you know all this before we began trying to have a baby?"

"No! I told you, a lot of the information didn't come to me until recently, in the last months. In fact, I only found out two weeks before my unfortunate *accident* occurred. I had no idea you were pregnant. As for my eyes, I'm trying to lead up to that, Dannie."

She looked at him, slowly shaking her head as she rested her hands protectively around her middle.

He exploded, making her jump. "Look, Dannie, I knew we tried many times to have a baby, with no success, so when I discovered . . ." He sighed. "Let me back up and tell you the rest of   it, up to and including how the plan for my death came about."

Chapter 18

1945, Wyoming, USA

"When they brought me back to the states, as I said before, I was debriefed. They sent me back to Francis E. Warren Air Force Base, in Cheyenne, Wyoming. There, a committee approached me who I thought were military, requesting volunteers for a *special* assignment which they said would only last for one year at the most. For participation in this assignment, they promised bonuses, which equaled three years' pay. It was hard to turn that down. All I could think of was that when I came home, we could fulfill some of our dreams.

"There were a total of twelve men, including me. We were transferred to this god-awful place, in the desert. The thought of earning so much money in such a short time was appealing. I had you in mind when I took it on."

"Didn't you wonder why I never contacted you?" Danielle inquired.

"No. They assured us they contacted any family members that needed to know. They said you understood that there could be no contact during the assignment, and you were assured we would never be in any danger for this."

Ethan continued. "Part of the trip to the assignment site they called a 'blackout' trip. We had no idea where we were going. They either painted or closed the windows in the military transport plane. I couldn't tell. They even took our watches from us. When we got there, they herded us into a bus with windows blackened the same way. The plane landed in a closed hanger, so we still could not tell where we were.

"It took several hours, from my calculations, to get to our final destination. The last few minutes of our trip, I could swear we were going in a downward spiral. I didn't find out until just a few months ago that we were."

~

The bus had only twelve passengers, all soldiers. The commanding officer who accompanied them on this leg of their journey got up and addressed the men.

"As you all know, upon accepting this assignment, it is on a 'need to know' basis, due to National Security. We'll take you off the bus, one at a time upon arrival, due to the sensitivity of this mission. This does not guarantee your participation. This is merely the preliminary. If they don't select you to remain, we'll take you back to Warren Air Force Base in Cheyenne, Wyoming. From there, you will prepare to muster out of the military with full honors, although, as you know, you won't get the bonus.

"You must all pass a physical, which will be extensive, and may require a number of days to complete. We chose you according to your records and actions in this war. If you have any doubts about participating, now is the time to say so. Are there any questions?"

None of the men spoke up. They were all ready to serve on home soil after the bitter and mercurial climate in the POW camp. Little did they know they had marched into something far worse than even Hitler could have dreamed.

All twelve passed the physicals and were now on their way to what they were told was guard duty at an experimental base, set up, 'somewhere in the desert'. The duties would include watch, with orders to 'shoot to kill' if anyone breached the perimeter limits. They were eager to go. Ethan remembered nothing about the next two years.

He knew he needed to wait before he told her about his ordeal in the desert. Ethan skipped ahead to how his *accident* was set up.

~

Ethan traveled to Washington, D.C. to go over an order for the VA hospital located there. There was some sort of mix-up with some of the critical surgical instruments they had ordered. The hospital contacted him at work. Since he had to go there anyway, he made it a point to work the VA hospital's psychiatrist into his schedule.

He arrived in D.C. toward evening, checked into a nearby motel, and then set up an appointment for early the next morning with the supply supervisor to try to straighten things out. He also made an appointment with Fieldgreave.

"Wait, Ethan. Fieldgreave is a psychiatrist?" Dannie interjected.

"Dannie, yes. He saved my memory. I'll explain more about him later." Ethan continued.

During the night he experienced horrific nightmares, some of which he refused to reveal to Danielle, even though she asked.

He left early enough the next morning to have breakfast before his appointment. When he got there, he met with Fieldgreave.

"Dannie," Ethan explained, "I had nightmares a lot even after the counseling sessions. I never let you know, because I knew you would worry. I wanted to know just what these nightmares were. They seemed so real, yet bizarre at the same time.

"Dannie, one night after waking from one, I went into the bathroom to wash my face. What I saw in the mirror scared me. This was just a few months before my accident; the same thing you saw earlier, Dannie. Anyway, Dr. Fieldgreave is the one who helped me remember everything that happened during my assignment. He hypnotized me, bringing it all back.

"Dr. Fieldgreave shared the sessions he recorded while I was under hypnosis," Ethan continued. "What we began was a sort of reverse debriefing sessions, so I would know what I needed to do before we had any children. Only it all came out after it was too late. Dannie, I promise, I never meant to hurt you.

"We only found out about your pregnancy after some of our people reported unusual activity from some of Tanas's agents who were especially focused on you. Did you know that your doctor's nurse was one of them?"

Dannie shook her head, and then shook it again. "One of 'them'. You make it sound like that science fiction book, 'War of the Worlds'."

Ethan knew she could not handle it if she knew how close to the truth she was.

"I think I've said enough for now, Dannie."

"I am much stronger than you think, Ethan," she said in a monotone. "But you're right. I am very tired. I . . . I think I'd like to take a nap, if you don't mind."

"I understand," Ethan sighed, feeling helpless. "You can use the bedroom. It will be much more comfortable than the chaise you were on."

She turned, looked at him, and then went into the bedroom without another word. Ethan sat at the table, drinking yet another cup of coffee.

He knew somehow, something had died in Danielle. He did not know if she would ever get it back.

As was his custom for quite some time now, after pushing the lukewarm coffee away, he knelt down on his knees and prayed for the woman he loved so much--and the child he had longed for.

~

Doctor Fieldgreave drove with purpose. He wanted to get to Ethan and Danielle as soon as possible. Even though the road to the lodge was barely more than a trail, he navigated it with expertise, even in the snow.

Ethan had no idea how long he had remained in deep prayer when he heard a car approach the lodge. As Ethan looked out the window, he saw Stephan bound from the car. He knew it wasn't the desire to get into the warmth, but something more urgent.

Ethan met him at the door.

"What's wrong, Stephan?" Ethan asked.

"I want to take you and your wife to a place in Wisconsin. A farm owned by a couple who are good friends of mine. They are, so far, unknown to anyone else. I heard through chatter that they are pulling all the stops to try to locate you. Ethan, if they find *you* they will also find your wife."

"How much time do we have, Stephan?"

"By my calculations, and from what I have heard, we have no more than twenty-four hours."

"Surely they couldn't find us here, Stephan," Ethan said.

"That is dreaming, my friend. Besides Ethan, your wife should be somewhere safe as the birth of your baby draws closer. She is strong enough to travel for now, and this place is not the best place for her to give birth--or for them to discover you both. Where *is* your wife, Ethan?"

"She went to lie down. She's absorbed a lot of information, and I haven't even touched the surface of what's going on. I'm afraid to tell her too much. I don't want her to lose the baby."

"Nor do we, Ethan. Nor do we."

Ethan knew the double meaning of his statement and shuddered at the thought of his son or daughter becoming their human guinea pig. Even knowing God was on their side did not allay his concern for his wife and child.

"Oh, God, my Father!" His heart cried out. "Please protect them from our enemies!"

~

Danielle was trying to find her baby, but didn't know where to look. She was asking people if they had seen her baby, but no one could help her. She found herself in a desert. The terrain provided no sense of direction. The people she was meeting in the desert seemed catatonic, yet seemed to move under a power not their own.

The first woman she met approached her. She seemed to be staring at Danielle, yet not really seeing her. The woman carried what appeared to be a Bible of some sort. On its front cover, the word Tanas, engraved in gold, was in the center.

"Ma'am, have you seen my baby?"

The woman refused to speak to her. She kept repeating a mantra. Danielle tried to get close enough to hear her whispered words, but a huge wind pushed her away.

The next person was an older man, apparently traveling with his wife and their three children. Like the older woman, they too, carried the strange book.

Another passed her by, this time a well-known movie star. Next, a man came who appeared to be a preacher. Many were following him, all of them with the same book.

She watched them as they all traveled, alone, yet together in the same direction.

Once again, she was crying out for help to find her baby when she saw what she thought was a baby carriage in the distance. She began running toward it. As she got closer, she saw more. Lying in front of the buggy was a huge dragon.

As she stopped, the dragon reared up on its hind legs. His head was large, with the same eyes she had seen in Ethan. The iridescent-green scales rippled in the dry, desert heat. His odor was a mixture of sulphur, smoke, and rotting flesh. His forked tongue slithered in and out as he spoke.

"What do you want?" it asked. "Have you come to see the thing we have created?"

One cold, smooth claw took her hand and brought her forward to see her baby. She wanted to jerk her hand away, run in the opposite direction, but morbid curiosity, along with something she couldn't quite get, held her in the dragon's grasp.

As she got closer, she became frightened, not afraid of the dragon, but afraid of this child. She knew she should not fear her own child, but she shuddered. She tried to back away, not wanting to see what she bore. Danielle knew she could never love this creature.

The dragon held her, brought her closer. As they stood before the buggy, she tried to free herself but he forced her head down, closer to the baby covered with a blanket. He reached down and uncovered it.

What she saw was hideous. The child had green eyes with the same serpentine slit. Atop its head were two tiny nubs where horns would eventually grow. Its skin was scaly, shimmering with the same iridescence that the dragon wore. Its tiny wails sounded more like the screaming of a banshee. One small-clawed hand reached toward the source of food--her breasts.

Her scream was primordial, savage.

Someone shook her violently. Was she in the dragon's mouth? She struggled against the sensation.

"Dannie. Dannie!"

She focused her eyes, seeing Ethan's face. The real Ethan. She finally escaped the terrible nightmare.

As Ethan watched the glazed look in her eyes fade, he spoke. "You were screaming." He longed to comfort her, but somehow he knew he was the cause of her nightmare. He just stood there, aching to hold her.

Since their initial embrace, a thick, pea-soup tension between them remained. They were strangers, yet oddly connected at the same time.

Ethan finally left the room.

~

Danielle could not go back to sleep. She kept seeing the dragon *and* that baby. She shuddered again.

Danielle knew she loved Ethan, but *who--what*--was he *now*? He looked like Ethan; he smelled like Ethan, yet something inside him had transformed him into a total stranger--maybe even a monster. Could she ever trust him again? How could their lives ever be normal after what they had been through over the past couple of years, after what he had told her--after what he had become?

Would they have to live on the run like fugitives? How could they possibly raise a child in any semblance of normalcy in their situation? Would these unknown forces snatch their child away anyhow; this strange group of obviously powerful people? What could she do? What could Ethan do? Was he simply insane? If he were, would he ever let her go? Would he harm their child? Did she even *want* this child?

She knew deep down inside that Ethan was not insane--at least, she hoped not. He appeared sane, yet only God knew what he had survived during his time in the POW camp and the years following. She pictured him demanding his husbandly rights. She ran to the bathroom and vomited, shivering uncontrollably.

For the first time in her life, Danielle entertained thoughts of suicide. She actually thought of killing herself and the baby, just to avoid what they might have to go through. As she sat on the floor in front of the toilet, she decided.

She stood up and peered into the medicine cabinet. There, she found a razor blade. She sat down on the toilet seat, looking from the razor to her wrist. She made the decision. In one smooth slice, she watched the blood flow, and it began to pool beneath her.

"Lord God, please forgive me," she said as she slipped away.

~

Ethan and Stephan were talking about Danielle's condition.

Ethan bathed her face with a warm washcloth, while Fieldgreave checked the bandages on her wrist.

"Stephan, I need to confess something. I secretly hoped she would lose the baby once I found out she was pregnant. I feel like such a monster."

"What happened to you was not your fault, my friend. What is done is done. However, I am not certain she will survive labor and delivery of this child while in such a state of shock. Perhaps once we are out of this lodge and with my friends, she will come out of this."

"Stephan, I hate myself right now for everything I've put her through. I worried that this would be too much for her to handle."

"Ethan, the mind is able to do amazing things in order to assimilate information that is too much to accept. She will eventually come out of this. I know she will."

"Well, I'm not sure what she will do once she finds out that her Uncle Charles and Aunt Hilda think she's dead."

"Ethan, remember--with God, all things are possible."

Chapter 19

Charles could not believe it when the fire marshal told him about Danielle. He just would not believe it. Not Danielle. Not after all she went through. Was God angry with her entire family for some reason? What really boggled his mind was the fact that he had completely serviced her heater and furnace in the fall. Could she have . . . ? No. He could not go there, either. He knew she had too much faith to do something like that. His sleuth-like mind began turning the possibilities over.

The fire marshal spoke to Charles. "Charlie, our initial investigation indicates a gas leak as the likely cause of the explosion. Her body was almost impossible to find at first. The explosion was severe. When we finally found her, she was so badly burned she was unrecognizable. We're pretty certain she died from smoke inhalation, but we won't know the results until the autopsy. I'm afraid the final identification won't be for quite some time. We'll need to send for her dental records in order to make a firm ID, Charlie."

"Jacob, she never went to a dentist. We could never afford that. I'll identify her myself."

Jacob Potter was beside himself. His close association with Charles made his task all the more difficult.

When Hilda heard the news, her body shook with grief. She had loved Danielle so much. She couldn't believe she was gone. "Charlie, I just talked to her a week ago. How could she be gone so fast? This isn't fair!"

Hilda remembered their final conversation.

~

"Aunt Hilda, you know when Junior is born," she said rubbing her belly, "he's going to call you Grandma, and Uncle Charles, Grandpa. After all," she had continued, "you *are* the only grandparents he will ever know."

"Oh, Dannie, I would be honored to be a grandmother to him or her!"

"Aunt Hilda, I want a boy so I can name him after Ethan."

"Charles would dote on him, Danielle, that's for sure," Hilda said humorously.

"I miss Ethan so much," Danielle sighed. "I long to be with him more every day. I want us to be together so badly, sometimes . . . sometimes, I pray and ask God to reunite us."

Now, Danielle has received the answer to her prayers, Hilda thought.

Hilda did not know just how right she was.

Wanda took the news hard. Danielle was the one she had counted on for so many things. She felt empty inside; lonely without her. She too, had a hard time accepting Danielle's death.

The funeral was simple, but elegant. Wanda and Hilda clung to one another for support, relying on God's strength as well as each other. One of the church choir members, tears streaming down her face, lilted *Amazing Grace* aappella.

Flowers were everywhere in tribute to Danielle's love for them. Roses, carnations, lilies, violets, and forget-me-nots, just some of the flowers, threatened to overfill the sanctuary.

The coffin, a beautiful finished pine covered with lace, lay on the bier, closed. A photograph of her sat on top of it.

Goodwin Medical closed for the day so that everyone she had worked with could attend the funeral of the woman they had grown to love and respect. Everyone said his or her good-byes and they placed her beside her husband, to remain until Resurrection Day.

Chapter 20

The trio left the lodge the morning after Dr. Fieldgreave arrived. He and Ethan set up the backseat of the car to make the ride as comfortable as possible for Danielle. Ethan assisted Danielle into the back seat. He tried to avoid looking at her vacant stare.

The trip would take almost twenty hours to drive from the Allegheny Mountains near Barnes, Pennsylvania, to Montfort, Wisconsin. October cold and more snow greatly complicated matters.

They packed several thermoses of coffee, sandwiches and cookies, among other snacks for the first leg of their journey. Ethan and Stephan ate breakfast before leaving the lodge. Dr. Fieldgreave left the key where his friend, who owned the lodge, indicated.

Ethan wished Danielle had learned the full truth of his ordeal once he got to the secret location. The ordeal he himself   had only learned a few months before.

Chapter 21

Doctor Fieldgreave pulled into the long driveway of David and Rose Trusdale around three a.m., to the sound of two barking dogs. The Trusdales greeted them as though they were family come to visit after years away. David and Rose introduced themselves and then promptly gave Ethan and Stephan huge bear hugs.

Afterward, Ethan assisted Danielle from the car and guided her into the house.

Rose quieted the two dogs, Teak and Goldie, as they all went into the huge farmhouse. David, Rose, and Stephan walked ahead of Ethan and Danielle.

To the Trusdales, who were privy to Tanas Labs and what Stephan was trying to accomplish, Stephan said, "I must tell you, Mrs. Anderson is in quite a state of shock with what she has discovered. Ethan does not know that you are aware of their circumstances. Please allow me to tell him in my own way."

The Trusdales agreed.

~

Danielle failed to notice the large woven rugs in the living room, which flanked the overstuffed sofa and matching chairs. She also didn't see the calico cat, cleaning itself quietly while sitting upon one of the large stuffed pillows that embellished the paisley print of the sofa. She would appreciate later, the handmade quilts and flannel sheets, which adorned the large, four-poster bed, set in the middle of the huge bedroom.

Rose helped Ethan put Danielle to bed. "Does she have anything to sleep in?"

"No, our . . . our home burned down. There's nothing left," Ethan said, embarrassed.

"Listen, I have whatever she needs. Hang on just a minute."

They managed to tuck Danielle into bed, and they left the room.

After Rose fed Stephan and Ethan, some serious conversation took place.

Ethan paced like a caged animal. He stopped and looked at Stephan. "She seems so pale. Stephan, she doesn't look good to me."

He ran his fingers through his thick hair, the impulse to pull it out taking strength for him to resist. "Stephan, I am so torn over this, I don't know what to do."

"I understand, Ethan," Stephan sympathized. "I am in much prayer regarding this situation. I have examined Danielle several times and I find her in reasonably good health. Ethan, I believe her condition is more emotional than physical. She will recover from this, I assure you. So please, try not to worry."

Somehow, this did little to ease Ethan's state of mind. Stephan knew this. He felt helpless to do anything more than pray, but he knew it was also the best thing he could do for his friend.

David and Rose had listened to a brief exchange between two very emotionally, spiritually, and physically exhausted men, over where they should go to escape Tanas's eyes.

David spoke up. "Look, Ethan, Stephan. Why don't you two get some rest before trying to make decisions right now? You are both so tired, you cannot possibly resolve any problems with an unclear head."

They knew he was right. They all went to bed.

~

Danielle awakened to the rich aroma of coffee, mingled with the savory smell of bacon frying. For a brief moment, she had the sensation she was back home with Uncle Charles and Aunt Hilda. She shook off the impossible dream and as she woke more, realized that Ethan had slept with her. He still had his arm around her waist, careful, even in sleep, to be mindful of the baby.

She eased herself out from under his embrace and then discovered a warm, wool robe lying on the bench at the end of the bed. She put it on when she could not find her clothes then ventured downstairs to the kitchen where she found a woman laboring over breakfast.

On the table sat a jar of honey, freshly sliced tomatoes, strawberry jam, and butter. Milk, in a large glass pitcher, was frosty from the cold of the icebox, which stood in the corner of the large kitchen.

Rose heard her and greeted her. "Good morning, Danielle. My name is Rose. We're friends of Stephan."

"N . . . nice to meet you too, Rose," Danielle replied, still disoriented.

"Would you like a cup of coffee?" Rose offered.

"Thank you, yes, please."

Once Rose placed the cup in front of Danielle, she studied the kitchen as she sipped the rich coffee appreciatively. Where the table sat, one could take in the panoramic view of the vast acreage that made up the Trusdale farm, through the large picture window, which created a canvas for the wintry scene. The rolling farmland slept under the white blanket, hibernating until spring.

Danielle took a closer look at the kitchen. The floor held pale blue linoleum, dotted with delicate white and yellow flowers. The wallpaper echoed the muted colors of the floor. Above the sink and stove, copper sheets of metal that protected the wall underneath from grease spills and splatters, glistened.

To the right of the stove, a large pie safe held home-canned peaches and other various home-canned foods. Sitting on the open shelf, a pie cooled for the noontime meal. The table was large, with a parson's bench on one side, and upholstered, straight-back chairs on the other. The matching chairs at each end of the table had arms for seating the patriarch and matriarch of the house. Though there were five place settings, they seemed curiously dwarfed by the table.

Rose began some small talk with Danielle, shaking her out of her musings.

"Danielle, I hope you're hungry. I think I fixed enough for an army."

Danielle offered a wan smile. "Thank you, Rose."

For the next few weeks, conversation with Danielle was almost impossible, but she seemed to be overcoming her state of shock.

The second night they were there, Ethan told Danielle that the Trusdales knew at least some of the story.

Then, with Rose's gentle coaxing and her obviously kind heart, Danielle became more of the person she had once been.

Rose, though young, had thick brown hair, speckled with gray. Today, she wore it coiled into a large bun on top of her head.

She and Danielle were in the warm kitchen, sipping coffee.

Danielle found herself opening up to Rose. She ventured to say she had few clothes other than what she had been wearing.

"Oh, Honey, that's no problem at all," Rose crooned. "I have a lot of maternity clothes I don't use. They should fit you just fine."

Danielle smiled and thanked her.

Rose said nothing and just smiled back, the smile not quite reaching her eyes, only a longing there, mingled with sadness.

"I love your house, Rose," Danielle said, changing the subject.

"Thank you. My David built this house himself with the help of his four brothers, of course. But he designed it." Rose sighed wistfully. "He built the house for a wedding gift to me. I was so pleased, so happy. We talked about the kind of house we wanted before we married. We determined to have a house designed for many children. Children just weren't meant to be, I'm afraid."

"May I ask why?"

"I'm not able to have children, Danielle. We tried for years. I became pregnant seven times. Seven times, I miscarried. The doctor finally told us I would never be able to carry to full term. He had told us I had a very weak womb. We tried to keep our last baby by me staying in bed, but again, I miscarried. I finally had to have surgery. The doctor did a partial hysterectomy by removing my womb. We thought about adoption, but it never seemed to work out for us."

"I am so sorry, Rose," Danielle commiserated, not knowing what else to say.

From the first conversation at the breakfast table, up to the time they left, Rose and Danielle drew close. They shared their life stories with each other.

~

The next two months passed in a hurry. The two women shared the keeping of the house, while the men worked outside, tending to the livestock, gathering eggs, and keeping the fences mended.

They celebrated Thanksgiving in the old tradition of having fresh-killed turkey, dressing, home-canned cranberry sauce, mashed potatoes, and giblet gravy. Home-canned vegetables accompanied the delicious fare. There were fresh baked pies for dessert, including pumpkin and pecan.

They gave a special thanks to the Lord on that day, for keeping them all safe, and asked Him to bless the life soon to come into the world. Ethan asked a special prayer for the divine protection of their child.

November brought with it a number of snowstorms, some of which drove all life indoors. Ethan and David transferred the livestock into the barns. Then the entire household huddled inside the warmth of the house. Some of the storms were "whiteouts," which meant zero visibility.

David, used to the Wisconsin winters, had prepared for such as this, so they stocked provisions. The men had chopped an ample supply of wood and David had gone into town and purchased plenty of coal for the furnace. The women kept the kitchen warm with constant baking. They baked bread, pies, and cakes. They placed the bread in the Westinghouse freezer that held a proud place in the kitchen. David purchased it as an anniversary gift the year before.

The men tended to the livestock during those fierce "whiteouts" by clinging to the frozen rope attached to the side of the house just outside the kitchen door. They attached the other end to the barn, right by the main door. This ensured their safety, as well as making the care of the animals easier.

As each day passed, all three sojourners regained health in their bodies, as well as their souls. The rich, home-cooked food, along with daily Bible devotions in the morning and chapter studies at night, brought on the renewal of their minds, spirits, and faith.

December arrived with more snow, followed by a few ice storms. Danielle had more difficulty getting around as her body grew heavy with the ripening child. Rose assisted her in every way she could.

Rose had never been the type of woman to make friends easily. She stayed pretty much to herself, all too often feeling the barrenness of no children. When they went to church in the warmer months, the women always seemed to talk about babies, their kids, and the rigors of motherhood. Rose felt so left out that she retreated into herself. The other women in her church prayed for Rose often. They were aware of her pain and longed to get close to her.

The night of December fifteenth, Danielle began experiencing some pains. At first, she thought she was in labor, but the pains subsided. The following morning, she awakened feeling better. It was the first of several false alarms.

Chapter 22

On Christmas Eve, at 3:30 a.m., Danielle Anderson delivered a healthy baby girl. At first, Danielle refused to look at the baby.

"Rose, I can't look at it. It . . . it's a monster!"

"Danielle, no. She's a healthy baby girl. Please look at her," Rose pleaded.

Slowly, Danielle turned to glimpse the child. There, she saw the most beautiful angel. She fell in love with her. Rose placed her in Danielle's arms.

Danielle could only stare at the tiny, cherubic face. She was beautiful. Her head, well-rounded, held a full cap of strawberry blonde curls. Danielle examined her. Her fingers and toes were normal; no claws, no scales like in her dreams. When the baby cried in hunger, Danielle eased her breast out and allowed her to suckle.

Everything Danielle had been through faded in the moment of this experience.

Weeks passed. Danielle still had not chosen a name for the baby and everyone wondered why. It did not take long for them to find out, but no one expected the bombshell she laid before them.

~

Danielle had become very quiet, introspective. Ethan began to worry about her. Rose, as well as Doctor Fieldgreave, assured him it was simply due to the birth of their child.

Since moving in with David and Rose, she and Ethan slept in the same bed, but no intimacy existed between them. Things were still awkward. They were not yet able to talk things over. Danielle had needed more time. She was still in shock over all that had happened.

"Ethan. I'm ready to talk, now. I never got to tell you what I went through during the time you were missing. I want to share it with you now."

Danielle told him about the officers that came to give her the news of him missing in action. How she had raised Cain with the bureaucrats in Washington to demand to know what they were doing to try to find him.

"I thought you were gone forever, or if you were found, they would find you dead. I was sick with worry the whole time you were gone."

"I have a feeling that part of the reason I'm even here now, is because of you, Dannie."

"Ethan, there is something else I need to tell you. I've made a decision. Please. Hear me out before you say anything."

"What is it, Dannie?" he asked, with a resigned sigh.

"Ethan, first let me ask you this question. How are we going to have to live from now on?"

"It's going to be very difficult, Dannie. We'll be on the run for quite a long time, maybe for the rest of our lives. These people are not ones to mess with. And I would even venture to say the fact that we are still free is a miracle in itself."

"Ethan, what you just said has finalized my decision. I need, desperately need, your support on this."

Ethan almost held his breath, expecting the worst.

She continued. "Ethan, as much as this is difficult to say, I . . . I want to allow the Trusdales to adopt our baby."

At what she thought was a concerned look on his face, she hurried before he could say anything.

"Look, Ethan. The way we will have to live, it's just not fair to our baby. Besides, this would be the safest place for her to grow up--in a normal, happy household--not running with us.

"I . . . I hate the thought of having to give up our baby, but I want what will be best for our child. Do you understand?"

Danielle fell silent as she waited for his response. Ethan did not explode as Danielle had imagined he might. He agreed with her, for it had been on his mind as well. He told her he would have never approached her with something like this, but had been praying about it, too.

Danielle went on to explain to Ethan the situation with David and Rose, the heartache of not being able to have any children of their own.

He put his arms out to her. For the first time in many weeks, they held each other, sharing in the pain of what lay ahead of them, and the heartbreak of their decision.

The next morning, they all gathered at the kitchen table and discussed this at length.

Rose and David both cried upon hearing the news.

At first, when David and Rose heard the offer, they refused, not wanting to inflict such a hurt on their two new friends, but after Ethan, Danielle, and Stephan presented their arguments, David and Rose tearfully accepted. There were tears of joy, mingled with sorrow, bittersweet, for them all.

For the next few days, the house became a bevy of activity, preparing for the nursery. David and Rose pulled out all the baby furniture they had purchased a number of years before after they found out she was pregnant with their first baby. She never thought she would ever need them, but she could not bring herself to get rid of them, either. Now she knew why.

Rose insisted that Danielle choose the baby's name. Danielle picked a combination name of her mother, David's mother, and Rose's mother. Margaret Elizabeth Isabelle Trusdale had entered the world at eight pounds seven ounces. Rose had taken her sewing tape and measured little Maggie. Her feet had hit the eighteen-inch mark.

No one need know anything about the baby's birth parents. Doctor Fieldgreave knew a nearby--discreet--colleague. His associate filled out the birth certificate, no questions asked. The birth certificate listed David and Rose Trusdale as Maggie's parents.

Rose experienced an awkward reluctance to take over Maggie's care. Danielle assured her it was fine. They finally agreed for both of them to care for Maggie. Rose knew Danielle needed time with her child before they left. The days she spent with Maggie would be the only memories she would have of her precious daughter.

Not long after that, Danielle developed a fever. Doctor Fieldgreave examined her.

Ethan, David, Rose, and Stephan stood in the hallway, talking about the results with the doctor.

"I'm afraid Danielle has contracted an infection. I will do the best I can. Rose, she cannot continue to breast feed. The baby could become sick from Danielle's milk. She has to go on formula immediately."

David and Ethan battled the winter storm and drove the ancient farm truck into town to obtain the formula for the baby despite the snow.

Over the next few days, Danielle went in and out of consciousness. She remained delirious much of the time. It would be weeks before she recovered enough to sit up in bed, or eat solid foods.

Danielle's recovery was slow, at best. Ethan, Stephan, as well as Danielle, knew they could not delay their departure any longer.

After much agonizing, Ethan and Dr. Fieldgreave decided to leave Danielle behind and send word to her later as to where to meet them. Ethan would make contact through some of their connections to ensure her safe trip.

Ethan and Stephan left on March first. Ethan agonized over having to leave Danielle. The last week they were there, they drew close once again, speaking of things previously left unsaid.

Rose and David insisted that the time they spend together should include Maggie. During that week, Rose served as a nursemaid, limiting her involvement with Maggie. She felt they needed this precious little time as a family.

~

On the night before Ethan's departure, he and Danielle finally talked things out.

"Dannie," Ethan began, "I want you to know that I never stopped loving you, ever."

"Ethan, I know. I still love you, too. Just try to understand that all this has overwhelmed me. As much as I love you, Ethan, things have changed forever. I just hope we can make it."

"We will, Dannie Girl. I know we will. I never meant for any of this to happen. Dammit! I wanted our lives to mean something--not this."

"I know, Ethan, I know. My heart aches over Maggie. I will never stop loving her, or missing her, Ethan."

"Dannie, me too, Sweetheart. Me too."

She wept in his arms until she finally went to sleep.

The following morning, goodbyes were said through tears, the agony each of them felt dominating the departure.

~

During her recovery, Danielle began to write in a journal, which Rose purchased for her at her request. In it, she wrote everything she had been through, as well as everything she knew about the secret place in the desert, about Ethan's ordeal there, about Maggie being such a special child, about her immense love for her baby. She wrote everything down, leaving nothing out.

Danielle told Rose about the journal, that she wanted her to keep it under lock and key until Maggie was old enough to handle it.

Danielle and Rose often discussed whether to tell Maggie they adopted her. Both women agreed she should know from as early an age as possible, even though it was an uncommon practice in those days. Their situation--quite different. Maggie thrived with two mothers who doted on her.

In late May, Danielle became ill again. She worsened each day. They contacted the doctor who filled out Maggie's birth certificate. After examining Danielle, he approached Rose and David.

"I'm afraid she had too rough a time when she delivered. She will not last much longer. I'm so sorry. Rose, she's asked for you, but please . . . keep it brief."

"I understand," Rose barely whispered.

Rose quietly approached Danielle, who seemed very pale. She had her eyes closed.

"Danielle?" Rose called hesitantly.

Danielle opened her eyes. "Rose," she said weakly. "I wanted to ask you something. If it isn't too much to ask, could you bury me here? This place has brought me more peace than I have known for a long time now. Even before WW II.

"Rose." She noticed Rose could not speak due to the tears running down her face. "You know that little orchard down by the pond, where we went to picnic a month ago?"

Rose simply nodded. Danielle reached up to wipe her friend's tears and continued, "I want to be buried there, under the large, shady oak near the orchard. But if you aren't comfortable with that, I can make other arrangements."

Rose finally found her voice. "Oh, Dannie, we'll bury you here, but only if the time comes. You're going to get better, you hear me?" Rose firmly told Dannie that she could entertain no other choice.

Danielle smiled at her friend. "No, Rose. I know I'm dying." At the look on Rose's face, she tried to comfort her friend. "Rose, trust me. It's time for me to go. I know this. And it's not a lack of faith. I'm tired. I'm ready to go home."

After hashing out the burial arrangements, they talked into the wee hours. Rose stayed despite the doctor's warning. Danielle had asked her to. Rose was like her own family. She held Danielle's hand for the rest of the night.

Around one a.m., Danielle drifted off. At four twenty a.m., she died peacefully in her sleep.

Rose and David buried their friend whom they considered sent by God to fill their broken hearts with an adorable little girl. Besides leaving her flesh and blood, Danielle left them with a piece of her unselfish spirit.

Her headstone simply read, 'D, an angel sent from God. Rest in Jesus'. One year after Danielle's death, the Trusdales received a telegram from a name that they had committed to memory, knowing it came from Ethan.

He asked in the telegram to send the package, which meant it was time for Danielle to join them.

Weeping, David sent a telegram back, telling him the package had been lost. Ethan knew his Dannie had died.

PART TWO

Maggie

Chapter 23

Maggie ran in from the flower garden, a small nosegay of pretty flowers hidden behind her back. She was now six years old.

"Mommy, Mommy! Look what I brought you!"

Rose never got tired of watching her daughter grow. Every little nuance of Maggie's precious life was a miracle to her grateful mother.

Maggie knew by now she was special, because she was 'dopted' as she told her school friends; that her Mommy and Daddy picked her special out of all the other little girls and boys.

Delighted, Rose took the nosegay of flowers and slid them into a vase, then centered it on the table. "Thank you so much, Sweetie. I love them. Now, would you be a sweetheart and go out to the edge of the field and get your father? It's almost time for lunch," Rose requested.

As Maggie left, Rose thought of how proud Dannie would be of her now and amazed at how much Maggie looked like her. Rose watched her skip out to the field. She turned and started into the house to finish preparing lunch, when she heard a car pull up into their long drive. Teak and Goldie, the dogs that protected the farm the night Ethan, Stephan, and Dannie showed up, still barked warnings. Older now, they seldom lumbered out to inspect visitors.

Rose wiped her hands on the dishtowel, laid it on the table and then went through the house to the front porch. As she opened the door, she saw two weary looking men emerge from a battered old car. She did not recognize them, but suddenly, the old dogs regained their youthful exuberance as they wagged their tails as though greeting long lost friends.

As Rose stepped out onto the porch, the two men walked toward her, their familiar steps crunching against the driveway gravel.

The older man spoke first, "Hello, Rose."

Her face bloomed into smiles at Dr. Fieldgreave's accent. She ran to both of the men she knew and loved.

In a reunion-like embrace Rose, Stephan, and Ethan wept and laughed with joy.

They were still hugging and laughing when David and Maggie came through the door looking for her.

Ethan broke from the hug first.

"David!"

David hugged his friend in wonderment. "Anderson! By God, I'd know that voice anywhere."

After a few more moments of hugs, greetings and back slaps, they went into the house. David sent Maggie to play while the grown ups talked. Stephan told David and Rose about the name changes and what they were doing now.

Ethan had obtained the name Joseph. Stephan had become Lemuel. They lived in Israel, though they did not say where. The serious conversation stopped for the moment.

Rose always prepared extra food for unexpected guests, so there was plenty to go around. Small talk dominated the visit until after they ate and Rose put Maggie down for her afternoon nap.

"Maggie, these are our dear friends, Joseph and Lemuel. They came a long way to visit."

Maggie greeted them and began to ask too many questions, her curiosity aroused. Rose had to corral her.

Joseph studied his daughter. By now, her once strawberry-blonde locks took on the color of corn silk, which Rose kept adorned with every color ribbon one could think of. Her clothes looked impeccable, the matching ribbons bouncing along with her hair as she walked.

Maggie came up to Rose and asked, "Mommy, can I go out by the pond to pick some flowers? I want to make another nosegay for supper."

"Sure, Sweetie," Rose said. "Supper will be ready soon, so don't be too long. And you know the rules about getting too close to the pond, right?"

"Yes, Mommy, I won't get too close."

After Maggie left, Joseph said, "You two have done such a wonderful job raising Maggie." He choked up a bit.

Rose saw the pride mixed with sadness, as well as the agony he was going through on the inside. She began to cry.

David broke the silence. "It has really been Rose, but you have to admit, she came from the best stock." He slapped Joseph on the back.

Rose regained her composure then said, "Nonsense, David. Who's the one who reads her all those bedtime stories? Who does she cry for when she has a nightmare?"

She turned to Joseph. "He's being a mite modest, Joseph. The sun rises and sets with that man as far as she is concerned and vice versa," she said, her tone bittersweet.

As though he was reading her thoughts, Joseph assured her, "Rose, I understand. Maggie would have never survived the ordeals we've faced, but the Lord has done marvelous things for Lemuel and me. We are now in the ministry of bringing the people of Israel to the Messiah. God saw fit to open the door for us to come back to the states, so here we are.

"David, Rose, I have hesitated to ask you, but has there been anything unusual about Maggie that you can tell? I mean, has she displayed anything out of the ordinary?"

David spoke up, "Physically, she's fine. She's had some the normal childhood diseases. The only thing extraordinary about her is that she is the sweetest, most precious gift we have ever been given." David finished, choking up. "But, there has been something going on recently, that Rose and I haven't been able to fix."

Rose began to cry.

"What is it? What's going on with Maggie?"

"Joseph, she's been having nightmares for the past few months. They seem to be the same ones, over and over. She wakes screaming, and I'm the only one who seems to be able to calm her down."

"I just hate seeing her so upset and not being able to do anything to make the nightmares stop," Rose said through her tears.

"Does she tell you anything about the dreams?" Joseph asked.

Rose cried even harder as she gripped her coffee cup.

"The only thing she does is ask me to kill the 'dragon man'. Rose and I are at our wits end with it."

Joseph closed his eyes. The thing he feared most had come true. Tanas was trying to contact Maggie.

"David, Rose, Maggie is being contacted. I know this from experience. What she's experiencing are psychic contacts, but with her age, the messages become distorted."

"Psychic contacts. Joseph, you make it sound so science fiction. It's like those fortune tellers at the carnivals." Rose choked her tears back and asked, "What can we do?"

"Unfortunately, Rose, this is all too real," Joseph said.

As Joseph saw the shocked look on their faces, he said, "There is nothing you can do to stop this. She'll have to fight him in her dreams. You have to tell her that in her dreams, she's strong and can defeat the dragon man. It's the only thing that will work, and it will stop the psychic contacts."

He patted Rose's hand. "Maybe I can help, but don't ask me any questions."

Rose and David agreed, knowing that Joseph knew best.

Maggie came skipping into the room just then, curls bobbing behind her. Everyone changed the subject until they could discuss it further. The men went on to talk about other things. David told them about his new tractor. Joseph and Lemuel went into further detail about their ministry in Israel. As they continued talking over coffee, Rose studied the two men she had come to love and respect. Though their faces were quite different, she knew them. They had found a plastic surgeon who agreed to change their appearance.

Rose got up and made some lemonade while the three men sat around the table.

Joseph asked about Dannie's beloved Uncle Charles and Aunt Hilda. They were doing well. They rather adopted little Blake, Wanda's son, as their grandson, since Wanda's parents died. They sold the farm after the fire. The money went into a trust fund for Blake until he was old enough to attend college. They felt Danielle would want it that way.

They found this out from a contact Lemuel had set up before they left. Lemuel wanted to make certain no one looked into Danielle's death.

Joseph avoided the subject, but he could no longer stand it. He finally asked about everyone. The last person he asked about was Dannie.

"Did she suffer? And where is she buried?"

Rose could not trust herself to speak, so David solemnly told him how she became sick again. He recounted how she died peacefully in her sleep, Rose by her side. They told him about her burial under the oak tree near the orchard. Joseph excused himself and went outside.

The others knew where he was going, and sensed that he needed to be alone for a while.

Joseph walked down to the gravesite where his wife lay sleeping. Sunlight sparkled on a pewter vase at the foot of the grave, which held fresh flowers. Peonies, tea roses, and chrysanthemums framed Dannie's small memorial yard. It had the unmistakable mark of Rose's caring hands. Small stones bordered the flowerbed she so carefully tended. The oak tree's shade covered the headstone and bathed it in muted blue tones. The grass, rich and green, made the small grave stand out, beautiful in its simplicity.

He knelt beside where she lay and wept. Grief, guilt, anguish, and anger all vied for prominence in his tears and face. His tears clenched, for he prayed his heart out to God to heal his wounds, and to help him forgive the ones who had brought all his grief about. Even so, he wondered if he ever could. After a bit, his tears subsided.

"Dannie Girl, I wish you could see our beautiful daughter. She is your image, with corn silk for hair. Her golden locks fall down her back in ringlets. You would be so proud of her."

He wept again, this time for the joy he felt in knowing they would some day be together.

For a long while, he sat there in that small sanctuary, communing with God and at times, speaking to Dannie about things that occurred since his departure. He knew he would share with David and Rose, but for now, he felt he needed to be near his Dannie for a while.

When he reached the house, the smell of chicken frying tickled his nose. It made his stomach growl in anticipation despite that just moments earlier he felt like he would never be hungry again. As he hesitated at the kitchen door, he saw a pie cooling on the pie safe, much the same as the first time they came to this home.

Before he walked in, he was determined to put on, if not a happy face, one that seemed normal. "Something sure smells good, Rose," he commented to her, as he wiped his feet on the rubber mat in front of the back door.

Rose looked up and her heart wrenched when she saw his reddened eyes. But she spoke with forced cheerfulness. "Thank you, Joseph. We're having fried chicken, mashed potatoes with cream gravy, corn on the cob, pinto beans and cornbread. I hope you're hungry!"

"Yeah. I am."

Rose smiled at him. Just then, Maggie came running into the house, the screen door making a resounding bang behind her.

"Margaret Elizabeth Isabelle Trusdale. You know better than to come into the kitchen without wiping your feet," Rose scolded with mock severity.

Maggie grinned. "Oh, Mommy. I forgot again," she said, laughing.

Rose smiled and said, "You'll learn, Sweetie. Now wipe your feet and go wash up for dinner."

Maggie skipped through the kitchen, her curls bouncing.

Joseph watched her again, proud of the carefree child she was. He imagined what she might be like had he kept her with him. He saw the children of some of the missionaries, and some of them had haunted looks in their eyes from having seen so much tragedy, devastation, and horror. He inwardly shuddered to think of those sparkling blue eyes, burned out from life's despair, becoming hollow. Having to live as a fugitive, more or less, would have been a devastating existence for her.

Once again, he thanked God for His protection over Maggie. He shook himself out of his brooding and concentrated on the two men who had just walked in from the field. Lemuel knew Joseph was upset after his visit at his wife's grave. "Joseph, are you all right?" Lemuel asked, concern in his eyes for his dear friend.

"I'm fine, Lemuel. God is good."

Rose broke the severity of the situation by rushing the men upstairs to go clean up for dinner. Maggie had already come back downstairs to help Rose finish getting everything ready.

All through dinner, Maggie kept them entertained with her little stories that she liked to make up. They all laughed until they cried over one such story about a chicken they had.

"This one is a real true story," piped Maggie.

Rose agreed that the chicken story was real.

As she listened to her precious daughter, once again, Rose thanked God for her. She always asked Him to protect her at all times, and she never tired of giving thanks.

Maggie was in first grade now. She caught the bus right at the end of their long driveway. She loved school. She was bright, with a love for learning new things. Her teachers were delighted with her enthusiasm. She was a straight A student, having a first grade reading level before she even started school. This was thanks to Rose and David for reading her some of the classics like Old Yeller, Little Women, and Black Beauty. Black Beauty had always been her favorite.

David and Rose truck-farmed their crops and made a decent living by it. David was a shrewd businessman, and had invested wisely. As a result, they never hurt for money, always making sure they had money to fall back on in case the year's crops failed. Their crops failed two years ago, but the loss never dented their savings.

Like any parents with some means, they set Maggie's college fund in place. They wanted her to excel in whatever she chose, and always encouraged her in whatever endeavor she became interested in.

Back when the rest of the family first heard of the adoption, they were all delighted and doted on Maggie, the only granddaughter in the family.

David and Rose traded visits to their parents' homes. One year they would spend Thanksgiving with David's family, and Christmas with Rose's, then the following year, it would be the opposite.

The year Dannie, Ethan and Stephan were there, they told the families the weather was too harsh to travel. The families understood. David also explained that they were expecting a private adoption and the baby was due in December. He would explain further, when he could.

Rose and David phoned everyone with the good news when Maggie was born. They decided that July Fourth would be the best time to introduce their new baby. Celebrations of the new life abounded in various parts of Wisconsin. Roses' parents, David's parents, and their respective siblings celebrated Maggie's birth. The mothers especially, were glad they named her after them.

They never spoiled Maggie in the way an only child often was, for her spoiling was love, not indulgence. They had been adamant about that. They did not want her to become shallow. She learned her chores at an early age, gathering eggs as young as four years old. Rose made it a delightful game, so it never seemed too mundane for Maggie. Besides, it was in Maggie's nature to want to help. Rose suspected that trait came from Danielle. Maggie loved doing other things to help Rose, as well as David. With Rose, it was hanging the laundry out to dry or planting seeds in the vegetable garden, or dusting the furniture. With David, she often went fishing with him in their well-stocked pond. She also helped him when he chopped wood for the winter. She would gather all the wood too small for logs and place it in a pile used for kindling.

Her favorite thing to do with her father was fishing. One day when they were out fishing, none of the fish had been biting, so she wandered off to the orchard. There, under the huge oak, she found the small, delicate headstone at the end of a carefully maintained grave. The grave bordered all the way around with baby's breath, delicate tea roses, and forget-me-nots. Within the border, the grave contained plush, manicured grass. A pewter vase held fresh gladioli surrounded by Easter lilies.

Maggie ran back to where her father sat. She asked him about the funny flowerbed by the oak tree. David explained that he and Mommy had a friend who lived with them at one time, but she had died a number of years ago. Since there was no date of death on the headstone, there would not be any need to go further as Maggie got older.

"Daddy, that is sad. May I give the Lady Friend flowers too?"

"Sure, Pumpkin, I think the lady would have loved that," David said with difficulty.

Maggie faithfully took flowers to the Lady Friend's grave every day from then on, except during winter.

All this they relayed to Joseph. David and Rose shared as much as they could with him in hope that somehow he could hold on to the memories of her to take with him when he left.

By the time Rose washed, dried, and put the dishes away, everyone seemed ready for bed.

~

Maggie was in the bad place again. She did not like the dragon man. She wanted her daddy to come get her. The dragon man was doing bad things to her--and to other children. She did not like the tubes and the strange pink water. She struggled to get free from dragon man, but could not escape.

"Come on, little one," the dragon man said. "I won't hurt you. This is good for you to help us."

Maggie screamed.

Joseph, as well as everyone else, heard the hair-raising shriek.

David found her sitting up in bed, tears streaming down her face. Joseph entered the room a second later.

"Daddy, please make the dragon man go away!"

David rocked her, looking up at Joseph for help.

"Maggie, I might be able to help you get rid of the dragon man. May I try?"

Maggie nodded.

"Will you trust me now, Maggie? I promise, you won't have to worry about the dragon man again, okay?"

Again, she nodded.

"Okay. Now close your eyes, and think of the pretty flowers that you love so much, and listen to my voice, okay?"

"Okay."

After Maggie went back to sleep, Joseph asked David to leave him alone with her. David left the room. Joseph settled in beside his daughter and placed his hand on her forehead. He closed his eyes and prayed he had the power to do this.

He was in Maggie's nightmare--the one he induced. He saw the lab where Tanas conducted the in vitro experiments.

~

Maggie sat in a chair, waiting her turn. Her eyes were saucers as she looked off to her left. Joseph looked in the same direction. There, he saw the figure; the dragon man. It was hideous.

He wondered why the creature could not see him. He saw his translucent reflection in a glass door, which separated the lab from a small office. He indeed appeared different. Joseph now sported huge wings, which spanned out behind him. His muscles were huge and bulging, and he wore an ancient-looking toga. His hair was the color of spun gold. In his hand, he held an enormous sword. When he looked down at himself, however, he was no different from what he could see. Perhaps God was allowing her to see him as an angel.

God was with him. He called to Maggie.

Maggie looked at Joseph and then slid off her chair and ran to him. She hid behind his wings, as Joseph fought the demon. The demon saw the power and might of his sword, and cringed.

In a voice that sounded like legions lived inside him, he cried, "We cannot fight that sword!"

The demon knocked the sword out of Joseph's hand. Joseph pushed Maggie into a corner behind him, careful to keep himself between her and the demon.

The slimy creature, a dark ash color, smelled of sulphur, smoke, and decomposing flesh. It could not have been any taller than four feet, but its long arms held deadly looking claws. Its eyes, the color of fire, glowed in triumph. It was going to win this one. The demon jumped on Joseph, scratching and gnawing on his shoulder, trying to gain the upper hand.

Joseph piggybacked the demon as he lunged for the fallen sword and grabbed it. In the motion, he knocked the demon off his back.

The demon kept coming, dodging the sword at every turn, managing to wound Joseph in the ribs and back.

Joseph called on God to help him.

Suddenly, the demon shrank back, whimpering and pleading with an unknown power.

Joseph plunged the sword deep into the dragon man's gut. The dragon man disintegrated right in front of him. Demonic laughter echoed and then faded.

Another one appeared in its place, facing Joseph. This one was taller and more dangerous looking than the first one. This one had a scaled body, a reptilian tail, and beady eyes with the now-familiar flame in them. Its hands did not hold claws; they boasted huge talons. In its hand, it carried its own sword. The sword, unlike the shiny glint of the sharp metal of Joseph's, showed signs of wear, rust, and decay--matching the appearance of its owner.

Joseph leaped away just as the second demon, now enraged, lunged at him.

Suddenly, Joseph and the demon both stood still, as Joseph's sword began to quiver. It elongated, and seemed to sharpen itself, until the sword was almost too much for Joseph to handle.

He beheaded the demon in one smooth stroke, its body crumbling before him. Its head exploded into a million pieces and vanished, hissing its final words: "We'll be back, just you wait and see. We'll come to get you, Maggie!"

Suddenly, Joseph and Maggie found themselves in a field of wildflowers. Joseph knelt down in front of Maggie. "Maggie, if you have this dream again, just call out to me and I'll help you, okay? Say my name and I will be here. My name is Rimon. Remember my name, it is important."

Maggie nodded and hugged him close. Joseph felt washed out by the time he completed his task. However, he felt good that she would never remember her dream, that it was he, protecting her.

Maggie slept soundly and did not waken again that night, or any other night. Her nightmares were over--for now.

~

The two men stayed three days, all of them crowding in as much time as possible. They all knew that somehow, they would never see each other again in this life. The day Joseph and Lemuel departed was fraught with teary goodbyes, hugs, and a commitment to pray for each other.

David, Rose, and Maggie watched until the car vanished from their view. The Trusdales were lost in their own thoughts, wondering how the lives of those two brave men would turn out.

Maggie watched with curiosity and a strange feeling of familiarity, though she would not understand why until she was older--much older.

Chapter 24

Joseph and Lemuel arrived in Jerusalem a week later. They settled into their ministry to assist in helping the few Jews who escaped the death camps during WWII. Some of them were shell-shocked. 'Shell-shock', the term commonly used for anyone who suffered from the ravages of the war during the era, seemed commonplace.

Joseph made it a point to visit these poor souls every day, speaking to them of the Lord--how they could have freedom from the oppression that robbed their peace. Many of the bitter refugees, having lost family and faith, spit on the floor at the sound of His name. However, Joseph and Lemuel were gently persistent. They knew there were other needs in the peoples' lives they needed to address first. Lemuel took care of their physical needs as they came up. They worked almost day and night.

Joseph offered services for Messianic Jews. This part of their ministry was particularly dangerous, as they had to have the services under covert conditions. If the Israeli Army caught them, they could send all involved to prison or deport them, perhaps execute them. Still, they pushed on, doing the work of the Lord.

On a spring day in mid-1958, Joseph met a woman who had been coming to services. She always sat in the back listening to this man of God. She normally left before the end of the service. This particular Friday night--Joseph and Lemuel insisted in keeping the Sabbath to honor the Jewish culture--she walked up to Joseph and told him she was sure he was telling the truth about Yeshua Messiah. She was ready to accept the Son of God as her personal Savior.

"Brother Joseph, I have suspected for a number of years that Yeshua was the Messiah. Yet my culture is so steeped in the Jewish religion, that it will not tolerate any heresies. In fact, my late husband tried to convince me of the true Messiah. They killed him for his efforts to convert the wrong person. I don't know who it was, but I do know it was a traitor. I now believe he died a martyr for the cause of Yeshua. And I am ready to follow in his wake."

"Praise His name, Sister," Joseph spoke.

"I am not quite sure what I need to do, since I have always followed Moses and the Law. Will you help me?"

The three of them got down on their knees while Miriam Goldstein prayed for Yeshua Messiah to come into her life.

They began a wonderful friendship that led to marriage. Joseph and Miriam served the Lord together. They adopted as many children as possible after Joseph explained that he could not father children (for he made sure he would not ever bring another child of his own into the world). As a result, they had ten adopted children.

When he and Lemuel had the plastic surgery, Joseph felt led to have a vasectomy. He was not sure he would ever marry again, but felt the Lord had prompted it.

She never knew about Joseph's past for he did not want to burden her, and with him being able to control his abilities--they had grown and developed over the years--he never worried that she might find out.

Joseph and Miriam continued to preach the message of hope to those who were in such need of Yeshua Messiah. They were still spreading the good news when they celebrated the millennium in Israel.

Chapter 25

Maggie grew into a fine young girl. The fresh air, the homegrown food she ate, as well as plenty of exercise, gave her a healthy glow. She learned to ride her pride and joy, Cheyenne, the palomino gelding her parents had bought for her seventh birthday. She and Cheyenne were close. When she was not riding him, she was grooming him until his coat shone like velvet. His corn silk mane and tail were soft and full from all the brushings she gave him. Her hair and his mane and tail matched in texture and color.

By twelve, Maggie entered Cheyenne in some of the local rodeo contests. She excelled in barrel racing. Cheyenne was in his element in this event. She and Cheyenne made a stunning show. Maggie chose her cowgirl outfit with great care, not opting for the flashy pinks, golds, and bright reds the other girls preferred. Her personality ran in other directions. She chose a buckskin shirt trimmed in cream-colored fringe, with matching pants. Her dark brown leather boots with turquoise beadwork completed the picture. She wore her long, thick hair in a loose French braid, which cascaded down her back and just touched the top of her boot-matching belt. Rawhide intertwined with the thick braid to the end, where it knotted.

She joined the 4H club, raising her own sheep, which was hard for her when they sold him. She cried all the way home, but her parents never berated her for her emotions. For they had animals on the farm they had grown attached to. It was hard on them when they had to sell or slaughter theirs, so they well understood. They always waited until her grief had been spent, then they would talk it out, until she was better. She knew she never had to put on airs with her parents.

Maggie's high school days flashed by. The long lanky girl emerged into college as a beautiful young woman. She had grown taller than both her parents, reaching five-feet, nine-inches." She still kept her hair long, in keeping with the sixties vogue. Her wardrobe matched the same style. However, that was where the similarities ended. Maggie became intrigued with politics in her high school civics class and decided on a career in the political field. Her philosophy about how to help Americans was a passionate driving force within her.

Graduating Valedictorian of her senior class in 1968, she went to work over the summer, earning money for extras she might need in college. Since she had her pick of universities, her logical choice was Harvard. There she studied with great enthusiasm, kept her grade point average as high as possible, which was a 3.8, and struggled with her social life, not wanting any serious relationships; yet she was approached over and over by the many young, cantankerous men, whose hormones seemed to be raging out of control. Maggie soon had the nickname 'Harvard Ice Queen'.

She became involved in Federal Law. The history of the founding fathers was fascinating. Although she disagreed with some of their extremist views, she understood the principle behind them. Some of the zealots of the new America went overboard, especially in religious ideology.

Even though Rose and David took her to church regularly, Maggie held different ideas about God, the creation of the universe, and nature. To say she was agnostic would have been incorrect. She believed in a Supreme Being, just not what the 'antiquated' Bible claimed Him to be. This was the only area where she and her parents differed, yet they respected her right to choose. She never fought going to church, as it had become habit over the years.

By her junior year in Harvard, she fully indoctrinated herself into Transcendental Meditation, yoga, and other Eastern religions of the day. She loved to feel she was one with the "Cosmos" and not just, as she put it, some sort of toy for the One God of the Universe.

She did not hold the same passion about the Viet Nam conflict as many other students, even though she felt it was senseless. During the Viet Nam era, she met Joshua Channing.

She had been walking through a crowd of demonstrators, and she bumped into him. While he was helping her pick up the books she had dropped, the police arrested the demonstrators. As a result, she found herself in jail, along with the others.

Joshua paid her fine. She offered to pay for lunch as a way to thank him.

Fortunately, Maggie and Joshua escaped the violent incidents that many young men and women participated in. Those were the draft dodgers, hippie communes, and free love groups.

The next summer, when Joshua got his 'greeting' from the President, he could not bring himself to dodge the draft.

While Joshua was on his tour of duty, Maggie immersed herself in her studies. She learned a lot the last year and a half she spent at Harvard.

She decided toward the end of her junior year that she could help others see the light, not by the juvenile protests that other students held, but as one of the *'Establishment'*. She would infiltrate their ranks, expose them for what they were, and legislate laws for the people and by the people. Her idealism would eventually change.

Margaret Elizabeth Isabelle Trusdale graduated from law school. Once again, she made her parents proud when she presented them with her diploma. After passing the bar, Maggie obtained a job as a junior attorney. Joshua entered the military. Soon after, they married.

To her mother's chagrin, they opted for a civil ceremony rather than a clergyman. Rose, being the kind of mother she was, bit her tongue, her attitude being, "It's her life, but Dear Lord, please help her to give her life to You!"

Chapter 26

Maggie and Joshua changed over the next few years. The responsibilities of marriage, coupled with their careers, matured them in ways nothing else could have. They soon put their college days behind them, tossing out most of the ideals and visions when stark reality hit them. They learned rapidly that life was much more complicated than the idealisms they once held dear.

Maggie still embraced TM, Yoga, and an Eastern religion she could accept. They enabled her to cope with the harsh world outside. She "zoned" out many times after making it wearily into the door of the brownstone they now occupied in Baltimore, where Maggie was hired as a legal intern. Joshua still did various tours, although by now, he remained stateside. They made Baltimore their permanent home.

Joshua only meditated in the small backyard, which afforded them some privacy. They had transformed it into a jungle-like setting, in keeping with their meditating practices. Their theory was, the more natural, the better, as Mother Nature intended it to be.

As the years slipped by, so did their resolve never to give up their belief system. Gone was the idealism. In its place were the social and career ladders they began to climb.

For Joshua, it was his military career. He moved up in the ranks with dogged determination, unrelenting in his quest to become a general before he retired. Although the military stationed Joshua in many parts of the world, Maggie declined to go with him due to her career. She was making a reputation for herself in a law firm that promised a bright future. Late December of 1981, Maggie announced she was pregnant. Although they had not planned on children, they chose to keep the baby.

On July 4, 1982, Leah T. Channing was born to proud parents Joshua and Maggie Channing. It was quite a struggle in the early years, due to demanding careers, but they managed to maintain both career and family.

Leah was remarkable in her learning abilities. She spoke her first word at the tender age of 6 months. Her first word was Mama. It was not the mumbled version most parents think is a word, but she clearly said 'Mama'. By three years, she could name the fifty states, recount entire episodes of *Sesame Street* and read some words out of the newspaper, all while her astonished parents sat open-mouthed.

Joshua and Maggie had her tested by a good friend who happened to be a child psychologist, one of the best in her field.

Panthea Poskinski was a wonderful counselor. She held PhDs in many areas. One of the techniques she used in therapy was what she called Relaxation Therapy. In this type of therapy she encouraged patients to go to a quiet, darkened room and allow themselves to mentally visualize a place they loved--a beach, forest, wherever they felt most relaxed. She also provided them with relaxation therapy tapes; some had sounds, a waterfall, or ocean waves gently lapping on the beach, sometimes music. This, she claimed, would allow anyone to self-hypnotize, to achieve the best relaxation. She was also into TM, much like Maggie, except she added her own technique to it.

After extensive testing on Leah, she concluded that Joshua and Maggie's daughter was an anomaly in the world of geniuses. She talked to them at length about her.

"Joshua, Maggie. Thank you for waiting. What I am about to tell you is something I find hard to believe myself. You have an extraordinary child. Not only is she extremely intelligent, she also possesses an extraordinary ability to recall anything, and I'm talking about recalling verbatim. I have never seen such ability in anyone before. She is going to need a lot of training in order to control her abilities. If she doesn't get the training, it could destroy her mentally. I know you want her to have as normal a life as possible. I must warn you, however, never tell anyone of her unusual gift. If it ever got out, she would become a laboratory rat."

She leaned toward them for emphasis after noticing the shocked look on the couple's faces. "Look. You have a child that could blow the gene theory all to hell. We have no idea about the magnitude of this. But for now, just let her be a child."

She sat back, waiting for it all to sink in.

Maggie, still shocked at what her friend told her, was speechless. Joshua spoke first.

"Doctor, what are you saying? I mean, aren't there a lot of kids who are geniuses?"

"What I am saying is, according to some theories, genes are preserved during development and are passed on unchanged. According to another theory, genes can and usually do mix their phenotypic effects in an organism, but themselves are not mixed and they're transmitted in an all-or-nothing mode to the next generation. I have never seen or heard of Leah's anomaly before. But I have seen, read about, and studied gifted children for twenty-five years, since kids are my specialty."

"Can you explain in plain English, Doctor?" Joshua asked.

"What it all means is that Leah should have your genes; yours and Maggie's. She has something different from either of you, according to your medical and family history. Basically, she's a possible link to proving evolution. I am also saying--no offense--that your daughter is a freak of nature that many scientists would love to tap into. Leah needs to live as normal a life as possible--for her sake."

"All right," Joshua said resignedly. "Whatever we need to do for our daughter to have a normal life; we'll do it."

"How could this happen?" Maggie exclaimed. "We're normal people! My parents . . . ." She paused. What did she know about her blood parents? Right then, Maggie vowed to try to find out.

Maggie and Josh entrusted Leah to their friend Panthea. She was Leah's mentor and teacher to all the ways of meditation, yoga, TM, and self-hypnosis. By the time she reached the age of ten, she was well equipped to handle her mental ability. She could, in effect, go into her own mind, catalogue, file, and put away anything she wanted. Her brain operated much like a computer. Part of the reason for this was an exercise that Panthea developed and taught Leah.

She and Doctor Poskinski would get together and she would lead Leah into an imaginary office, complete with a file cabinet, desk, and chair. This set up her "file" system, so she could keep her thoughts, ideas, and memories in order, to pull out the "file" and look at it, then file it away after she was finished.

The only drawback to Leah's gift was her difficulty in separating her emotions from the memory or event she pulled up. It took two summer trips to the Orient to study with a Master Zen Buddhist to learn to have complete control over her emotions. Panthea went with her, taking the opportunity for a hiatus from her practice. Though Josh and Maggie agreed with some reluctance, they were grateful once they saw the results.

Leah was not looking for popularity like most girls. She was somewhat shy by nature, but her shyness gave the false impression of aloofness. She had some friends, but she chose them carefully--methodically. They were some of the top students in her classes, yet she did not choose them for their academic abilities, but their common interests. As a result, she had a close circle of good friends, rather than superficial ones that the popular girls had. She liked it that way.

~

Not long after the visit with Panthea, Maggie underwent three grueling months searching for her roots, but came up with nothing. For years she gave up, until one fateful day, it fell into her lap.

Maggie had just seen Leah off to college for her sophomore year, when Maggie's mother, Rose, became gravely ill. Maggie rushed back to Wisconsin to be by her side. She was there for eight very eye-opening weeks.

Chapter 27

Maggie took care of her mother for the first week, until she could hire a private-duty nurse. Maggie had insisted that she herself would take care of bathing her mother, as Rose was a very modest woman. The nurse's duties were to administer medications, check her vital signs, and report to the doctor, as well as help Maggie to change her mother's sheets.

Rose suffered from heart disease for a long time now. She had had an acute attack of angina and, luckily, had made it to the hospital after calling 9-1-1.

Maggie reached the hospital in record time. As she stepped into her mother's room in intensive care, she was shocked to see her once-vivacious mother lying there, helpless.

Rose had taken a sedative, so Maggie went in search of her doctor. When she found him, he told her the bad news.

"Maggie, I'm so sorry. She only has a little time left. I've done all I can do."

"How much time does she have, Doctor?"

"With her heart in the shape it's in, it's hard to say. She could survive several months, but that would be pushing it. The best thing you can do for her now is to hire a private nurse as soon as your mother is able to go home."

Rose was in the hospital for over two weeks and then sent home.

During the first several weeks, Rose poured her heart out to Maggie. She told her about her natural mother at last. She wanted Maggie to be aware of where she had come from. For years, the fear that Tanas would discover her existence haunted her. She wanted Maggie to begin to watch out for herself and Leah.

"Mother, why didn't you tell me about all of this before now?"

"Please forgive me for not telling you sooner, but I thought I was protecting you better by not revealing the secret. The less you knew, the better off you would be; but I have very little time left. I did not want to die with this on my conscience. Besides, I know with all the new technology, along with the freedom of information act, the risk has become much greater for you and Leah. There's something else I need to tell you about."

"What's that?"

"Maggie, do you remember the two men who came to visit when you were five? One spoke with a foreign accent."

"Do you mean Joseph and Lemuel?"

"Yes, that's them. I'm surprised you remember their names." Rose took a deep breath before she continued.

"Maggie, Joseph was your father."

"Oh my God, Mother! I can't deal with this right now, I just can't," Maggie cried.

Maggie ran from Rose's bedroom. She took a walk down to the orchard to calm down. She strolled to the grave for which she had always had a curiosity. It dawned on her then; the woman buried here, had been her natural mother. Somehow, she knew it. After placing flowers on D's grave, Maggie walked back to the house.

Rose looked up as Maggie entered her room. Maggie took Rose's hand and held it.

"I hope you don't hate me, Maggie," she pleaded grasping her daughter's hand tightly in her own.

"No, Mother. I could never . . . I love you for trying to protect me. However, isn't it all just a little too much to believe? Is it possible my natural mother had mental problems?"

"No, Maggie! She was a smart, vivacious woman, caught up in something she couldn't deal with. I think that giving you up, and all that had happened just wore her out. She loved you above all else, Sweetie. She only wanted to ensure you had a good life. Remember, I lived with her for quite a while, so I would have known if she had been mentally ill. She was the most rational and logical person I've ever known!"

"Then the woman buried near the orchard; she was my mother?"

"Yes, Maggie, she was."

Maggie now had more questions than she had answers about her past. "Maggie, one more thing; there's a journal in a plastic bag, in the bottom of the large cedar chest in the attic. It's under my wedding gown. It will tell you all you need to know about your natural parents. Your . . . Danielle wrote it. That was your mother's name."

Rose was tired by this time, so Maggie left her to rest, and meditated on the fantastic story her mother had confessed.

~

Maggie reminisced as she pored over the family mementoes. Yellowed photographs of smiling faces graced with youth, stared out at her. Her mother's wedding gown, which she herself had worn proudly, still wrapped in tissue inside a protective plastic cover near the bottom of the huge trunk. As she dug down to the bottom, tears welled in her eyes as she drifted back to a life filled with happiness and few responsibilities. A corsage from her first prom, dried by Rose and faded now with age, brought that night back in detail.

~

"Maggie! Hurry, Dear! Your date is coming up the drive!" Her mother called outside Maggie's bedroom door. Maggie sat there, palms sweaty, her nervousness showing in the slight shaking of her hand, as she applied the final changes to her make-up. "I'll be ready in a minute, Mother!"

Rose grinned to herself at the nervous tone of her daughter's voice. She relished all these moments of her daughter's life. Once again, Rose offered a silent prayer of thanks and praise to God for her miracle child.

These moments were also bittersweet for Rose. This moment meant her daughter would be too soon grown. Before she knew it, Maggie would be married with babies of her own.

Rose sighed, and swallowed the lump that threatened to choke her. She sternly ordered herself not to cry. She knew, however, she would not listen. She had not been able to hold them back before, so she knew she wouldn't now.

Rose took pictures, much to Maggie's embarrassment. She looked beautiful in her prom dress, a spaghetti-strapped bright blue gown with ruffles at the breast and hem. Maggie wore her hair up in a French twist, popular for the era. Her corsage was blue orchids, adorned with baby's breath and delicate white satin ribbons. Maggie's escort was too nervous to pin it on her, so Rose did the honors for him. The finishing touch to Maggie's ensemble was a white lace shawl her mother let her borrow to ward off the evening's slight chill.

Maggie remembered the prom itself. She and her date were dancing when the emcee stopped the music. A drum roll sounded and then he announced the king and queen of the prom.

Her friends had nominated Maggie for prom queen. She did not expect to win, but hoped she would.

Sarah Hawthorne won queen, and Maggie, Michelle Jennings, and Melissa Thornton won as her ladies in waiting.

~

Maggie shook herself out of her memories and continued to dig toward the bottom of the trunk. She finally found the journal. She took out the small book and reverently rubbed the cover, hesitant to open the first page. Laying the book down, she then tucked everything back into the trunk. She picked up the book and carried it downstairs.

After fixing herself a cup of coffee and a sandwich, she went into the living room, curled up on the couch and proceeded to read the journal, written by the stranger who had birthed her.

> *Maggie, this journal I am writing is hard for me to do. As I lie here in bed, I see you, so tiny, sleeping like an angel in your crib.*
>
> *You are so beautiful. I cannot believe God has blessed me with you! Oh, my Precious One! If only things could have been different. I would be raising you and living with your father. We could have had such a wonderful life together.*
>
> *I try not to cry, as I think about life without you. I can hardly bear it.*
>
> *But I am not writing this journal to lament over my own heartache. I am writing this for you, so if the time ever comes when you need to know what happened, you will at least have some knowledge so you can protect yourself. I do not know if, or how, you are affected, but as I glance over at you again, you seem to be a normal, healthy, little girl. I pray you are.*
>
> *Honey, I know this is all going to sound bizarre, but I know in my heart it is all true. I could not believe it at first. I thought your father had gone mad. After he explained everything, it took me some time to come to terms with it all.*

Maggie studied Danielle's handwriting as though she might somehow connect with the selfless woman who gave her life. Danielle's handwriting was beautiful. Her letters slanted to the right, with delicate curves in small, old-fashioned cursive.

Maggie had no photos to look at, but if she had, she would have been astonished by her resemblance to her mother. Except for her hair color, she could have been Danielle's twin.

She stopped reading, her eyes misting over with tears. She now felt a connection with this woman. It was almost spiritual. She put the journal down, tried to drink the rest of her coffee, and finish her chicken sandwich, which was her favorite, but she found herself unable to swallow any of it. The lump in her throat was taking up all the space right now.

She checked her wristwatch. She was due to relieve the nurse for just a little while. It was time. Reluctantly, she rose from the sofa and then climbed the stairs to sit with her mother. She absent-mindedly rubbed the banister of the stairs, something she had done most of her life. She gently opened the door to her mother's room, relieved the nurse, and sat quietly as her mother lay sleeping.

Maggie ached to talk to her, for she still had so many questions, but Rose had been so upset just from what she had told her, she would not have risked it for anything now. She knew she would only learn of her parentage by the journal waiting for her, which was tucked away inside her pillowcase on her bed. She had thought about bringing it with her, but again, she did not want to risk upsetting her mother, so she tried to lose herself in the novel she had left on the bedside table.

Maggie took a shower and changed into her nightgown after the nurse returned. Now propped up in bed, she continued reading the journal where she left off.

> *If you are reading this now, it means Rose is dead, or near death, for she vowed to never let you read this unless she could no longer watch out for you. Where shall I begin? I suppose I shall start with the beginning.*

Danielle took her from when she first met Ethan, to when she found out she was going to have a baby; then she wrote about everything that had happened to Ethan overseas and at Tanas Labs, and finally ended her journal with her love, prayers for Maggie's protection--and a plea for forgiveness.

Maggie, shocked by what she now knew, wondered if she could ever live with this horrible secret, but she knew she must, at least for a time.

Chapter 28

Maggie was engrossed in the journal searching for anything she could identify--a name, place, something. She felt like she was reading one of her husband's science fiction novels. Josh loved them. She could not share this with him, however. She felt too much pain to share this even though they kept no secrets from each other.

She still wasn't over her mother's death, and it had been eight weeks. Her mother's death, coupled with what she recently learned, left her reeling with questions--and no answers.

She arranged to take a leave of absence, which, of course could have jeopardized her position as a senator, but she just couldn't seem to get a handle on everything that went on in the last four months.

She was seeing her friend, Doctor Poskinski for her unbearable grief. She still revealed nothing of her mother's journal, even to Panthea. Doctor Poskinski knew she was holding back, but attributed it to the discovery of her adoption. Many adopted patients in grief counseling, felt their grief a bit harder than children whose natural parents had died. Doctor Poskinski was a very patient woman, so she allowed Maggie to take her time.

After five months, Maggie returned to work. Only this time, she had another agenda other than the business-at-hand. She began making what she thought were discreet phone calls; always from a pay phone knowing Washington's tendency to tap the phones on Capitol Hill, especially after Watergate and then the World Trade Center bombing in 1995. She wasn't going to take any chances.

She had been trying to gather various bits of information on her father, Ethan, as well as Danielle, with little success. Danielle had been born and raised in Bridgeport, Pennsylvania.

Of course, she had explained all of this in her journal. However, Maggie wanted tangible proof of her existence. She had not yet managed to obtain Danielle's birth certificate, her social security number, or the address of the couple who had raised her.

Chapter 29

Maggie was on the phone again with the hall of records in Bridgeport, PA searching for any records on her mother. She was on hold, drumming her well-manicured fingernails on her desk, the clicking sound somehow easing her frustration.

"I am so sorry to have kept you on hold, Mrs. Channing. We seem to be having an unusually busy day. Now, how may I help you?"

"Do you have anything on a Charles Sykes or a Hilda Sykes? It's spelled, S-Y-K-E-S."

"Sure, I'll look it up. Please hold."

After another interminable amount of time, the court clerk came back on the phone.

"The only information I can release to you is the fact that he was the County Sheriff at one time. His date of death is March 23, 1961. His wife, listed here, died ten years ago due to natural causes. Any other information on Sheriff Sykes is sealed. There was also an adopted daughter listed. She's deceased as well."

"Can you tell me anything about the daughter?" Maggie heard paper rustling.

"Let's see. Oh, yes. In the case file there is mention of her. She was at least seven months pregnant, and it seems she died in October of 1950 from a gas explosion in her home. I'm sorry. That's all I have, officially."

"Can you possibly tell me why the judge ordered the files on Sheriff Sykes sealed?"

"Ma'am, I'm unable to give out that infor . . . okay, I can tell you now. We're not supposed to reveal this, but I'm alone now, so I can talk. The judge, who was a close friend of Sheriff Sykes, ordered it sealed due to an unusual amount of activity."

"Are you telling me that others have made inquiries into this case and file?" Maggie asked incredulously.

"Yes, and that's extremely rare, even for Sykes," the girl explained. "I *will* tell you something that's been a rumor here for years. This has to be off the record. Sheriff Sykes was arrested and tried for child molestation and murder in 1958."

"Was he convicted?" Maggie asked, her heart pounding.

"His case was tried in the fall of 1958, and Sykes was sentenced to the gas chamber. He never made it. Senator Channing, Sheriff Sykes hung himself in jail after they convicted him. He never stopped saying he was innocent. Some of us feel that someone really murdered him. That much of the case I can tell you only because you're a senator. If you were anyone else, I wouldn't tell you even this much."

"Can you tell me when the first inquiry was made into his record?"

"There was an inquiry made on March 23, 1998, by a Mr. John Smith."

"Can you please tell me one more thing?"

"If I can, sure."

"Is there any way I can get this information faxed to me?"

"I'm sorry, no. I have strict orders not to release this information. If anyone found out I told you anything, I would lose my job. Since I was alone for the moment, I wanted to tell you as much as I could. I *am* sorry. That's all I can do."

"Thank you. You've been more than helpful."

With that, she hung the phone up, still discontented with the fact that she came away with little more knowledge than when she started.

Accepting the fact that she was not going to get much further, Maggie decided to tell Joshua what was going on. With making that decision, she went out to their backyard. It was large, with a manicured lawn, flowerbeds trimming the privacy fence, a huge deck that surrounded their Olympic-size swimming pool, and an adjoining hot tub installed under a redwood gazebo. Joshua was doing the weekly pool maintenance.

Saturdays around the Channing house were not typical of most affluent people. They preferred to take care of as much of their home as their schedules allowed. The only thing they had no time for was the lawn care. Maggie did some gardening, but not as much as she wanted.

Joshua looked up as Maggie strolled outside. He thought she was beautiful. She still had a slim, youthful figure, evidence of her daily workouts. Her hair had not yet become gray. Now, the sunlight bathed her hair in pale gold as she walked toward him. At the moment, she wore a serious expression. Joshua stopped work, knowing that she needed to talk by the expression on her face.

After she spoke to him, they went inside, fixed iced tea and sat in the comfortable breakfast nook in the corner of the large kitchen. All family discussions took place here. Over the years, they made plans, settled debates, and finalized family decisions at this very table.

She tried not to burden him with this, but not because she was prone to keeping secrets. She never kept anything from him before, and she could not put her finger on why she kept this from him so far. Now, as tears rolled down her cheeks, she shared the awful secret that Rose had revealed.

Joshua looked stricken at first, then, when he thought it all over, he realized why Leah had such remarkable abilities. He said as much to Maggie.

"My God, Maggie! Do you realize what this means?" he asked, after saying so.

Maggie looked up at him, concern written across her tear-stained face. "Yes I do, Josh. Our daughter might be in danger if they ever find out about her. That is, if it's all true."

"Exactly. Honey, why did Rose keep all this from you for so long?"

"Oh, Josh, I'm not sure. She told me she thought she would be protecting us more by not telling us. I'm still having a hard time with it all. She knew about Leah. She was just so old-fashioned when it came to the ways of the modern world."

Joshua asked for the journal that Rose gave her. Maggie got up and came back in a few minutes carrying the worn book. Maggie sat silent as Joshua read the journal. After reading only a third of the way through it, Joshua spoke.

"Maggie, I do have some major connections in the Pentagon, you know. I can nose around, do some research. I was never involved in Tanas, so I only know what I've heard. What I have heard, is that they've been restricted to carrying out top-secret projects for military purposes, such as weapons, and anti-aircraft missiles, as well as some state-of-the-art aircraft technology. However, I can dig as deep as I need to. Maggie, maybe our daughter is just a fluke of nature. Maybe your birth parents were a bit . . . eccentric," he finished hopefully.

Neither of them believed Josh's last statement, but both were desperate for anything that would cast another reason on why their daughter had been born so unique.

Finally, Joshua told her he would begin looking into it immediately.

"Thank you, Honey!" Maggie said as she reached out and took his hand, grateful for the understanding man he was.

With the secret released, Maggie was able to concentrate more on the other matters relegated to her. She felt safer knowing Josh was handling the situation.

Chapter 30

Adam Hanson read then reread the report the intelligence agent brought to him. He was still pissed off about the most recent failures. He could kill Scott all over again with his bare hands. An in-house investigative team came across some old records of one of the first doctors assigned to Project EVAH.

Hanson could not believe his eyes. There was actually a possible success out there. Unfortunately, the trail stopped cold at the death of the woman who had supposedly been Danielle Anderson.

By design, Tanas carefully stored samples of tissue, blood and other physical evidence, frozen in sealed, cryogenic containers from as far back as the beginning. Danielle's tissue and blood samples, they obtained through the nurse that had worked for her obstetrician. They were now carefully stored in the cryo lab, safe. Since there were no living relatives of this Danielle Anderson, they were able to exhume her body. Luckily, they had contacts everywhere.

After exhuming her body, Hanson waited impatiently for the results of DNA testing. Hanson was proud of perfecting the method for extracting DNA no matter how old the body was. So far, it was his crowning glory. His ego, however, hated that the world knew nothing of this accomplishment.

In the report, now in his hands, were the findings. The woman they had exhumed was not Danielle Anderson.

He could not keep from reading it repeatedly. The real Danielle Anderson would have been seventh months pregnant with a healthy embryo. She might still be alive. Did he dare hope her child made it alive?

He sat at his massive mahogany desk formulating a plan. He thought about it for a long time, wondering if Tanas would approve, though it might be hugely expensive, an unprecedented undertaking, not to mention risky due to the unusual activity that would ensue. He decided to call an emergency meeting with the executive staff, along with Tanas's High Council. This was too important not to.

The meeting took place in the rarely used boardroom.

"We have something of the utmost importance to decide, ladies and gentlemen," Dr. Hanson began as he addressed the board members and his staff.

"We could be on the threshold of success, or we could be chasing ghosts. One report has surfaced that is extremely hopeful. A woman by the name of Danielle Anderson--reported to be dead only months after her husband, Ethan--is not dead. As you know, he was among our first test subjects during WW II. Recently, he was located in South America, and then only by a fluke. He had the onset of senility, or Alzheimer's disease. It's also possible he's suffering from the long-term effects of the testing we performed on him back in the forties. We don't know for sure, yet.

"Anyway, he was taken to the doctor by one of his adopted sons when he began to rant about conspiracies, the end of the world as we know it, among other things. One of 'ours' was waiting in the same doctor's office and struck up a conversation, or at least tried. All he got out of him was his real name. He'd been going by the name of Manuel Gonzales and spoke fluent Spanish. Our guy heard enough of what he was saying to know this man knew what he was talking about. He immediately called us to inform us of the situation.

"We arranged a trip for him to the states. We have some great advances in the field of Alzheimer's disease here. It didn't take much to convince his son to agree to it. He obviously loves his father very much. He's now in the same place he was in the beginning, but, we went to the trouble of making sure he thought he was in his own home. It was expensive, but we thought it might be worth it. We were afraid he might go off the deep end if he recognized our base.

"This was three days ago. We're now awaiting DNA testing to ensure that he is Ethan Anderson. We should know within the week. He revealed much to us in his mumbling and ranting. We learned that his wife, Danielle, didn't die as we supposed, but lived at least as far as he knew. We did some checking and found out the woman buried is not Ethan's wife. Now, we must try to find her if we can."

He paused for dramatic effect, and then dropped the bomb. "People, she was seven months pregnant with a healthy child. We must find that child and any children he or she produced."

With his last statement, everyone began talking at once.

"We have to find her if we can," someone called out. Others concurred with the Tanas member who spoke out. The meeting lasted well into the evening. They ordered dinner from the complex's food center.

By 10:30 that evening, the Tanas High Council decided they would not spare any expense in finding him or her. Even though the chances were slim, there was still a chance.

Three days later, they realized Ethan was still at large.

Fortunately, the investigation did not cost them much. It did not take them long to find the child either, but it was   not by their methods. Maggie herself, alerted them to her whereabouts.

Chapter 31

As Maggie tried to gather all the information on them she could, Tanas followed her trail. She had thought she covered herself very well. Tanas had many ways to track people, even when she and Joshua thought they were covered. Once they found out who she was, it was easy--too easy--to get her DNA, especially since she was a government official.

At first, they checked her medical files for any anomalies. There were none. All her medical records were as normal as anyone else's. She had suffered the usual childhood diseases--chicken pox, measles, colds, flu. Maggie even needed extensive treatment for anemia.

None of these findings did them any good. She would not have had any illnesses or diseases at all. She'd had one pregnancy, Doctor Hanson read, bolting straight upright in his chair. "One pregnancy, one full-term birth. Sex: girl, five-pounds, eleven-ounces; eighteen inches long. Leah T. Channing; born July 4, 1982." On the page's lower right corner, the agent had scrawled, *Medical records on daughter enclosed; addendum--you might be really interested in her medical files.*

As he poured over her records, his face became increasingly animated, like the drawing of a cartoon character coming to life on film. As he got deeper into her file, his eyes lit up. He'd found what he wanted.

No illnesses, no childhood diseases, no nothing. Very unremarkable medical history. Every checkup resulted in a clean bill of health. He vaguely wondered why her physician never got suspicious, but it passed into the dark recesses of his mind, to never be remembered, as was all information he deemed unimportant.

He jumped up from his desk, called his secretary on the intercom, and growled for her to get in touch with Agent Nicholls to have him come to his office immediately.

He finished barking at her with, "And I mean damn fast."

Agent Nicholls knew Hanson summoned him for something important. The secretary had quoted Doctor Hanson verbatim.

Agent Nicholls arrived in short order.

"Yes, sir?"

"I have an assignment for you," Doctor Hanson said.

Doctor Hanson gave agent Nicholls the dossier he had prepared for him, after he removed what he wanted to keep from Nicholls. Nicholls went over the information thoroughly. After he finished, he looked up at Hanson.

Hanson knew not to disturb Nicholls when he was gathering information on a subject. He shook his legs in a subconscious effort to control his short temper. He was chain-smoking Winston cigarettes and his ashtray filled up fast. The circles of smoke he blew spewed out like smoke stacks from a diesel as it raced its engine. The only time he did not smoke was when he was engrossed in one of his projects.

Agent Nicholls sat back and lit one of his cheap cigars, knowing that Hanson hated them. He did not like Adam Hanson, but also knew Hanson would never say anything to him, for he was the best in the business. Hanson did not like Nicholls either.

Nicholls was loyal to no one, but also knew never to risk the repercussions he would endure if he ever betrayed Tanas. Because of their tenuous relationship, each one seemed gleefully to stretch the other's patience to the breaking point, yet without crossing over.

"Well, Hanson. What do you want to do about this one? She has a pretty interesting dossier, if you ask me." Nicholls sat back and put his feet up on the corner of the desk.

With a controlled voice, his teeth set on edge, Hanson said, "I didn't ask you, Nicholls. What you are to do with this one is to locate her and bring her back in one piece. Moreover, she had better not have even so much as a tiny scratch on her. Am I understood?"

"Sure, Hanson. This one'll cost Tanas a pretty penny. I can tell just by your attitude, as well as her dossier, that she's special. Am I right?"

Doctor Hanson did not respond to Nicholls's last statement. This told Nicholls all he needed to know.

"There is another matter we need you to take care of," Hanson said. "One Senator Margaret Channing. She knows too much. We have to eliminate her. Most likely, we'll have to delete Colonel Channing, as well. We cannot take any--and I mean *any*--chances of the locals getting suspicious about the unfortunate *accident* the Channings will have. I don't want to know how, where, or method. I just want the usual confirmation that it is done."

"Sure, no problem. We succeeded with Kennedy, didn't we? A senator will be a piece of cake. To this day, no one has been able to trace the real power behind Camelot's demise. Who knows, maybe one day, it'll be Caroline's turn."

Nicholls was ice cold to his very core. It showed in his eyes. Since the eyes are the window to the soul, his showed clearly that he did not have one.

After Nicholls left, Doctor Hanson went down to his lab. He booted up the computer, entered his password, and proceeded to work, a faint smile of satisfaction on his face.

Chapter 32

Leah came home, having completed her junior year at George Washington University. She enjoyed the summer respite from the rigors of classes, though she breezed through every course she took. She swam with her friends, went to the lake, and worked part-time in a clothing boutique owned by her parents' best friends.

Leah, always independent, insisted on working to earn money for her first car. She announced this when she was thirteen. Leah took on a paper route, babysat, and did other odd jobs for three years prior to obtaining her license. By the time she reached her sixteenth birthday she purchased a used Cabriolet convertible. Josh and Maggie presented her with a brand-new gas card in her name, along with an insurance policy good for one full year, gifts for her accomplished driving skills. She accepted the gifts graciously.

Joshua and Maggie had always tried to dote on her, but she'd never had any of it, even when she was little. She was strong-willed at times, but only if what they asked her to do seemed illogical. "Because I said so", was never good enough for her.

She wanted to know *why* she could not do a certain thing. The early years with her were a mixture of awe and pride, marred by battles and frustration. Luckily, they had Doctor Poskinski as a buffer. She set to right many of the conflicts that arose during the first years of struggle.

The next few months were uneventful in the lives of the Channing family. They all went about their business and social obligations. But in late fall of 2001, the bottom began to fall out.

September 11 devastated the Channing family, as it did the entire nation. Both Maggie and Josh had to handle some of the crises. Maggie, in her capacity as a senator, went to Washington to assist in the efforts to find out what had happened. Joshua left to help at the Pentagon, assisting in the investigation, while at the same time grieving over lost comrades.

Shortly after September 11, Frank, a close friend of Josh's, died after borrowing his jeep for a fishing trip. The jeep careened out of control and flipped down an embankment, killing him instantly. The accident investigators deemed faulty brakes responsible for the fatality. Josh knew this was wrong as he'd had the brakes worked on just a few weeks prior to Frank's death. He wondered how such a thing could have happened, and continued to make inquiries, in spite of dead-ends he kept running into. He had one more option.

Joshua was on the phone in his study talking to another good friend, Colonel Boseman, in his Pentagon office. He explained what he wanted.

"Josh, I have no idea what you're talking about."

"Howard, I'm only asking you to see if military records show anyone stationed there, posted as a perimeter guard during the latter part of the 1940s. You can't do that? How would it threaten National Security?"

"Josh, okay, I'll discreetly look into it, but I make no promises. Understood?" Howard conceded.

"Thanks, Howard. You have no idea what this means to me."

"By the way, Josh. Why do you need this information?"

"For a friend, Howie. For a friend."

"I'll get back to you on this."

Howie hung up the phone before Joshua had a chance to thank his friend again.

Howard Boseman punched the keys on his secured-line cell phone as he leaned back in his office chair. He rubbed his forehead as he placed the phone to his ear. When the voice came on the line, he spoke abruptly.

"We have problems."

After he explained the situation to the man on the line, he waited.

"What do you want me to do about it, Colonel?" the disembodied voice asked.

"He's one of my best friends, but we can take no chances. Eliminate him and his wife. Make it look good. I hate having to make these decisions.

"Damn!" he exclaimed, as he hung up the phone. Though he despised what he had to do to his friend, he knew he had no alternative. He had hoped Joshua would have given up already; he had hoped his friend would not place him in this situation.

~

Joshua was reading more of the eye-opening journal penned by the mysterious Danielle. He knew Maggie was unable to glean much information on this woman's existence in Bridgeport. He decided to make a trip up to Pennsylvania during his two-week vacation. He would leave two weeks after Leah's graduation in May. It would take that long to schedule his vacation time and make travel arrangements. He searched for Maggie to inform her of his plans.

When he found Maggie and told her his plans, she jumped up and gave him a hug and a kiss, thanking him for his support.

~

In an undisclosed location, the agent on duty dialed a number.

"We need to act fast, Sir."

"What is it?" the man on the other end asked.

"We need to get rid of the Channings soon. Why it hasn't already been done is beyond me."

He briefed his boss on the latest development in the Channing household.

"You get it done before he leaves. Do it shortly after the daughter's graduation. Just make sure the vital package is not in the house when it happens! Any mistakes in this and heads will roll--literally!"

"Yes, Sir."

Chapter 33

As Leah T. Channing sat on the stage of the auditorium at George Washington University, she waited for the commencement ceremony to begin. She was to give the valedictorian speech for her graduating class.

As she sat there, she searched the first few rows reserved for the families of those who were to speak during the ceremonies, looking for the three people she loved most. She smiled when she saw them sitting side by side in the second row. She studied their faces as she watched them talking to each another.

Her father, retired Colonel Joshua Channing, still as military as ever, was aging nicely. Still well-built, tall, with broad shoulders, trim waist, and muscular legs, he appeared younger than his years. His ebony hair was now softened by streaks of gray scattered throughout. His eyes, a pale blue, always twinkled as though he might be on the verge of laughing. She thought of the many nights when she was small. He would come upstairs to her room, a book of fairy tales in hand, and lie down beside her and read a bedtime story to her until she was almost asleep. Then she would feel his comforting hands gently pull the covers up and tuck her in. She would wait until he left her room and then snuggle under the blanket, sniffing the pillow he'd sat propped up on, breathing in the faint scent of his cologne. She remembered every little detail, as was in her nature.

She looked at her mother. She was smiling as she listened to something her father was saying. Margaret, known by her friends and family as Maggie, though a statuesque five-foot-nine, seemed short when she stood beside her husband. She had hair the color of corn silk, with vivid blue eyes that spoke of a woman well-satisfied with her life, marriage, and career. A senator for the state of Maryland, her political career began as a city Councilwoman many years before. Leah thought how, though her mother had a busy career, she never felt neglected. She remembered many afternoons, coming home from school, the smell of homemade cookies in the air. She remembered school plays, her mother clapping the loudest; slumber parties on the weekends; many late-night talks, whispers in the dark about secret things. Margaret Trusdale-Channing was her best friend and confidant.

Little did Leah know the boiling cauldron of change, tragedy, and mystery that lurked under the surface of the seemingly calm Channing couple.

She moved her attention to her fiancé, Richard Slazenger, an attorney for the Washington, D.C. law firm of Wagner, Howell, & Jamison. He was still a staffer, having obtained his law degree just one year prior to her graduation. He was six feet tall, with dark brown hair the color of chocolate. His eyes were such a dark brown they appeared almost black. He had a stocky build that evidenced rigid workouts.

She and Richard had planned their lives so carefully. They were going to be married in June of the following year.

Leah held a passion for law over the years. After discussing this with Richard, she decided to wait and begin law school a year after they were married. They wanted time to adjust as well as save money. She had already lined up a job as an assistant to the curator of the Museum of Natural History. She would start her job the first week after graduation.

She caught the attention of her family and smiled at them.

Leah heard the Dean call her name and she gave her speech without incident.

The celebration dinner took place at Mona's Cajun Cuisine, their favorite place to eat out, not to mention that Leah's best friend Mona, owned the place. They loved the original Cajun food that Mona served with a flair and style all her own.

Mona became her best friend during her first year at the university. Leah met her at the restaurant she owned. They were as different as night and day, but their differences seemed to draw them to each other. Mona told Leah her life story--being raised in an abusive home, being put on the streets when she was fifteen, finding herself rescued by Gateway, a private home for throwaway kids. She received love, counseling, and a free education from private donations, which kept the home running. After graduating culinary school, she bought her restaurant by saving up every cent she did not absolutely need. It took her ten years to achieve her goal, but she did it and was proud of her accomplishments.

Leah was so excited about the life she would soon have. She and Richard had a rare and wonderful relationship. They fit so well. They complimented each other.

She thought back to the first time she ever saw Richard.

Her favorite place to relax was an off-campus gourmet coffee house called The Grinder. She went there to indulge her craving for cappuccino. The Grinder was a large place, dotted with tall tables, matching bar stools completing the sets. Other areas were reminiscent of old- fashioned parlors, complete with reproduction Victorian-style furniture. These areas complimented large, low tables adorned with antique reading lamps, giving the place a relaxed, intimate atmosphere, ideal for studying for finals. Soft, piped in jazz completed the ambience.

She walked in, placed her order, and sat down in one of the parlors, choosing a corner of one of the large sofas. She began studying her Latin. He walked in, his hair disheveled from the strong breezes that day. He wore a long-sleeved flannel shirt and snug jeans. His hiking boots completed his outdoorsy look.

They saw each other at the Grinder off and on for several weeks before he struck up a conversation. They discovered they had a lot of hobbies and interests in common. They took their time getting to know each other, becoming friends. They grew in love, rather than fell into it like so many people they knew, yet there was always an underlying passion kept under control.

She switched gears and brought her thoughts back to the present after having pulled out that particular file, and stored it away neatly.

She was looking forward to her life.

PART THREE

Leah

Chapter 34

Leah worked late and was tired. She turned off the computer, satisfied with the data she'd entered for the new acquisitions for the museum, cleaned up the remnants of the deli sandwich she'd had delivered, then proceeded to lock up.

She took her time in leaving, though she was tired. She loved to linger over the wonderful antiquities there. There were artifacts dating as far back as the early settlers. Other areas of the museum housed reminders of the cost of gaining the freedom most people took for granted. She finally reached the door to the parking lot.

She stepped out into the warm, dark summer night. Checking her watch, she realized it was well past ten p.m. As she made her way to her car, she noticed several parking lot lights were out near where she'd parked, casting darkness around her vehicle. Even with all the lights on, the lot was dim at best. Her boss apologetically told her the city utilities had been promising to correct the now defective lights for months. She wished she had not parked her car near the bushes at the street side of the parking lot.

As she started to walk down the steps of the employee's entrance, Leah thought she saw a shadow near the bushes to her right. She turned to look, but saw nothing. She was unusually jumpy, her extraordinary senses aware of danger; yet, she could not see anything out of the ordinary.

She stood on the steps for quite some time, searching the night for something hidden. There were cars parked along the street that ran behind the building, but there were always cars parked along there.

She started walking toward her car, hesitating as the little hairs on the back of her neck began to rise. She berated herself for her jitters and then walked, more determined, toward her car, fishing her keys out of her purse on the way.

The two agents sat in the sedan, watching their prey. They used unconventional state-of-the-art equipment. The senior agent in the driver's seat used a four-in-one night vision monocular. The video camera adapter recorded its subject.

His partner looked like the serial killer during the climactic scene with Jodie Foster in *Silence of the Lambs*, in his infrared night vision goggles. The straps, which held the goggles in place, ran over the top and down the back of his head, and joined the two side straps, one over his ears and the other underneath.

They knew she might have extremely keen senses, maybe even strong psychic abilities. Though it was mere speculation, Tanas wanted to take no chances. This one must be a "live capture". Hanson had driven that point home to the two agents assigned this project, with the promise of severe consequences should they fail.

They scarcely breathed as she stood on the steps looking like a beautiful animal, poised for flight at the slightest evidence of danger. They watched as she walked down the steps. The two agents saw her clearly. Holding their breath, they hoped she had not sensed their presence.

She headed to her car.

They exhaled and then breathed deeply at the same time.

"Good," he said. "We'll follow her until we're sure she's home, then we can do what we have to."

His partner nodded.

"We have to remember to be careful with this one, though," the partner spoke. "She's the only successful result we've ever had. He said not to damage her in--"

"Look!" the driver exclaimed, interrupting as he pointed toward the bushes by her car.

She had just opened her door when there in the shadows, a dark figure rushed her, grabbing her from behind. They watched her go limp, apparently from chloroform or some other drug given through a cloth placed over her mouth and nose.

Holding her with one arm, her attacker reached down and opened the back door with his free hand, and placed her in the back seat. Then he retrieved the keys that had slipped out of Leah's hand, got into the car, and drove away.

In his hurry to be on his way, he scraped his knuckle on the rough surface of the parking lot. He searched for a piece of napkin or tissue to stop the bleeding, but only after putting a little distance between him and the relative risk he had taken to get the girl.

"Damn!" the driver said, striking the steering wheel with his fist. He'd stopped looking through the stationary monocular in the excitement, trying to see with his own eyes.

"Who in the hell was that?" he continued. "Did you get a good look at him through your goggles?"

"Yeah, but I couldn't tell who he was. He had on a ski mask."

"If he harms her in any way, we are yesterday's news!"

The agent started the car. They followed her car as it headed toward the thoroughfare.

Somehow, they lost her car. Traffic was heavy, usual for Friday night in Washington, D.C., and they were worried.

The agent in the passenger seat leaned over to a modified laptop attached to the dash, pushed a button on the keyboard, then leaned back, satisfied with the reassuring dot on the screen moving along a detailed grid map on the monitor.

"We got her," he assured his partner.

They watched the monitor for some time, following the path the car took. The pulsing dot became stationary fourteen blocks from where they were. They drove, careful to maintain the traffic speed, confident they would track their prey down. When they reached the alley where the car had stopped, they found it abandoned.

"Damn!" the driver exploded, "He must have had another vehicle to put her in!"

The driver yanked a cell phone out of his pocket, dialed a number and spoke into it.

"We need backup here, now! Send a wrecker."

~

The man looked back at Leah, satisfied with his work, yet despising the necessary tactics. He drove on in the old, nondescript Suburban, heading south. He knew she would be out for at least twelve hours. That would give him plenty of time to get out of the state. He would have to keep her unconscious until they reached Mexico. Then, he would tell her about her extraordinary past, her roots--the whole thing. He felt for the CD in his pocket and glanced down at the laptop computer sitting in the front seat. Peter knew that if it were not for the information he had on him, he would never convince her of the truth about why she was so different.

Early the next morning, before she had a chance to awaken, he pulled into a deserted rest stop and administered another dose of the drug to keep her asleep. He was careful to stay off the main interstate roads, opting instead for the lesser-used two lane highways that snaked across the country.

She was in the back of the Suburban, under the floor in a false bottom where he had removed seats. Looking at it from the outside, no one would suspect there was a false compartment in there. A small air vent patched into the main air conditioner. This would ensure that the captive would not suffocate and would stay comfortable. After closing the compartment and the back door of the Suburban, he hit the remote lock on the control pad he kept in his pocket, enabling him to leave it running and locking it at the same time. As a result, the Suburban was very deceptive in appearance. No one would ever suspect the high-tech devises that he'd installed.

Satisfied with his ministrations, he walked over to the vending machines, got a cup of coffee that he used to help him gulp down No-Doze, then got back into the SUV and headed back out.

~

The wrecker got to their location quickly. The agent told the driver to take the car to the designated warehouse. As they approached the door, it opened. The wrecker pulled into the bay and stopped. Men wearing surgical gloves and carrying fingerprint kits approached the car. The wrecker driver, another Tanas agent, donned gloves and dug into the open trunk, searching for any clues he might find. On one wall of the small warehouse appeared to be a laboratory. There was a sophisticated computer equipped with a high-tech scanner. Along with the elaborate computer equipment was a long table, complete with a large microscope. It looked like one of those forensic labs one sometimes saw on the episodes of those "Forensic Stories," which aired on Court TV, TLC, and the Discovery Channel. However, no forensic lab had anything as technologically advanced as Tanas's equipment

As the agents searched the car, they collected various samples in tiny vials. They would then take the vials to one technician, who would transfer the contents onto a microscope slide. A special device attached to the microscope read the data on the slide. Once he completed this, the technician punched the data into a keyboard then downloaded it onto a CD. When they finished collecting all the data, the lab chief took the CD over to another operative, who scanned the data. Within a few minutes, he found what he had been looking for.

"Bingo! Gotta match here. I know who took her."

They all gathered around the man, looking at the monitor. There he was, complete with picture, fingerprints, hair samples, blood type . . . and his DNA pattern.

Peter Wiler had been very careful about not leaving fingerprints on the vehicle, but what he had never been privy to was the fact that Tanas had covertly managed to obtain everyone's DNA, blood type, hair samples--just about everything they could, to ensure they would never have trouble finding or identifying any agent.

"Dammit! I was afraid of this," said the agent in charge.

"He was one of our best agents, too, until he got religion. Now he's become our worst enemy. We can't allow him to go through with his plan. If he does, it will blow the lid off the entire operation. Now we have two problems, men," the agent in charge said.

"One, we still have to get that disk back from Peter Wiler, especially now since he has her. She could very well break the codes on that disk. We have to make sure Peter Wiler dies, and we have to get the girl . . . alive and well."

An eerie silence fell over the agents as they contemplated the ramifications that this incident would cause, especially when they would have to report to Tanas. Tanas had been able to keep the lid on what was going on for more than fifty years without incident.

They had searched for Peter Wiler for over a year now. How one man escaped with a copy of the encrypted disk, they never could figure out. Most of their agents made CIA operatives look rank, but Peter, by far, had been their best agent.

The few agents who, when Tanas was young, had attempted to leave, never made it out alive. Up until a year before, no one dared try to leave since those unfortunate few became painful examples of what would happen to deserters.

Peter Wiler was a quick, proficient learner. All the skills he mastered impressed many of the mentors and teachers assigned to him. His psychological profile proved him devoted to the cause. He truly had believed in the goals of Tanas. He proved his loyalty when his boss assigned him to kill one agent who attempted to spill the story to the press. Little did the agent know that they had people everywhere, including much of the media. Peter never blinked when the agent fell, the surprised look on his face frozen in death.

He and Peter had trained together, roomed together, and had become as close as any two brothers might have been. Yet Peter felt nothing but disdain toward him as he had begged for his life.

Peter developed a coldness about him during the years in Tanas. He learned to control his emotions so well that most of the time he felt nothing at all. This made him more dangerous than many of the agents that graduated through training. Now Peter Wiler was a major threat to the cause. They had to eliminate him while at the same time maintaining Leah Channing's safety. She would be a most important key to the future. Peter Wiler proved to be elusive in every way, as though some force had been keeping him hidden from the high-tech resources at Tanas's disposal. His intense intelligence training had proved to be their downfall . . . until now.

"The way I see it, he's got at least ten, maybe ten and a half hours on us," the agent in charge continued. He looked at the two agents who had followed Peter and the girl. They knew they had made a deadly mistake in losing the girl; especially now.

"We cannot assume," he concluded, "that he will let any grass grow under his feet before he gets out of town. We will have to bring in more agents to find them."

The hunt began.

Chapter 35

Peter knew he needed to keep moving, but he had to make one stop first.

He pulled into the almost invisible auto repair garage located in one of the many small towns of eastern Tennessee. One had to live in the area to know it existed. The garage sat on one of the many back roads that snaked their way through the hilly, Tennessee countryside.

After Peter got out of the Suburban, the mechanic closed the overhead and placed the "Out to Lunch" sign on the front door then locked up. Peter and the mechanic, Zachary, talked in low, earnest tones.

"I knew it was risky when I got her," Peter was saying. "I spotted two of them in a car parked down the street from her job. Thank God they didn't recognize me. I was wearing a ski mask. I'm afraid that won't last too long, though. There have been national headlines, reporting Senator Channing's daughter's kidnapping and possible murder. Everyone is looking for her now."

Shaking his head, he continued. "I don't look forward to telling her about her family and friends. They were all at her parent's home when the explosion took place. I know Tanas had something to do with it. It was gruesome at the crime scene. I was there. Of course, no one knew who I was. She doesn't even know, yet. Poor kid!"

"I understand," Zachary replied. "It's gonna be awfully hard on her, ain't it, Pete?" the old man said.

"Yes, it is," Peter replied. He stood there, working his jaw muscles as he thought about the difficult task still before him. He finally spoke again.

"I hope you have something for me, Zach. You know what I need."

"No problem, Pete. Give me just a minute. I think I got just the thing for ya."

Zach went to the end of the garage toward the back. He slid open a door to a small room which held some old tools, a few tires, and some cleaning equipment. He reached down to a piece of flat rubber, lifted it up out of the way, and slid open a trap door that appeared to not even be there. Within fifteen minutes, he was back up with a packet of information and a theatrical makeup kit.

One hour later, an old preacher in a rusty looking farm truck loaded with Bibles and other items, headed for the Mexican border.

~

Even though he had become acquainted with many of the border guards, not one of them would recognize him now. He was not worried about it, but this made things much easier as he passed through into Mexico. The officers frequently changed stations, so he felt that his chances of not running into one of the border guards he knew would be good. He also had God on his side. As he neared the border, he began to pray.

"Father, You know I have obeyed Your call to this mission. I ask You right now to help me through this border. Blind the eyes of anyone who would be Your enemy. I ask You in Jesus' Name, Amen."

Peter got through the border and the two other check points inside Mexico with no problems.

Leah was well ensconced in another compartment within the truck bed, under the items. Though it was not as comfortable as the jeep, he knew she would be all right. He neared the town of La Paz when she began to stir.

Leah stirred in her cramped quarters, not knowing where she was, still very groggy. She felt the vehicle's rhythmic movement. She knew her mouth was taped shut so she could not scream. Her hands, she discovered, were tied up, yet comfortably so. She was bouncing hard, but someone had gone to the trouble of cushioning her to absorb the shock. The real shock was yet to come.

Peter was still very much the old preacher who had left Tennessee when he got Leah out of the back of the pickup. Still disoriented, she stumbled against him. He grabbed her to support her. Before she could get her wits about her, he covered her mouth again. Oblivion came.

Leah awoke once again, this time with a splitting headache. She found herself inside an adobe dwelling with terrazzo tile floors, some antiquated furniture, and an area rug in front of the bed where she lay.

She got out of bed gingerly, for she felt like someone had beaten her up. She was sore all over. She attempted to locate anyone who might be in the house. From the coolness in the home, she knew there was air conditioning on.

She found the large living room, where the décor was southwest design. The room was long and narrow with low, comfortable chairs and a matching sofa. There were Southwest design end tables, and a matching coffee table. On one end of the room was a large alcove with a sizable desk and chair.

At the desk, a man hovered over a laptop computer, accompanied by some very sophisticated, state-of-the-art communication equipment. In addition, it had a phone line, a small micro-satellite dish, and a scrambler device.

Leah, who never lost her head even in a situation such as this, approached the man to find out why he had kidnapped her.

He looked up as she approached.

"Who are you, why did you kidnap me, and what do you plan to do with me?" With that, she folded her arms and waited.

"Look, Ms. Channing. I will explain it all to you soon enough. Trust me that I will never harm you. I am not out to hurt you. I am here to keep you safe and to save your life. I know you must have quite a headache. Is there anything I can get for it? I promise it will only be aspirin or Tylenol."

He waited for her to respond.

"Okay, but then you *will* explain yourself."

Her emotions battled her intellect. She knew instinctively that he would not hurt her, yet she did not want to appear too trusting. Leah knew she would find out soon enough what his motives were. She had to be patient.

Two hours later, with some coffee, Extra Strength Tylenol, and some much needed food, he began to explain to her, along with the evidence he had brought, about her life, her family, and why she was being sought by Tanas. At first she thought he might be insane, but she could not refute the evidence he showed her. Now her abilities could come to light. She had no choice but to trust him. Though she did not want to believe such an outlandish story, it all made sense to her on some gut level.

Three weeks after arriving in La Paz, the two settled in at one of the ranches. Gone were the comforts of the adobe home. Here to stay was a mere existence. She now had just a makeshift bed in which to sleep. Her entire family was gone. She knew if Tanas caught her, they would subject her to anything they deemed necessary to assist in their cause.

Doctors, lawyers, politicians, some media moguls, as well as many other facets of the business and political world were involved. Some thought the project was an honest, upright, operation. If they ever found out otherwise, the western world's economic system would indeed collapse.

Many of the participants, however, knew all too well what was really going on. They were believers, passionate in their quest to assist in eliminating all undesirable humans that could not stand up to the test that the entire world needed to pass. Roswell was not a myth. What really happened there during the so-called weather balloon mishap was the dawning of the new age. It would be an age that one day in the future, would challenge some of the most religious zealot's faith; more so than in any other time in history.

~

Leah was lying on her makeshift bed, trying without much success to sleep. She had not had a good night's sleep in what seemed to be a lifetime. She was always on her guard now, in spite of the carefully selected men placed outside the shack she now called home.

Currently, she lived in one of the many anonymous "ranchos" outside the small town of La Paz, Mexico, under an assumed identity. Even though the many precautions were for her protection, she still felt like a prisoner. How long had it been since she could run free, or take a walk downtown, go shopping, or do just anything she wanted? She wondered how much time she had left, how long it would be before they found her. She let out a sigh as though it was an effort just to breathe.

Leah wondered where Peter Wiler was. He had brought her a box of brunette hair dye the day before, told her to use it, then left.

After she applied the dye, she finger-dried her short curls. Even in the ancient mirror in what one could hardly call a bathroom, she had been shocked at her transformed appearance. Gone was the woman that used to stare back at her.

Leah T. Channing had managed to reach five-foot-three inches in height, and there she stopped. She had a petite build, which complimented her pixie-like appearance. Her hair was blonde and curly, which she wore short. With her mischievous, almond-shaped blue eyes, framed by thick, long lashes, one could picture her as a beautiful fairy, frolicking through some mystic forest, her resplendent, translucent wings flowing behind her.

Now she had an even more ethereal look to her, enhanced by the dark circles under her eyes, pale skin, and now very dark hair.

She turned over in her bunk, trying to get more comfortable. She was still in shock over everything she had learned. It all still felt unreal, illogical to her very logical mind. Yet she could not refute the evidence of her unique existence.

When Peter Wiler had first told Leah about the secret to her past, she thought he was a lunatic. The evidence he produced afterward made her blood run cold.

She also knew nothing would ever be the same again. There was no one else left in her life, except Peter Wiler. Who she was and what she was had cost her the loss of her entire family. Her parents, her best friend, and her fiancé, everyone she knew and loved; gone. Now there were people who were looking for her, not to question her about the deaths of her family but to dissect her, to find out how she worked. Peter Wiler vowed not to allow that to happen.

Peter Wiler.

Peter Wiler was an enigma, the only person she had not been able to figure out quickly, but so far, he had proven she could trust him. But could he protect her indefinitely? Only time would tell--whatever time they might have left.

She wondered just how much time she had. How long could Peter go on protecting her? How long before she was no longer safe?

Chapter 36

Leah's existence was not what she would have wanted for her life and she hated not being in control. She had learned to exert so much control due to her mental abilities, that it became almost second nature.

She decided that Fate, or Karma, or something was against her all of a sudden. She never grew up believing in the traditional God that the church taught. Her logical mind could never accept that theory. She learned the traditional teaching but the first few classes in religion turned her off the subject. How could she believe in a God who allowed so much evil to happen? If He were the God of the Universe, then He could have done something long before now. Leah would soon discover He already had.

As she was thinking about all that had happened to her, Peter Wiler came into the house. Gone was the old preacher she had first seen. At first she was startled, not knowing who he was. Startled by her own reaction to his rugged good looks, she reined her thoughts in like always, filing the emotions away whenever things got too intense.

His eyes were the most startling blue she had ever seen. His face, weathered by all he had been through, added to, rather than diminished, his looks. His hair was the color of rich chocolate. Coupled with his deep olive complexion, he made quite a package.

The moment he spoke, she knew it was Peter.

"I thought you were old!"

"I'm sorry for the charade but it was a necessity in order to get across the border into Mexico. Too many people would have recognized me otherwise."

Life became as normal as possible under the circumstances. Peter attended services at one of the small non-conforming churches on the ranch. Mexico, steeped in the Catholic religion, mixed with a lot of superstition and witchcraft, often created bondage for the Mexican people. Churches like *Iglesia De La Dios en Christo* (Church of God in Christ) were rare although more of them were cropping up. The hearts of the Mexican people remained attuned to the truth when they could hear it. This created powerful prayer warriors.

The local president of the church ran the ranchero. He served as pastor, mayor, and local law.

Peter invited Leah to go on numerous occasions, but she refused each time, adhering to her beliefs.

This began to change as she watched the poverty-stricken people rejoice in each and every day they were given, sharing what little they had to the strange mujer (woman) that wandered into their midst.

One Sunday morning she decided to go and see what secret they held. She wanted to find out how they could be so happy and content in their lack. Leah needed no interpreter to translate. She learned Spanish in college. She did not know some of the words used by the locals, but she learned their meanings quickly, as was customary for her.

The services began with singing and dancing, which was new to Leah. The few services she had ever attended were stiff and stifling. It had all seemed so ritualistic that it ruined her for a long time. She had no idea that God was orchestrating her life, preparing her to face her destiny, her future. She had no clue as to how strong in the Lord she would need to be to face the future.

Had she known, she might have decided that dying was a better alternative.

There seemed to be no time limit on the service that day. She felt an unseen force leading the simple people. It was puzzling, yet the intrigue of it fascinated her. As she sat and listened to the pastor, his words began making sense.

He spoke in Spanish. "Good morning brothers and sisters. I am so pleased you have come today. I want especially to welcome our friend, Senorita Smith to the services. Today, I wish to speak of why things happen to us that seem like they are not fair, or that God should not allow them to happen.

"God is a God of love, yes. He is also a God who keeps His word. What does this mean? To answer that, first let us go to His written Word. Please turn to the New Testament, in the book of St. Luke, chapter 4. Jesus Himself was tempted in the wilderness. Lucifer came to Him three times and tempted Him with all the pleasures of the world. He enticed Jesus to eat bread if He claimed to be the Son of God. He told Him to cast Himself down from the mountain because God should protect Him, if He was the Son of God. He showed Jesus all the kingdoms of the world in their entire splendor, and said if He would bow down to His enemy, he would give Him all of these things.

"Jesus told him to leave Him alone. He would not tempt the Lord His God, nor would He live by bread alone, but by every Word from the mouth of God. He let him know that He would worship God only.

"Let us not forget that Jesus knew He was to come to earth to experience all the things we go through. He is not a God who does not know our pain, but a God who has gone through it already. He is the only man ever born who has truly walked a mile in every man's shoes.

"You say, 'Well if God loved us, He would not allow bad things to happen.' But I remind you that He did not promise us that this life would be easy. He said as much that we would suffer persecution and know tribulations. That we would find ourselves facing perils and temptations just like the ones He overcame. In Luke 4:33, He said to be of good cheer even through tribulation, for He has overcome the world.

"As you all know, we suffer sometimes from diseases we have inherited from our ancestors. Things like the weak heart, or like Brother Gonzales who has the diabetes. Or even more so, the ones who have not tasted the freedom that we afford to worship God in Spirit and in truth. I am speaking of the ones who are still in bondage to the traditions of our people. We suffered oppression. We were deceived--persecuted when we did not deserve the punishment.

"We are now new creations of the Lord. He has brought us a cure. That cure is Himself.

When the world was created, there was nothing wrong with anything. The world was perfect. Adam and Eve were perfect. Yet they sinned by their own free will. Let us liken sin to an incurable disease. When we became diseased with sin, we inherited it from them. They were the first created in the likeness and image of God. God, their Father, created them with free wills. He wanted them to obey Him and to commune with Him. He wanted to gain their trust and love. These elements were there, but He wanted those to mature and grow.

"Adam and Eve decided they wanted to partake of the forbidden fruit. This was the fruit from the tree of knowledge of good and evil. God allowed them to take any other fruit in that garden, but they chose the one fruit that would forever separate them from God. If one thinks of this in logical terms, it is the only thing that makes sense of all that is unfair in life.

"God loves us all, but if He were to make us no more than robots, then the love would not be genuine. It would be against our own free wills. Think about this, my hermanos y hermanas . . . How would *you* want to receive love? Whole-heartedly, or because the person was programmed to love you?

"I know I would want that love to be freely given."

Leah walked away from that service in deep thought. She longed to go for a walk to ponder the preacher's message. Should she defy Peter's admonition not to venture off alone?

One thing she knew was that she would need solitude to come to a conclusion. She waited until the daily siesta that shut everything down in the heat of the day. She was going to pray to this God to speak to her. If He spoke to her, then she would know it.

Peter stayed close to Leah, however. She knew she would have to be extremely careful to be able to go for a walk. Eventually he would need to bathe, or relieve himself. Her chance came the next morning right after breakfast. She knew the guards kept vigil outside the door, but maybe she could manage to get out the window that was little more than a small hole in the wall. She measured the opening with her eyes. She was sure she could do it.

Peter had gone to take care of some things with the admonition for her to stay put. He told her the guards would not allow her to leave. It was not that she was in trouble, but Peter knew what she could face if she got lost or worse yet, if someone from Tanas found her. He also knew their time here was limited. They needed to move soon.

Leah climbed out of the window as quietly as she could. It was a tight squeeze, but she managed. Slipping to the ground, she surveyed her surroundings, careful to tread lightly. She got her landmarks and began her walk.

~

Peter met with the man known only as Hector. He was the only human smuggler he trusted. Most 'coyotes' had ulterior motives and could not care less about the poor souls desperate to find a better life for their families by fleeing to the U.S. Many who fled Mexico never made it alive. They traveled in hot, smothering trailers, attached to big rigs. Many times they had no air, no water or food. Many of them were unaware that they needed both to hopefully survive the trip. Some of the illegal immigrants simply disappeared, for if they died on the way, they were tossed into the desert of Mexico where they became sustenance for the wild life that survived in the rugged terrain.

There were times when the border patrol arrested the human traffickers. When that happened, the immigrants had to go back to Mexico and the cycle would start again.

Hector was different. His charges always made it across. A small, nondescript mission right across the border was set up to assist those who needed the work in the U.S. in order for their families to survive in Mexico. They took menial jobs, backbreaking positions that many U.S. citizens would never take.

Peter and Hector spoke well into the afternoon. Peter did not worry about Leah as he thought she would be unable to get away.

~

After Peter completed all the paperwork for their trip to Brazil, he headed back to the ranch. Donned in his old man persona, he ventured freely, passing those who would have known him immediately had he not put on the disguise. Many would have sold him out to anyone who paid them. Under the circumstances, their hunger called for desperate measures. Others were simply greedy. As he approached the ranch, *El Presidente* stopped him, excitedly waving his arms.

Chapter 37

"They did not go anywhere. I know these men and they want to keep the senorita safe."

Upon hearing this, Peter went into the small ranch house. Immediately, he knew she had managed to leave through the window. Now he had trouble.

"Pedro, take your men and search the area. I'll go to the woods behind the house. I think she may have gone for a walk. I want every possible man on this. We must find her."

Peter felt Tanas's pincers close in on them. He knew they were going to find them soon. It was as if he could smell them long before they reached him.

For two hours the search party tried to find Leah. They were unsuccessful. By the time they got back to the ranch, Leah was at the small desk in the house, poring over Peter's Bible.

"Leah! Don't *ever*--and I mean *EVER*--go off alone like that again! Do I make myself clear?"

Her head jerked up at the harsh way he spoke to her. She resented it. Although she knew logically that he was right, she had a perverse desire to defy this man, this stranger who had rescued her from a fate worse than hell.

She stuck her chin out and told him, "I needed some solitude, Mr. Wiler. I cannot stand having people around me all the time. I cannot bear this much longer."

Peter just stared at her. Finally, he spoke again. This time his voice was soft and reasoning, although inside his patience had worn thin.

"You need to realize the situation, Leah. There are those who would stop at nothing--*nothing*--to get to you. They would not think anything of destroying this rancho, the people here, including the children, to ensure your capture. Do you want that on your conscience?"

"No, I do not! Do you think for one moment that I have not thought about that? My mind is very logical. I think about all possibilities and probabilities in any given situation. I was taking a minimal risk. I think if they were close enough to know where we are, they would have already made their move."

Exasperated, Peter rubbed his hands over his eyes before speaking again.

"You don't know these people like I do. They are not above bribery or any other means available to them to get information. I can tell you that not all of these people are like the ones in this ranchero. There are those who out of desperation would sell their souls to feed their families. We need to sit down and have a long talk about this. You really need to understand what Tanas is all about. I have not told you everything, Leah."

~

The operative was in Matehuala, San Luis Potosi. He knew he should be close by now, but he was not having any luck finding a native that was willing to talk. He ventured in to a local cantina and ordered a beer. As he sat there drinking it, an old man bellied up to the bar. Ordering a beer for himself, he glanced at the American in the business suit, who looked as out of place as a bum at a gala wedding.

The suit had no idea the old man recognized him.

The old man leisurely finished his beer. Once he was done, he walked out with a deliberately slow gait. Outside, he got into his dilapidated old produce truck and headed for home.

Leah was enjoying a rare bath at the home of El Presidente, relishing the clean water afforded her.

Most people in the ranchos hauled water from a community well or tank. The water that they hauled once a day was used for everything from drinking to washing dishes and watering their livestock. They wasted nothing. They could not afford to waste anything. They usually worked from dawn to dusk in order to feed their families. They hunted for meat, often bagging the field rats that roamed the rugged mountain deserts. It was a mere existence.

By now, Leah knew what sacrifice went into providing her with such luxury. She had been simply washing herself off as best she could. She hated it. She also needed to re-dye her hair. The blonde was beginning to show. She had just finished her bath when Peter drove up, still in his old man persona. It was the only way he would venture into town.

He did not even say hello.

"Pack your bags. I have the documents we need to get out of here. They are now in Matehuala. They are closing in. I only saw one of them. I got a tip from one of my sources that he was inquiring about us. He claimed that we were fugitives and that he needed to bring us in and get us extradited to the states. So far, he has not been successful in his pursuit."

This alarmed Leah. She packed in no time flat. Peter had brought her the hair dye and she was ready to go within an hour. Before they left, Peter altered Leah's appearance to match the documents and other information to ensure safe passage.

Peter did not tell her their next location. She did not even ask, although she was curious.

There had been times since they had been together that he frightened her. She suspected he did this to ensure that she cooperated in every instance. She knew her life depended on him.

They headed toward South America. Peter knew the Federales would closely examine documents in and out of the border. His contacts were very good. These were 'coyotes'-- men who made their living assisting people out of the country. Most of them were in it for the money only, not caring what happened to these desperate people.

~

He had played a part in the arrangements of some of Tanas's subjects, arranging for them to live out their lives in anonymity. What he later discovered was that he had really arranged for their further indention into some horrible conditions. Some became sex slaves for foreign officials. Others went into even worse conditions, sold as victims for snuff films, tortured, raped, and eventually murdered. These films sold worldwide over the Internet and both the FBI as well as the CIA had problems finding the root that perpetrated this heinous market.

Unfortunately, there was a tremendous market for humans. From extensive investigations through the FBI and other government agencies, there were key cities that had a propensity for selling and moving these victims. Dallas ranked seventh on the list of cities that had problems with human trafficking. It was a daunting task to catch these criminals.

Peter knew of just a few 'coyotes' who were Christians. They worked to transport humans, but to rescue them from brothels or other equally cruel situations. One such 'coyote' was Manuel Diego, who took many risks to rescue such women and children. The children were the high paying commodity.

Manuel had witnessed many miracles in his quest to free these victims. There were times when the border guards did not see anyone, even though they were in plain sight. Other times, the guards would begin to arrange to search the vans and then become interrupted by a commotion elsewhere.

Other people would have never taken a risk like this. However, Manuel listened intensely to the voice of God, relying on the Holy Spirit to lead him. God never misled him in his efforts.

Peter knew him well. He had found refuge in his home after he fled Tanas. He learned much from his friend and brother in the Lord. His discipleship was intense and thorough. His discovery of what the Lord had done for the world and especially for him personally, saturated his very soul, filling it with such gratitude and awe of what God had done for him that he would never look back.

In the beginning, Peter had a hard time believing that God would forgive him for all of the horrible things he had done in the name of so-called freedom. Manuel had gently led him to the full knowledge of just how much God loved him. When Manuel felt Peter was ready, he took him into Revelations, which foretells the end of the world, the return of Christ, and the thousand-year millennial reign. When Peter read some of the things in that prophetic book, he began putting many things together that he had learned from Tanas. He kept many things to himself for quite some time. When he finally shared the things he had learned with Manuel, Manuel gave him a word. He told Peter that God had chosen him to fight in the end times for those lost souls that had fallen victim to Tanas.

He further speculated that Tanas would herald in the Antichrist.

~

Part of the success of his recruitment into Tanas had been the way he grew up.

Peter grew up under his father's cruelty. His father was not physically abusive, but Peter was always just under satisfactory with anything he did, according to his father. No matter what Peter accomplished, he could have accomplished more, or he could have done something different. Furthermore, Peter's father seemed to loom large before him, making a lot of money, accomplishing many great things. Peter knew he would never live up to his father's expectations. This had been one of the major things he had to overcome in his relationship with the Lord. The Lord led him out of that stronghold.

Peter grew up, because of the cruelty, to be an overachiever. He went all out in everything he did, yet still sought to do things better. He studied martial arts and earned his black belt, becoming a three-time champion in competition. He went to college and studied criminology, intent on becoming a law enforcement officer.

Tanas often recruited through their contacts in law enforcement. Peter proved to be one of the most promising of any recruits ever approached. One of the things that appealed to Tanas was Peter's family background and the psychological report on him. Most police academies required a comprehensive psychological exam to ensure that the cadet would be a viable part of any police department. Although some questionable things came up on Peter's report, the bottom line was that he would make a dedicated officer.

A few weeks prior to graduation, the CO called Peter into the academy office. There, he met with two men who identified themselves as agents with a special government force. They said they needed more men like him who would be willing to dedicate themselves to the ultimate safety and freedom of the United States of America.

"Peter," Captain Rogers stated, "this is an opportunity of a lifetime. You will be serving your country in a way that you would never otherwise serve. I would advise you to take it. I certainly would if I were eligible."

Peter wanted more information on this "special" force before making his decision, but Captain Rogers assured him that this was a topnotch group, so elite that most FBI and CIA agents were unaware of it.

One of the suits said, "This force is high security and to really be informed, you must climb several levels before you get involved in the meat of the operation. To give you an overview, we are dedicated to preventing certain catastrophes that would be devastating to our country. From your profile, you seem to be very patriotic. This is tantamount to your entry into Tanas. At this point, you are on the top of our list for entry. We only allow a few to join our team. We do have other academies to visit prior to making a final decision. If you are interested, then we need to know within an hour. We need to continue on to the next academy."

Peter did not even have to think it over. He made the decision. He wanted to serve his country in any way he could. He knew there were many things that the public was unaware of. What he did not know was just how much remained unknown from not only the citizens, but also much of the government itself.

By the time he knew the real agenda, he had been convinced that it was right.

Captain Rogers had been an operative for Tanas. He recruited only one outstanding cadet each year. He felt that Peter was the most desirable candidate Tanas could have ever received.

Peter's time in Tanas taught him a lot. He now used his knowledge to his advantage and Tanas's disadvantage. This fact is what made him the most dangerous enemy Tanas ever went up against. He had the power to destroy the world's economic system, so tied up were Tanas's many contributors and other entities that secretly supported them.

~

Peter and Leah arrived in Venezuela three days after their departure from Mexico. It had taken some time to come up with the proper documentation for them to pass the borders. Venezuela was beautiful indeed. Though Leah had traveled extensively, she had never been to South America. It had a rugged beauty all its own. They had a harrowing trip through Columbia, encountering violence on the way. Columbia was at war with the drug lords, and at one point they had to run for their lives.

The only thing that saved them was the fact that Peter had some connections due to some of the operatives located there. These operatives had been established back when Ethan and Stephan began their crusade against what was coming soon. Globally, there was a force that Tanas had to deal with all these years, and they had been a pain in the ribs of it. They were always in battle. Some of the subjects that were lost seemed to have disappeared off the face of the earth. That was of nominal concern to Tanas as they had successfully wiped out the subjects' memories of their experiences, anyway.

What they did not know was that from the testing and other horrible things they had done to the subjects, they would pose the most dangerous threat to Tanas than any other enemy.

Peter and Leah arrived in Puerto Carreño, Columbia on the third day. There, they met the guide who would lead them to a small village in the foothills of the Andes Mountains.

"Leah," Peter admonished, "Some of these people here are so far behind the times that their views on women are very different from ours. You must obey my every command, and as hard as it may be, do not argue with me or even look like you might defy me. Understood?"

Leah had learned to trust him much more, and knew he was right. She had read about the fate of some of the women who defied the men in that region. She was not about to risk her life.

"I understand, Peter."

They arrived at the small village shack that afternoon. The air was a bit cooler, but nothing like Leah had expected. She'd thought it would be much colder. Of course they were nowhere near the peaks, which even now, in the middle of summer, were covered with snowcaps.

They camped there for three weeks without detection. When no sight of the agents from Tanas came around, they felt safe enough to continue their long journey.

Their final destination was to be in a remote location in the southernmost tip of South America. She knew that Peter wanted them to be as remote as possible. They were going to Chile. The final stop would be in a small village in the mountainous region near Puerto Aisén, Chile. This ramshackle village held its own secrets. There was a sophisticated control center deep in the belly of the mountain range. The center, built with funds secretly left by the late Howard Hughes who knew what was going to happen, housed some of the most sophisticated computer and communications systems money could buy.

The complicated acquisition of the equipment had taken over three years to put together. Many of the components they purchased through black markets, underground organizations, and individuals above suspicion. Overall, it had the look of a command station for NASA. In fact, some of it they acquired from the same manufacturer of a lot of NASA's equipment through a network of people in the company's hierarchy. No one ever questioned the procurements of the components.

A missionary who had discovered, through divine revelation, what was to come, ran the center. He had been a close friend of the eccentric Howard Hughes. Of course, since such mystery surrounded the recluse, no one ever knew of the close friendship of the two men. Everyone thought Howard Hughes was insane, but in reality, he was a Christian man, devoted to assisting in any way that he could. His notorious treks on his bicycle were no more than helping those less fortunate than he.

Peter and Leah arrived in Chile, via their guide. Once they reached Puerto Aisén, they sped away in a special jeep with dark tinted windows. From the outside, they looked simple. From the inside, the passengers could not detect where they were going. A privacy glass separated the front seat from the back seat. Thus Peter and Leah were transported to the secret site. They could not speak to the driver nor could they stop until they reached the center.

~

Leah was past exhaustion when they arrived. A woman who spoke fluent English escorted her to a comfortable room within the compound. When she reached her room, she would have never thought she was in such a remote location. Her room reminded her of some of the hotel suites she had stayed in over the years. In the center of the room, a king-sized bed was adorned with what looked like a handmade quilt. Soft, fluffy looking pillows rested against the headboard. The adjoining bathroom was also modern, complete with a garden tub. Placed in the linen cabinet above the commode, huge towels neatly folded, awaited her use.

Leah wondered how this place could house such luxuries, but she was too tired to ask.

She slept for quite a long time. When she awoke, she felt refreshed and energized. The hot bath she'd taken the night before had relaxed her and she'd fallen asleep almost before her head had hit the pillow.

She had just gotten out of the shower when a knock came at the door. Outside was the same woman she had met the night before. In her arms she held a tray of food, which smelled delicious. The scent of strong coffee was permeating the room. At the sight of the food, Leah's stomach began to rumble.

"Maria, thank you so much! How did you know I was awake?"

"Senorita, I just took a chance that you would be up. I am here to serve you in any way that I can."

"Well, Maria, I am not used to having anyone wait on me, so don't put yourself out on my account."

"Oh, it is my pleasure, Senorita. I am happy to serve you. It is as unto the Lord. This is my calling. When you are finished eating, I will take you to Senor Peter. He is waiting for you. There is a telephone for your use by the bed. You cannot call out, but just dial seven to reach me when you are ready. Oh, one last thing Senorita Leah; you will need something warm to put on. It is very cold in the tunnels. Do you have something?"

"What tunnels, Maria?"

"Where we are going is not the same way we came to your room. Those are hallways, which are always climate controlled. Where we are going is much different."

"All I have is what I brought in my backpack. I do not have anything that would pass as warm clothing."

"What is your size, Senorita?"

"I'm a size three, at least according to American clothing. And please, just call me Leah."

"Very well, Leah. I will bring you something when I return."

"All right, Maria. Thank you again." With that, Maria left.

Leah enjoyed her breakfast. The tortillas were unlike anything she had ever tasted in the states. Her eggs were delicious and spicy yet not too hot. She had fresh fruit along with her coffee, which tasted freshly ground from coffee beans right off a mountainside.

By the time Leah finished her breakfast, Maria had returned with some clothes that fit Leah perfectly. Her pants were fleece-lined, and were a rich burgundy. Her flannel shirt was feminine. It was a burgundy and white plaid, which complemented her face. Gone now were the dark circles under her eyes. The stress lines that had dominated her face had all but disappeared.

Here, she felt safer than she ever had before. Here, she was in a refuge.

Peter was waiting for her in the command center. When she walked through the heavy metal doors, she gasped.

"Leah, I would like for you to meet Dorian. He is the man in charge of the command center."

"It's very nice to meet you, Leah."

"It's nice to meet you too, Dorian," she said as she shook hands with him.

As they sat down in a sitting area complete with comfortable couches, Dorian explained what was going on. Peter had not divulged the entire operation to her, yet she was not surprised by the compound.

"Leah, many years ago, your grandfather was, as you know, subjected to something that no one had ever been subjected to before. He was the only subject out of all the others that did not go insane, was not murdered, or committed suicide."

After a nod from Dorian, a door opened and out walked a man who appeared to be in his early to mid sixties. He was somehow familiar to Leah, yet she knew she had never met him. She felt an immediate connection, not yet knowing why. Not only was there the emotional and mental connection, there was a strong spiritual one as well. It almost overwhelmed Leah initially.

"Leah," Dorian began, "I want you to meet your grandfather, Ethan."

Leah now knew the reason behind the strong connection. Ethan just stood there, looking at his granddaughter. They were looking at each other, until emotions took over. Leah ran to Ethan, threw her arms around him and began to weep.

"Oh, Leah!" he cried. "Praise God you are safe. Thank the Lord you are finally here."

"I can't believe you actually exist," Leah spoke through her tears.

The two left to another room to become acquainted privately, while Peter and Dorian began to go to work on the encrypted CD.

Leah and Ethan started out speaking to each other but shortly after they began the conversation, each one fell silent; yet, their minds were more than active. There was something wonderful happening. They were speaking to one another mentally. There was no need for verbal communication. The communication they were having was perfection. There was no awkwardness, no time to try to get to know one another. It came as naturally as breathing.

Unlike some of the science fiction movies where the person finds out that they have the ability and they have no control at first, this was just another ability, which had lain dormant until just the right time. Within a few minutes, they knew all there was to know about each other, even down to spiritual beliefs, the doubts and fears, the very heart of them.

She and Ethan both stood up at the same time, left the room, and joined the others in the command center. Ethan was the one who would explain what had occurred in the room.

"I want to say here and now that *no one* else can know about this. This discovery is exactly what Tanas was after the whole time. Imagine an entire race with the ability actually to read minds. There would be no stopping Tanas then," Peter admonished.

Ethan and Leah's ability was something he knew instinctively that Tanas was not yet privy to. He knew this would be a great advantage to him and Leah for their defense against Tanas, as long as Tanas did not know. If they did somehow find out, there would be nothing, nothing at all that would stop Tanas from trying to capture him and Leah. They would not spare anyone. At this time, Tanas only hoped. He shuddered to think of all the damage Tanas would do if they knew for certain.

Chapter 38

Dr. Hanson was on the phone. The voice on the other end of the line was Nicholls. His report was not good. He had been unable to find any trace of Leah.

"Hanson, we lost her in Old Mexico. It's as if they vanished into thin air. We have a number of those renegade, Bible toting *coyotes* in custody. By the time we're through with them, we'll know exactly which way they went. One of my associates is very adept at getting information out of anyone, even the most devout of the Jesus freaks."

Dr. Hanson felt his face flush at the news. He did not care what Nicholls did with those radicals, but he wanted Leah found alive and well. He was afraid she might be brainwashed by them before he could get to her. He also knew if she was, it would be next to impossible to gain her cooperation.

"Nicholls, I do not give a damn about the coyotes or what you have to do to them to get the information I need. Just get it done fast!"

"Hanson, don't get cranky with me or I'll disappear and you will never know where the girl is," Nicholls said lazily.

With that, Hanson took a deep breath and said for Nicholls to contact him as soon as he had any word.

The next call that came in made Hanson furious. He did not like the news at all. He hated it even more than the news about Leah's whereabouts.

The man that they had was not Ethan, but Dr. Stephan Fieldgreave. Fieldgreave had given no useful information before they killed him. For the rest of the day, Hanson made everyone around him miserable. Everyone cringed when he approached, for they knew he was out for blood.

Chapter 39

Leah and her grandfather spent much time together after their initial meeting. They were both grieving over the loss of Maggie, as well as Rose, David, and everyone that they loved.

Ethan told Leah that they needed to continue holding verbal conversations as much as possible. It would be too easy to fall into mental communication forever, for it was so effortless, so easy. The only time that he would allow it would be in an emergency. Leah knew that even though it would be safe enough to communicate mentally, she obeyed her grandfather.

A few days after they had arrived at the facility, Leah, Peter, and Dorian were hard at work, trying to decipher the CD. Peter was about to give up. Dorian had become frustrated.

Leah said, "Let me try something." She went to the computer, laid her hand on the CD ROM drive, and just sat there. Everyone quieted, waiting to see what would happen.

Ten minutes after she had laid her hand on the CD ROM drive, she abruptly took her hand away and began typing. The group had never seen anyone type so fast before. They could not keep up with the things she was entering. Another ten minutes later, the computer screen went blank. They all stared at the monitor.

Suddenly, the screen flashed on the 'code accepted' window. Everyone held their collective breaths while Leah hit the enter key.

Another file window came up. The prompt told them to enter the code to open the file. Leah went to work again. This time it was a little harder to decode. When the screen went blank again, she held her breath. It was another dead end.

Leah knew what this was. She said as much.

"This is a maze encryption. The beginning of it is pretty easy to break, but as we go in deeper, the codes become more difficult. This could take some time. Grandfather, do you think you could break this?"

"I can try, Leah. This is one of those times when we need to communicate. That way, I will know all you know about computers. It will make it easier for me."

Peter and Dorian looked at each other. They knew enough to remain silent.

Within fifteen minutes, Ethan was hard at work at the computer, deciphering codes. His abilities had matured greatly over the years.

He was hacking into the main file when the screen lit up. On the screen a skull and cross bones flashed and it said, "You have reached a dead-end. You must now go back three files. The code for that file has changed due to your mistake. You have only three more chances. If you go beyond the fourth mistake, the files will be deleted."

~

Ethan had spent an hour decoding files. He had reached the twentieth file. He was evidently tired. Again, Leah took over.

The entire process took more than two days with Ethan and Leah working in shifts, each telepathically sending the codes they had used to the other. Finally, Leah entered one last code.

The screen lit up and all sorts of binary codes flashed on the screen. Then the screen went blank again. Again, everyone held a collective breath.

The screen began flashing binary language so rapidly the human eye could not read it.

The screen went blank again.

When the screen came up again, it showed the information they had been searching for.

Names, companies, governments, all showed up on a list. Under the heading of the companies were more files, listing key contact people in each organization. These files were not encoded. Beside each name was a list of funds donated to Tanas. There were major food companies, beverage companies, tobacco companies, many famous worldwide. Huge conglomerates were listed along with all the subsidiaries they owned, some of which had been sheltered until now.

One such company, which had a reputation for advocating strong family values, had been secretly funding terrorists. How the CIA and other intelligence organizations did not find that out was in the notes for that file. It seemed they had the endorsement of a government entity-- one that had a lot of power--one that could actually make or break a company.

The shock of realizing just how widespread the conspiracy was caused them all to fear for the world. They could not believe how much secrecy there was, yet that secret was still intact.

One company name kept coming up as the root company. The company name was Destiny, Inc. After searching in their database for further information, they could not find any record of the company anywhere. They searched Wall Street and other resources, to no avail.

Tanas was the only other binding entity listed with every other company on the vast roster.

"I now wonder how many random murders, robberies, and other things have actually been connected to Tanas," Peter speculated.

"I can't believe all of this!" Ethan exclaimed. "I was the guinea pig for all of this; to initiate the super human race that they desire to create. Damn them all to Hell!"

Peter touched Ethan's arm. Ethan looked at Peter, a desolate expression on his face.

"Ethan, it will be all right. We now know who our enemies are. We now know we cannot trust anyone, not anyone at all. It is all under control of Tanas. All we can do now is to inform as many believers as we can."

They all knew there would not be many Christians who would take the information seriously.

Leah was reading an agenda file. She had a shocked look on her face as she read further:

> *Agenda: Interoffice memo: To all key agents:*
> *One Leah T. Channing, only child of Margaret & Joshua Channing; Key subject for Project EVAH. Subject must be captured at all costs.*
> *Viability: Confirmed. DNA retrieved from medical lab verified: Alien and human DNA co-existing.*
> *Abilities: Unknown, approach with extreme caution.*
> *NOTE: Do not under any circumstances injure subject.*

"Oh my God!" Leah breathed. "Grandfather! Do you see this? Am I part alien?" she asked incredulously.

"I am afraid so, Leah. No one knew that you were. Your mother turned out perfectly normal. I found out recently that what happened to me at Tanas was among the first experiments in splicing human genes with alien genes. We thought that it never took. I was the only success they had and they lost me. That was a miracle in itself. Now they have my good friend, Stephan, and they think he is me. He suffers from Alzheimer's now. They won't get anything much out of him."

Peter looked at Ethan. "Ethan, does he know where this location is?"

"No. I only found out about it recently when I ran into Dorian. I got his name from a contact over in Israel, so as far as I know, he has no idea about this place. At least he never mentioned it to me."

Dorian looked up sharply.

"Peter, the contact that gave you the information had been in contact with Stephan a few years ago. Ethan, he never told you?"

"No!"

"We most likely have been breached, then. We're going to need to abandon this location. Everyone get packed up quickly and meet me in the emergency exit tunnel."

With that, everyone scrambled to get everything they would need for the next escape. No one took anything but sturdy shoes and clothing, backpacks, water, canned food and some mules. They were all going to be traveling higher into the mountains. Dorian would lead the way.

Three days of climbing, camping in caves that only the locals and they knew, had worn them out. They finally reached the old monastery high in the Andes. They all knew this was just a stopgap for them. They would all eventually wind up in the hub of the Christian underground, located in Israel.

Chapter 40

The military regime arrived at the secret location in the Andes. They had to use explosives to get through the main door into the tunnels, but had it done in no time at all. The soldiers pushed forward into the compound. They set C4 at strategic locations throughout the entire facility. They confiscated every bit of data they could find on all the computers, took the hard drives and stored them in the military trucks they had arrived in.

What they did not know was that once they tried to open the data in the hard drive, a sophisticated virus would destroy all the information on all of the computers they'd taken.

Shortly after they had finished their business in the compound, they set off all of the C4 by remote. They knew they would have to be quite a distance from the location, due to the threat of an avalanche. The mountain range rumbled at first, creating what they perceived as an earthquake, which was common. They passed off the huge avalanche as a direct result of the quake. They determined that the quake's epicenter was in the same location as the avalanche.

~

The group, who had been at the monastery for five days now, felt the quake. They all knew that the command center was no more. They felt that it was again time to go. They gathered their meager belongings and rendezvoused with the freighter that was to take them to a location near Rafah, located near the Gaza strip.

They arrived at the port of Comodoro Rivadavia on the east coast of Argentina.

The captain of the freighter had known Dorian for many years and had helped him recover many of the victims of the vast human trafficking trade. He was another sort of 'coyote' who wanted to do his part for Christ. It was agreed that the men would bunk with the rest of the crew of the ship, but Leah was to stay in the captain's quarters, and it was made clear to all that she was to be treated as though she were the captain's daughter, herself.

The journey took more than three months, the ship stopping in various ports to either load or unload its vast cargo. Leah made herself useful by assisting the galley cook. She enjoyed the cuisine of the Argentineans. She learned the language without any problems.

One week, there were stormy seas. During this time, Leah spent her time in bed in her quarters. She was not fond of the motion of the ship. Peter found some Dramamine and gave her some. This alleviated much of the motion sickness she experienced.

The rest of the voyage went without incident.

As they neared Portugal, Spain, they ran into a problem. Officials wanted to search the ship for anyone who might have stowed away. They were looking for contraband as well. This was in part due to the close proximity to Israel and countries that harbored terrorists.

As they boarded, they asked the crew if they knew if there was a woman aboard. The crew responded that none of them had seen anyone aboard that they did not know, and that the ship had an all male crew.

They hid Leah in the cargo hold. The officials never found her.

As they went through to the Mediterranean Sea, closer to Israel once again, they were detained. The Israeli Port Authority to port at Tel Aviv ordered them.

There, they subjected them to a thorough search. This time, they found what they were looking for.

They took the entire group from the ship and escorted them to the Port Authority office to answer to the charges of illegal entry. The officers that had taken them into custody refused to speak to them. They all sat in the back of an enclosed van, with no windows or air conditioning. They all sweltered from the heat. The guard that sat in the back with them would not even look at them.

Peter found this behavior odd. He and the others were soon to find out why.

The van headed away from Tel Aviv. The route they took went north-northeast of the city. Once they were well out of the city, they stopped on a deserted side road. The driver, whom no one had yet seen, got out of the van and came around to the back. He opened the door. With the sun behind him, the group could only see his outline.

In a commanding voice, he said, "Come out of the van."

They all scrambled out of the van and it was not until Peter turned to face him, that he recognized his old friend, Barak.

Peter and Barak went back a long way. When he had first joined Tanas, Barak had schooled him in the then rarely used Hebrew language. Since then, the Hebrew language had experienced a surge of popularity. It was the major language spoken in Israel, replacing much of the Aramaic that had been spoken for centuries.

They hugged each other and exchanged hearty back slaps. Peter and Barak had lost contact after Peter became a Christian. About the same time, Barak learned and then embraced the Messianic faith. Many of the people who had once held him with high regard ostracized him. He had grown rapidly since his conversion. He was now head of an underground movement to help thwart Tanas's massive plan.

An old bus met the group while they were catching up and introducing themselves. It looked decrepit and had some people in it with chickens, goats, and various other items in tow. Once again, Leah found herself in a secret cargo hold underneath the ancient bus, only this time she was not alone.

They arrived at another deserted monastery, high on Mt. Morah, just east of Nazareth. There, they remained for a long while. They had to establish false IDs and learn Hebrew, which only Leah did not know. The rest of the group received refresher courses on a language they already knew.

The day after they arrived, Leah was well versed in the written and spoken forms of Hebrew. Everyone marveled over Leah's ability to assimilate information quickly, and how she adapted to situations with such ease.

Peter and Barak both knew how valuable a commodity she was to Tanas. She and Ethan both needed guarding at all costs, for their capture would mean the downfall of the world and Christianity especially.

"Peter, we need to talk," Leah informed him one day. "I am very concerned about my grandfather. He seems to be having some health issues at the moment. I'm afraid something terrible is wrong with him. Is there anyone who can look at him? I only found out that he was having some pain in his back and arms by accident.

"Remember in Peru when he was so adamant about mental communication? Well he was 'hiding' some of his thoughts. I had been able to pick up quite a bit from him, you know, small conversations. Peter, I concentrated on that area of his body today and got a picture. It was as if I could see into his body. Peter, my grandfather has cancer. I know it as sure as I know anything. He's dying, Peter."

Peter could not speak at first. "Leah, do you realize what this means?"

"Yes, Peter, I do. It means I'm losing my grandfather. It also means that my abilities are advancing rapidly, which frightens me. I do *not* want this! Not any of it!"

She broke down then and cried.

Peter took her in his arms and held her while she spent the emotions she had kept in check all this time. Even now it was controlled, but he knew instinctively that she needed to get it all out. They stood there for quite some time until she pulled away and looked into his eyes.

"Peter, I know what you're feeling. I feel the same way. What are we going to do about it?"

Peter lowered his head and kissed her. It was gentle at first, but then it became passionate, fierce. She responded back, a passion stirred within her as she had never known, not even with Richard.

They finally broke the kiss and embrace in an effort to gain control. Neither of them wanted to take it any further now.

"Leah, I have loved you for some time, now."

"I know, Peter, I know."

They decided to confront Ethan about what was happening to him. They sought him out and learned the truth. A doctor had diagnosed him with lung cancer over a year before. He told Ethan that he might have two years, depending on how fast the cancer grew.

"Peter, Leah, I'm getting tired. I know I do not have long. I'm sorry I kept it from you, but I wanted to make sure that you were safe, Leah. Once I found you, I wanted as much time with you as possible without this hanging over our heads. It took a lot of effort for me to keep it 'hidden'."

Peter knew they needed some time alone, so he left in search of Dorian.

~

For the next few months, Ethan was able to fight off the disease using mind control with Leah assisting. Still, the disease raged on. His ability had become weakened over the years and his body ravaged by the things they did to him at Tanas. Leah still had some limitations, so she only managed to prolong his life for a little while.

Ethan and Leah spent a lot of time together after Ethan made her stop the telepathic healing. He told her he was ready to go home.

"Leah, I want to fill you in on everything that you do not know," he said to her one day.

"I want to make sure that you are prepared to face what is going to become your destiny. Leah, they will ultimately find you. Do you know that?"

"Yes, Grandfather. I do know that. I'm just not sure I want to survive long enough to be found."

"Leah, you really cannot fight this. This is inevitable. Do you realize what you are a part of ? Do you know why you were born?"

"Not really, no."

Ethan began to speak to her in detail. "Leah, how much have you read the Bible?"

"Very little, why?"

"Well, you are a part of something that is bigger than you, bigger than Tanas, bigger than life. There is an end-time prophecy in the Bible that speaks of a man who will rise to power. He will become the leader of the world. This man will become the Antichrist. He will not be ruthless or cruel at first. He will have a lot of charisma, a lot of charm, not to mention his super-human qualities. Leah, it is your destiny to bear this child."

Leah just sat there, a look of disbelief on her face.

"Grandfather, you cannot be serious! You mean you actually believe all of that? I know a lot of people who studied the Bible very intently. They all agreed that it was full of metaphors, analogies, and myths. I have to agree with that, even though I have never personally studied it. It is hard to reconcile in my mind that everything that the Bible says actually happened. It is highly illogical, some things physically impossible, things that defy physics. I just cannot accept them. Do you understand?"

"Leah, is there any way you can set aside your logic for just a little while? I do believe if you do, you will begin to see the logic of it. See, the whole world is upside down. In the beginning, it was not so. When man fell from Grace, the entire world suffered. Not just man, but beast as well. Leah, think of all that you can do with just your mind. This is what man was like before the fall. His mind defied reason. His mind defied physics. His body did not grow old and die at that time.

"You well know that old age was proven to be a disease, rather than just the way it is. Scientists have discovered that God created the human body to continue, to go on regenerating cells, and the heart made to last forever. It should never have to stop. And I know that you know the heart is still a mystery to the scientific world. They still don't understand why it beats. They don't know the logic of the mechanisms of the workings. This is because God created it to beat. He created it originally, to last forever.

"Leah, please. Study the Bible for yourself. Look deep into it. Allow it to take you to places you have never been before. You are going to need the help of God to get through everything. Do you understand?"

"Oh, Grandfather! Now I'm confused. I'm not used to this feeling-- this emotion. I'm not comfortable in this new place. But I will do as you say. I may seek out some help from Peter. He's knowledgeable in the Bible. I don't want to tire you with this."

"Leah, I am more than willing to help you. If I should start feeling tired, then I promise I will let you know. Okay?"

"Okay"

Ethan and Leah spent the next few weeks studying and debating over the Word. She made every effort to dismiss the logic her mind wanted to insert, and she was finally successful. Peter joined them for many sessions and by the fourth week, Leah realized that they had been right all along.

She made a profession of faith, accepting Christ as her Savior. She felt a strong release within her--one she had never known before. She was elated, enraptured, by the freedom she felt.

The Holy Spirit began working in her immediately. He reached the place that no other had ever been able to reach. He reached into her very soul. He gave her insight into the love of God, as no human had ever been able to do. Leah became strong in the Lord and in the power of His Might. She felt the Holy Spirit, learning the new and wonderful language of Him. She often spoke in the language and utilizing her knowledge of Hebrew, she found a Bible in the Hebrew language and pored over its contents.

She could now see the history of the world not as a growing event, but rather, one that was winding down, getting ready to be re-birthed. She knew she would become the unwilling mother of the Antichrist. She prayed for strength.

Their stay in the sanctuary lasted another three months. One month after Leah's conversion, Ethan died. They buried him in an unmarked grave in the cemetery that previously had been used for the monks who had lived there at one time. There he would remain until the day of   the Lord's return.

Chapter 41

Peter and Leah, once they received their papers, left and went into Nazareth. There they found a small section of town that was mainly Messianic. There, they established contacts. They both found jobs, living quarters and a home-based church to attend. Even with all of that, they knew they had to be careful at all times.

They decided not to pursue their relationship due to the inevitable. Peter knew that he would never have a normal life with Leah, and she knew that as well. They lived very low-keyed for six months.

One day, another of Peter's contacts got in touch with him. They met on a deserted road outside of town.

"Pete. Glad you could meet with me. There's something I need to warn you of. Tanas has called out some agents to Israel. I don't know how they found out that you and the girl might be here, but I think you had better leave. I arranged for you and the girl to travel to Switzerland. One of my own contacts will meet you there. A facility there can give you new faces and even alter your fingerprints. I've already made all of the travel arrangements for you both. You need to leave by the end of the week. My sources say that the group of agents will be arriving by the first of next week. Peter, you know they will stop at nothing to find her."

"I know, Phillip." He sighed heavily before continuing. "Phil, how for the love of Pete, are they getting the information? Have you been able to find out?"

"No, Peter. That's the frustrating part. Our organization has a mole, but he or she has been elusive so far. We are working on it. I'm sorry."

"As soon as you find out, contact me and let me know."

"I will, Pete. I will." Phillip handed the itinerary to Peter and then left.

By the time Peter got back into Nazareth, it was rush hour. He found Leah at home, eating dinner.

"Leah," he began. "We're going to have to leave again."

He went on to explain to her the meeting that had taken place--where they were going--and when they had to leave. He left her with the extra copy of the itinerary that Phillip had enclosed.

"Leah, we must not delay this. We need to leave as soon as possible."

"I understand, Peter." With that, they arranged to meet on the specified day and place for their departure.

They left Israel aboard a chartered boat. They took the route to northern Italy. From there, they went across the border into Switzerland.

~

Leah was sleeping on the train. She was beyond exhaustion. Peter watched her sleep. He felt so badly about all that she was going through. He knew that inevitably, they would take her. He just wanted to delay it as long as possible.

He was trying hard not to become bitter over this. His was a difficult job at the least. He knew in his heart that even if it were not Leah, eventually someone would give birth to the Antichrist. These were indeed, scary times. What the world, secular and Christian alike, did not know was that time was coming to an end; time as the whole world knew it; the economic structure; the religious vein; the whole world was getting ready to emerge into the Tribulation. Only those who were fighting for the cause knew what awaited everyone else.

He felt a heavy, heavy burden. Why had God picked him to protect her? How had his life become so complicated? He knew the answers, but asked the questions in his mind anyway.

He sighed and then tried to sleep.

The train was approaching Geneva. From there, they would board another train, which would carry them into Zunich. Peter thought how ironic it was that they would be stopping at a city that prided itself on creating the Geneva Convention*, the original advocate of the abused, sick, and wounded. Well, he was abused, sick and wounded, but they could not help him. The only One who could was God.

Peter had been dozing when the conductor announced the city stop. As he looked outside, he appreciated the pristine, snow-covered scene. It was a reprieve from all of the things he had on his mind. Now, he concentrated on the beauty of the untamed landscape.

The train traveled on through the foothills of the Swiss Alps. Once again, exhaustion took over.

The next morning, while they were eating in the food car, the announcement came that they would soon be in Zunich. From there, they had to make it through Germany and then on to Denmark.

Germany was not unlike traveling through other free world countries now. Going through customs at the border was routine. No one questioned his or her visas. They traveled through the countryside of Germany, again by train. They reached the city of Kiel, built near the Klaipėda seaport in Lithuania.

Kiel, a modern city with many wonderful tourist attractions including yachting, was beautiful. With the Baltic Sea nearby, the tourists could afford a wonderful view of the emerald sea. All of the beauty and culture of Kiel was lost on the travel-weary couple. All they wanted was to reach their destination.

The contact arranged for them to rest in Kiel for two days. They were booked at a modest motel, under assumed names.

Leah had been in her room long enough to put her things away. She was just about to shower when Peter knocked on her door. She wrapped her robe around her naked body and looked in the peephole of the door. There he stood, waiting for her to answer.

---

*Author's Note: The creation of the Red Cross was spurred by the publication of *Un Souvenir de Solferino* (1862), an account by Jean Henri Dunant of the suffering endured by the wounded at the battle of Solferino in 1859. Dunant, a Swiss citizen, urged the formation of voluntary aid societies for relief of such war victims. He also asked that service to military sick and wounded be neutral.

In 1859, Societe Genovoise d'Utilite Publique, a Swiss welfare agency, formed the organization that became known as the Red Cross. The next year, delegates from 16 nations met in Switzerland, and the Geneva Convention of 1864 for the Amelioration of the Condition of the Wounded and Sick of Armies in the Field, was adopted and signed by 12 of the nations represented. It provided for the neutrality of the medical personnel of armed forces, the humane treatment of the wounded, the neutrality of civilians who voluntarily assisted them, and the use of an international emblem to mark medical personnel and supplies. In honor of Dunant's nationality, a red cross on a white background--the Swiss flag with colors reversed--was chosen as this symbol. Almost all countries and their dependencies have signed the original Geneva Convention, its subsequent revisions, and allied treaties such as The Hague Convention for naval forces and the Prisoner of War Convention (although not always ratified). The International Committee of the Red Cross was awarded the Nobel Peace Prize in 1917, 1944, and with the League of Red Cross Societies, in 1963.

As she opened the door, she noticed he had food with him.

"Peter! I was just about to shower, but the food smells wonderful. I am famished. I can shower after we eat. Excuse me while I get something on."

She rushed out of the room and into the bath area, which had a private dressing room attached to it. Peter absently noted that her room was a mirrored image of his.

When she came out, she had on a pair of sweats and a sloppy t-shirt.

Peter placed the food on the small table situated by the large picture window. The view was not as spectacular as some of the five-star hotels by the sea, but still, the scenery was nice.

They ate their food after they said the blessing over it, and praying for protection for the rest of their journey.

"Peter, I am so tired," Leah said after they had eaten. "At this point, I wouldn't care if I were captured," she said dejectedly.

"Leah, please don't say that! I know you've been through a lot, but please, don't give up now. We're almost there. Another few days and we'll be in a place where we'll be able to stay for as long as we want. I promise."

Leah looked at him gratefully.

"Peter, I really want to wash away some of the road grime. Then I'm going to take a hot bath and go to bed."

"I know the feeling, Leah. I'm going to go to my room and shower, then go to bed myself. We have some things to do tomorrow, though. We'll be out most of the day. Be ready around eight a.m., okay?"

"Where are going?"

"We have some contacts we need to see. We need the papers for the last leg of our journey."

"All right, Peter. Good night," she said as she closed the door to the man she loved.

After Leah showered and soaked in the tub, she felt more relaxed. Even so, she tossed and turned in her bed for most of the night. She cried to this new Savior that she had come to know only recently.

"Oh, God, please help me! I need Your guidance and instruction. Please help me to not have to go through the horrors of Tanas."

Long after her agonizing cries to the Lord, she fell into an exhausted sleep.

The next morning, Peter came for her promptly at eight a.m. She was ready. Peter said nothing about the dark circles under her eyes, or the lines of exhaustion that marred her face.

He tried to remember what she had looked like while he was observing her in the museum. He had never revealed to her that he had been watching her close up. He had been there every night for several weeks, watching her; learning her routine. He remembered the soft look on her face as she caressed the artifacts that she often viewed each night. The unabridged admiration in her eyes for the history that she carefully watched over, and which she loved.

Now, she was not even an echo of her former self. Gone was the confidence he had seen in her; gone was the vivaciousness, the sassy quality she once had. He hated what was going on with her now. He wanted to make it all go away. He knew he could not ever do that.

"Peter, are you going to stand there all day?"

He shook himself out of his musings. He briefly wondered if she had been "reading" him.

They met their contact after having breakfast. The contact told them that they really needed to confine themselves to their rooms. It seemed that someone had leaked that they were somewhere in Germany, but no one knew exactly where. If they stayed inside their rooms, they should be safe.

"Peter, all they know is that you and Leah were going to be in Germany. They don't have the information as to your assumed identities, nor do they have your itinerary. So as long as you stay out of sight as much as possible, you should be fine. Are there any questions?"

"None that I can think of, Hugh. If I do, I know how to contact you, okay?"

"Okay."

With that, they all parted ways.

~

The ship that ferried them into Sweden was nice and the trip was uneventful. They arrived at the port of Limhamn, on the western side of Sweden. From there, they took yet another train to Stockholm.

Stockholm was their final destination. There, they met their final contact, who would keep them advised of any information they would need in order to survive.

The second week after their arrival, they met with one of the most prominent plastic surgeons in the world. He was very adept at his craft. Within one month, both were in the recovery stages of their alterations.

Leah emerged from her now-healed face, a different person. Gone was the pixie. Now she was more patrician in her looks. There were more angles to her face. They actually elongated her face to a minor degree. They straightened her nose. They raised her cheekbones, making them more prominent.

They received their new names along with all the necessary documents proving their identities. Peter was now Anthony Ethanburg, and Leah was now Alexandria Swanson.

Chapter 42

After their recovery, they at last had the freedom to live a somewhat normal existence. For the first time, they considered marriage. They now felt safe enough to want it for themselves. After several weeks of prayer, they felt that God's blessings were on them to do so. They were married in a small chapel in Stockholm, eight months after the surgery was done.

They moved into a small flat on the outer edge of the city. Peter found a job, provided by the contact.

When Hugh found out about their marriage, he was against it at first. After seeing them together, he could only admire their courage and faith in God. They had assured him that they had prayed long and hard about it and felt that God had given His blessing on the union.

Leah and Peter decided that children would never be an option. Due to her special circumstances, she could never consider giving birth to a child. She would never want her son or daughter to go through what she went through.

Tony and Alex, as she had decided she wanted them to be called, had an intimacy that surpassed anything that either one of them had ever known. One evening during Bible study, Leah approached Tony about something she had been thinking.

"Tony, I've been thinking about a possible solution to our dilemma concerning my getting pregnant . . . ever. I know it would be a drastic measure, but what would you think of me having surgery to prevent me from ever having a baby?"

Tony just looked at her.

"Tony, honey, what I'm trying to say is, once I have surgery, I'll no longer be a viable commodity for Tanas. They would have no more reason to want me, would they?"

"Alex, they have the capability of producing your offspring by cloning techniques. They would not care if you had no more reproductive organs or not. Honey, I don't want you to go through anything like that, not ever. Do you understand?"

Alex nodded her head.

"Tony, Honey, I need to tell you something, then. Tony, I'm pregnant."

His face turned white. He stared at her for the longest time.

"Alex, are you sure?"

"Yes, I am, Honey. I am so sorry! I know we took every precaution, but it still has happened. What are we going to do about this?"

The two talked about it well into the night. They made the heart-wrenching decision to terminate the pregnancy after praying about it at length. The next day, Tony phoned Hugh so he could make the arrangements.

Hugh would hear none of it. It went against all he believed. Tony said the same thing to Hugh, but argued that this circumstance was so different. He had to allow them to do this, or they would seek a doctor on their own.

~

The creature knew she was pregnant. He could feel it. He also knew the child was female. That would never do. He could tell the child would not pose a threat to the Project. He would allow her to go through the joy of motherhood now. This way, when she did come home, she would not fight nearly as much.

He was disappointed in the fact that she was fighting what was to be the inevitable. Her human emotions had tainted her brilliant mind. This would not be so for the male child she would bear for the cause.

The only thing that frustrated him about her now was the fact that she continually blocked her mind to her specific location. Even as he invaded her dreams, she was aware of his tactics on a subconscious level. She still did not know consciously that he had been invading. She would soon find out though, so he had to tread lightly from here on.

Wherever she was now, he knew she felt safe. She would soon lower her guard. He also knew she was the only one so far that knew she was able to do much more than anyone could possibly imagine.

He would soon have her back. He knew it would not be much longer now. He would bide his time until the female child was born. The child already was fighting its own destruction. She was already developing nicely. Although she would not have nearly the same powers as her mother, she knew when she was in danger, even from the womb.

He narrowed the filmy matter that served as lids over his bulbous eyes, situated far apart on his over-sized head. She would make an excellent breeder as well.

His serpentine tongue flicked in and out, already tasting the soon-to-be-won victory.

He summoned the good doctor. He liked to summon him. The otherwise rude, belligerent doctor was putty in his hands.

He thought about everything that had taken place over the years and achieved with light speed. All these years and they thought they had achieved all of this themselves. Knowing that he had been the one to implant thoughts and ideas in the minds of these hapless creatures, he realized he was a genius--knew what he was--had known it from the foundations of the earth and before that. He had been the king of space until He exiled him to this miserable planet. However, he had gotten his revenge the first time he had convinced one of the humans to defy the One.

He was glad the human had done so. How else was he to achieve all of this? He would finally have this planet all to himself. He would rule these idealistic creatures. Once the man-child was born and grown, he would enter him and take control. It would be easy enough because he would implant him from the womb.

He sensed that the good doctor was near. He morphed into humanoid form within seconds.

The door opened and Dr. Hanson stood there, waiting for permission to enter.

The now human-like creature looked ordinary in his business suit. His hair, a salt-and-pepper gray, was smooth and slicked back. All of this served to provide him startling good looks.

He was highly respected in this state. He never revealed his other persona to anyone, or they would surely destroy him, if that were possible.

If they knew his 'real' nature, it might even backfire on the plans he had cultivated for so long. Everyone seemed to think that angels were all light. Most people would run to their nearest church to give their fragile hearts to the One, if he revealed his true form. That would never do.

"Dr. Hanson, come in," he gestured as the doctor stepped through the door. "I wanted to let you know that you are doing a wonderful job in your field. However, I have some of my own operatives working, and they have informed me that the female subject is with child. We do not yet know if it is male or female, but we are going to wait until its birth, and then we shall make our move if we can narrow down her location. As you know, where I come from, we have the power to enter into the minds of some. Some of you here are not so easily readable. I do not like this, but once we have the model specimen that we have worked for, for so long, then we can begin to assimilate everyone into the peaceful existence you all need and want. Once this is achieved . . . well, I certainly don't need to tell you, Dr. Hanson, do I?"

"No sir. You don't. I know that you, as an ambassador to our earth, have helped us to achieve wonderful things over the years. I want to apologize right now for our misuse of the wonderful technologies which you, as a representative of your planet, so kindly offered."

"Nonsense, Hanson. There is nothing to apologize for. We did not specify what you or your race had to use it for. I am simply glad I am here to assist you in the evolution of their uses for peace on earth."

'Peace on Earth'. He had heard that phrase once before. He inwardly shuddered. He hoped never to see Him again. Somewhere inside his mind he knew he would, but he was too vain and self-centered to acknowledge that they would meet again. Besides, the creature was self-delusional, too.

For millennia, he had been going back and forth in his energy form trying to deceive, with limited success, but when the humans began to believe in the alien theory through books and movies (an invention he really had appreciated) he began to add a new element to his already elaborate plan. Now, here he was a beloved creature, an ambassador to assist the small planet in achieving a peaceful state. He was sure to reign and rule the earth as he had always dreamed.

Chapter 43

Leah/Alex and Peter/Tony were in the doctor's office, waiting for the results of the doctor's tests. They finally called her and told her she was pregnant. She had explained to the doctor that she and her husband had decided not to have the baby. This was something the doctor addressed immediately.

"Mrs. Ethanburg, I have to tell you that I discovered an anomaly in your blood work. If you choose to terminate this pregnancy, you might not survive. We have discovered that you have a very low platelet count. Any type of invasive procedure could kill you. As it is, even if you keep the baby, we will have to use methods to prevent anything from happening during the delivery. By the time our treatment can be effective, it will be too late to terminate the pregnancy. We cannot treat you until the second trimester, or it will affect the baby. The choice is now up to you."

Leah knew that her own child was manipulating her system. She knew this instinctively. She sighed. "Doctor, how much time do my husband and I have to discuss this and make a decision?"

"I would say another month is all you have."

"Thank you, Doctor. We will let you know soon," Tony interjected.

Once they reached their flat, they discussed it further.

"Tony, I know something that I need to tell you. Honey, this child is fighting for her life. She does not want to die. I have felt it for a few weeks, but thought that maybe it was just me."

"Alex, I believe you're right. We both know that there could not possibly be such an anomaly under ordinary circumstances. We'll keep the baby. I would be willing to bet that once we let the doctor know, your platelets will go back to normal."

"I know, Honey. I know."

Alex's pregnancy went off without a hitch. Tony loved watching her develop. Loved feeling the baby kick. As predicted, Alex's platelets went back to normal after her fourth month of pregnancy, without needing any treatment. The doctor was surprised, but then passed it off as just an unusual result of her body trying to adjust.

Tony and Alex loved the experience of the growth of their precious daughter. They relished in the wondrous changes, the miracle of growing life, the feel of the baby kicking, listening to her heartbeat, and talking to her.

Tony especially loved to sing to her, putting his face close to Alex's now swollen belly. The baby would respond, kicking and squirming at the sound of his crooning. She seemed to thrive on it.

~

Sarah Christiania Ethanburg was eight pounds, four ounces, and had a full head of brown hair. She was a delight to her parents. They doted on her, providing her with Bible stories, tapes, and Christian music, which they played in her room all the time. They both knew she would notice everything rapidly, much like her mother had done as a child.

A year went by without incident in the Ethanburg household. Alex had allowed her guard to drop, things had been so normal.

Even Hugh had not sent any activity reports since the birth of Sarah.

Sarah was dedicated to the Lord when she was only three weeks old. She never even cried when everyone in the small non-denominational church celebrated her birth and dedication. She smiled at everyone who held her; she exuded charm that was rare in a baby so young.

As Sarah's first birthday approached, Tony and Alex planned a big party, inviting all of her Sunday school friends from church to attend. They had some twenty-five children at the party. Most of the children were her same age, so it was interesting to say the least. Cake landed on both children and parents. Sarah had cake all over her cherubic face, wreathed in smiles.

Two hours into the party, there came a knock at the door. When Tony opened it, there stood Hugh, whom Tony invited, but thought it wiser not to attend, just in case.

"Hugh, it's good to see you. I thought you weren't coming, though," Tony greeted him.

"Tony, this is an official visit, I'm afraid. Somehow, they found out where you were. We still don't know who the leak is. Every attempt to locate or find out who it is leads to dead ends. Tony, I think it goes beyond any mole, or traitor. We think that somehow Alex is transmitting your location. Though to whom, we don't know, but it would have to be someone with the same 'gifts' as Alex."

They had stepped outside to talk uninterrupted.

Tony closed his eyes. He knew immediately why they had been able to hone in on their location. They had let their guard down too easily. They had become so used to the feeling of being safe, that they thought they would be immune to anyone finding them.

"Hugh, I'll go and break up this little party. I'll think of something."

"No, don't do that. Just allow the party to die down. There is no imminent threat to you right now, so you have a small window of time. I have what you need to escape into another country. I'll contact you later this evening."

With that, he left.

Tony went back into the apartment. Alex saw the look on his face and she knew something was wrong.

"Honey, come help me serve the coffee, would you?" Alex asked.

When they got into the kitchen, he told her what had happened.

She cried. She cried a lot since her daughter's birth. She knew it was everything that had happened in her short life. She did not suffer from postpartum depression like other mothers.

The party broke up around one thirty, a little before Sarah's naptime. Once all of the guests were gone, they talked about what they were going to do. They prayed for a long time together. They decided that they would assume new identities, for them as well as Sarah.

Alex vowed never to let her guard down again.

Chapter 44

Hugh showed up right after supper. He told them to have everything ready by Sunday night. They would be leaving first thing Monday morning.

That night, after they had gone to bed, Alex began having a nightmare. This one was particularly bad. She was standing before a creature, a small gray being with bulbous eyes and a slit for a mouth. It was speaking to her mind. She could not move. Even though her abilities were strong, this one had even more ability than she did.

What he was saying she knew were lies, yet she could not get away from him.

"Leah, you must help your fellow humans. You are their only hope for survival, peace, and freedom," it was saying. "We are not out to control you. This God of yours is a lie. He does not exist. We are the ones who created you and everything in this world. Leah, we *are* God. We visited this world when it was nothing. It had nothing to offer. We did this so that someday we would expand beyond our world and be able to bring a Universal growth. Without growth, the Universe would collapse. You must reach out and embrace your destiny, Leah. You are the mother of the future. Come, come to us, Leah."

He began asking her about her precious daughter, and how did she feel about her daughter becoming one of the special mothers? He knew she would still not remember her dream, but he allowed a vague recollection, which would upset her mind.

She screamed 'no'; she did not realize she was screaming aloud.

Tony woke her up. Her scream had been blood-curdling. He worried that her screams had disturbed the neighbors.

She was still asleep, yet she was crying. Her crying was not just tears, but also a primeval, gut-wrenching sobbing that came from the bottom of her soul. He just held her, not even trying to wake her. After a long while, she calmed down. She settled back to sleep.

Tony eased himself out of bed to go check on Sarah. She was there in her crib, fast asleep. She was on her stomach, her bottom sticking up in the air. She had thrown the covers off sometime during the night. Tony covered her up and went back to bed.

The next morning, Tony asked Alex if she remembered her dream.

"I do have a vague recollection. Not of the dream, but of enormous fear. I know it's there, but for some reason I'm unable to remember. I've never had this before. I'm not used to having memory lapses, even in my dreams. This is different. Honey, I know this dream was implanted. It had to be. I always remember my dreams; every detail of them," she finished with a concerned look on her face.

Alex prepared breakfast while Tony began getting ready for work. As she was pouring the orange juice, she suddenly felt extremely uneasy. She had such a feeling of panic, that she wanted to run away right then. She felt an overwhelming, protective instinct for Sarah.

Tony came in to the kitchen to eat, and Alex came right to the point.

"Tony, honey; we need to leave sooner than Hugh told us to. It's not a definitive feeling I have, but a sense of foreboding. We need to leave here by Friday or it will be too late."

"What is the foreboding you're feeling, Honey?" Tony asked.

"They're closing in on us, Tony. We need to leave quickly, or we'll wind up in their hands. Please! Contact Hugh immediately. We need the papers sooner than Monday."

Tony got up, called in sick, and put in a call to Hugh. He was unable to reach him.

~

The agent was by the phone in Hugh's living room. Hugh lay dead on the floor, his fingers and knees broken.

The agent was thinking, *That little twit refused to give out any information to me. He cried to this Jesus that they all seem to believe in, to take him home. I was the one who took him 'home'. Now he's simply no more.*

Right after that, the phone rang. The agent knew not to answer it, letting the answering machine pick it up. There was Peter, leaving an urgent message for Hugh to contact him as soon as possible.

When Tony hung up the phone, the agent looked at the caller ID and then made a phone call from his cell phone. After he reached the person he wanted, he repeated Tony's phone number. Within a short time, the agent had the address where Peter, Leah, and their baby were living.

~

Tony came back into the kitchen. He informed Alex that he could not reach Hugh. He had tried his home phone and then his cell phone. He knew something was terribly wrong.

They left immediately with only the clothes on their backs and their Bibles. Alex always had Sarah's diaper bag ready in case of an emergency, so the baby had plenty of clothes, diapers, and food. They drove northwest out of Stockholm toward Haga.

Hugh had Leah commit to memory, a contact there in the case of an emergency. Once in Haga, they contacted Hans Lichtenstein. He had some emergency items they would need.

As they walked in the door to Hans's home, he greeted them like old family.

Leah had been very quiet since she'd told Peter they needed to leave immediately. She would not speak at all. Even when Sarah began to whine, she ignored her. This was so unlike the usually doting mother.

Peter picked his daughter up and soothed her, but she would not quiet down. He did not know what to do. He tried to get through to Leah, but to no avail.

"Honey," Peter implored. "Please say something!"

She just looked at him and shook her head. Hans did not know what to make of all of this, so he just stood there.

"I'm sorry, Hans," Peter apologized. "Please, can you help us?"

"I am one of very few people that Tanas knows nothing about. I will show you to your room, and then we can concentrate on your wife."

During the exchange between Peter and Hans, Leah had taken Sarah in her arms and was holding her tight. Sarah immediately quieted. Leah then placed her back in Peter's arms. Sarah remained quiet the rest of the time.

Peter knew there was something very strong and significant going on in Leah's mind. She seemed to be in a trance, but she was fully aware of what was going on around her. Once they got into their room, Leah seemed to come out of whatever it was that had her so preoccupied.

"Peter, I was contacted!" she exclaimed once they were alone. "They were trying to penetrate my mind to expose where we are now. I had a hard time fighting them. Oh, honey! They are going to find us. We will never truly get away. We must try, however."

~

Things settled down after that. They had dinner with Hans and his family. The cuisine was delicious. They had Swedish meatball stew, home-baked bread, and apple strudel for dessert. The two men sat around the dinner table while the two women became acquainted.

Hans's children, four girls and one boy, had dragged Sarah into the living room and they played with her, toted her around, and were delighted with her antics.

Helga was privy to the goals that Tanas had set. She was not, however, privy to the full details of the role Hans played in the scheme of things.

Leah knew that Dorian had spread the word among all of the contacts he had. Somehow, he had managed to convey the messages even after the command post in Argentina had been destroyed. This was how they had been able to stay one-step ahead of Tanas for so long.

Peter and Hans were discussing the route they would take once they left Haga.

"I will rent an auto for you. You will travel north on E4; from there, you will travel the coastline until you come to Umea. You will take E12 to Holmsund. There, you will contact Enar Alexander, who will have your proper papers ready for you. You will board a ship bound for Finland. The ship will port at Oulu, Finland. There, you will contact Justus Gailmon. From there, he will instruct you. Are there any questions?" Hans finished.

"There are none that I can think of, Hans."

"Good. We will all get a good night's sleep, and begin tomorrow morning."

~

Peter and Leah, along with Sarah, reached Holmsund within a few short hours.

There, they met their contact. Within four hours, they were aboard ship. It did not take long to arrive at Oulu.

Peter went to call Justus. Within twenty-four hours, they would be ready to continue their journey.

Justus told Peter, "There is a modest hotel within ten minutes of port. I have made reservations in my name and informed them that you are relatives come to visit. Do not speak English. Use the Swedish language to communicate. They will ask your names. Do not use your first names, but use the surname Alexander. They will accommodate you until I can arrive."

Once the trio was settled in the comfortable room, Tony ordered dinner for them. They were all tired and fell into exhausted sleep.

The next morning a call came in, waking Tony and Alex. It was Justus. He was waiting for them in the coffee shop downstairs. Over breakfast they learned who they would be, and where they were going.

~

His operative was lurking outside the hotel. He knew they were in there. He also knew that they were in the coffee shop, having breakfast. Sir had told him not to confront them, or to call in a capture. He wanted, needed them to feel safe once again. This was going to be a successful capture this time. The operative closed his mind. He did not want the female to sense any danger.

He chuckled to himself. He had a millennia experience duping unsuspecting subjects. His favorite assignment had been that one disciple who had sold out the Master. Only he hated knowing that He was the Master.

They all knew who He was, but cringed and quaked every time anyone mentioned His name.

Judas, however, had been putty in his hands. He knew he was going to die. He had been so weak.

His lifetime study of Judas had provided him the needed tools to use him for the plan to kill the Messiah. It had worked until they all found Him right there, in the Dark. His Light shone so brightly that He blinded some of them.

What he had detested was the fact that some of the captives were set free due to His preaching the good news of His death. How could He have thought that His death was good news? Did He not know that the world despised Him? Did He not realize that the very ones who had adored Him before, were the very ones who helped to crucify Him?

They found out soon enough that He would rise again. He had fought Sir and won the keys to death, Hell and the grave. They had all moaned in defeat.

The good news had been that, in spite of His rising, the dead rising from their graves, and the five hundred or more people who saw Him ascend, there would still be many who would fail to believe.

However, when He came to the Dark, He had arrived there well after the Great Tribulation. He had arrived in the time of the final battle.

This was a touchy subject with Sir. Sir never would admit defeat.

The biggest problem for them--the ones who roamed the Dark--was the delusion of victory; the deception of feeling that they could win, when they were already defeated.

None of them remembered the time in the Kingdom. They had been well-loved and cared for until they listened to Sir. Then they all fell as lightning from the sky. The battle had been raging since the dawn of time. How long the Dark ones had waited for this!

The kingdom of Dark operated much like the Borg on *Star Trek: The Next Generation*. They were a collective. They all assimilated into one collective form. This was how they gained access to so many at one time. His thoughts were becoming distracting, and he received a harsh reprimand from Sir. These reprimands were always painful. He knew he had better remain at the assignment before him.

He honed in on the female's thoughts. He knew she was in turmoil; knew what she was thinking and he did not like it at all. If she succeeded, then they would all be in trouble.

He conveyed his message to Sir. The possibility of her going through with her plan disturbed Sir.

This would never do.

Chapter 45

Leah had been thinking about it for a long time now. It was the only way she knew to stop them from succeeding with their evil plans. She knew somehow, Peter would forgive her, but would he forgive her for the other thing she was planning? She felt that there was no other way. If she did one thing and not the other, it would be moot.

A part of her asked the question, "Are you insane?"

She was not listening. Sarah was. She was listening intently. She did not yet understand the word suicide, or mercy killing, but she felt the badness of it. She knew it was something bad that Mommy was going to do to her and to herself. She did not like it. It made her feel too sad.

She did not want to go to heaven yet. She was too young. She could speak already, but she thought anything other than Dada and Mama would be too much for her parents right now. However, she now had no choice if she were to prevent this bad thing from happening.

Once the breakfast was done and they had returned to their room, Sarah spoke for the first time.

They had gone back to their real names, leaving Sarah's name as it was.

"Mama, you don't do the bad thing!"

Peter and Leah stopped in their tracks. They were speechless.

Leah knew immediately that her daughter was far more advanced than she had been at the age of one. She now knew that her daughter had thwarted her plan.

Peter asked her what Sarah meant when he could find his voice.

"I . . . it was . . . nothing," Leah finished lamely.

"Leah, were you actually considering what I think you were considering?" he asked incredulously.

"Oh, Peter! It was the only thing I could think of that would solve this entire situation. There is something wrong with me lately. I . . . I can't think straight anymore. I'm not used to this . . . this chaos in my mind."

"Do you think they're getting to you?" Peter inquired.

"I don't know," Leah cried as she threw herself on the bed.

Sarah toddled up to her mother and put her tiny arms around her neck. She patted her with her little hands. "Is okay, Mommy. God help you. I know He will. I asked Him."

Leah cried even more when her one-year-old daughter was speaking words of comfort to her. It was not just the fact that her daughter had developed speech at such an early age; it was the fact that she knew her daughter would be a much more viable subject for Tanas.

For the first time in Leah's life, she did not know what to do.

She felt a fear and panic that she could not shake off. It was deep in her soul. The fear was so deeply embedded within her that she knew she would never be able to rid herself of it.

After crying, she turned to Peter and said, "Honey, I think we should just give up. Nothing is going to save us now. It's over."

Peter did not see it that way. He contacted Justus and told him what had happened, about Sarah, and about the state that Leah was in. Peter asked him if there were any way to expedite the papers needed to get them away from there any sooner. Justus told him he would let him know as soon as possible.

The family, once again traveled to another country. This time they were traveling back to the U.S. Justus told them that Tanas would never suspect that they would come back home. They had more false IDs, passports, and birth certificates. Sarah did not yet know English since they had not raised her around it. She still spoke Swedish. She would need to learn English as soon as possible. This was not a difficult task, given her advanced mental capabilities. She learned within two weeks, which was how long it took them to arrive in New York City. They hoped that New York was large enough that they could become lost in it.

~

The Johanssons settled into one of the barrios of New York. Peter found a job as a mechanic, one of his many talents. He worked for a small mom and pop operation that serviced commercial trucks for various local delivery companies. He worked long hours, but managed to get home by seven each night. His days began around five a.m. Many of the trucks simply needed an oil change, or a lube job. Others needed tire rotations, or new tires. The smaller jobs he saved for later in the day.

Leah remained home, caring for Sarah, teaching her how to "block" when she needed to.

Sarah was a rapid learner. She had a vast command of language by the time she was eighteen months old. She knew all of the presidents of the U.S., could recite the Constitution verbatim, knew all of her ABC's and her numbers, and could spell small words.

Leah knew she was going to grow much more powerful than she, so she decided to arm her precious daughter with anything and everything that she could think of in order to protect her from the evil.

Peter, Leah, and Sarah had been in New York for over a year when the bottom fell out. Leah had not had any dreams, or premonitions.

Sarah was developing beautifully. Her hair had gotten longer and thicker. She was so intelligent that it sometimes frightened her mother.

Peter was doing very well at the mechanic shop. The company had promoted him to shop supervisor. He was making very decent money.

It was in the fall on a cold day. Peter had just gone out to get the paper. He was going to go back up to the apartment and have breakfast. He bent over to get the *Times* out of the machine, when he felt a stabbing pain in his neck. Sudden darkness hit him.

Leah was stirring the eggs when she heard someone come into the apartment. Sarah was still asleep.

"Peter, honey? Is that you?" she called out.

Almost immediately, she knew something was terribly wrong. She felt the same pain in her neck as Peter had. She called out Sarah's name before she gave in to the blackness.

~

The agents had it all set up. At that time of the morning, only the street cleaners and bums were up and about. The building that they lived in had an underground parking garage. They had placed the van in there, waiting to transport the trio to it.

They took the family down in a garbage buggy, the kind that had plenty of room in it. They were dressed in the uniform of the garbage company that serviced that building. No one would suspect anything if they were spotted.

All three would be out for a long time. They had more drugs to administer to them when they roused. It would be a long trip. They were concerned about the baby, but they knew what they were doing. Neither of them wanted the wrath of Dr. Hanson. They knew better than to botch this up. Besides, they were the best in the field.

The agents made it out of town around ten a.m. In a deserted location, they transferred the small family to a military bus with sealed windows, and painted the camouflage that was typical of military vehicles. They made them comfortable in the bunks that had been placed in the bus. Sarah had a crib-like bunk, so she would not fall out. That also enabled them to keep from restraining her. The couple was strapped in much as one would be on a gurney.

They slept for hours before they began to rouse.

"Be sure to give the baby the right syringe," the one agent stated as the other was preparing to administer the drugs.

"I will," the other one shot back. "I know what I'm doing, besides, they are clearly marked." He held up the syringes to show his partner that they were indeed marked.

"If we screw this up, we won't ever forget it, even if we die."

The agent with the syringes let out an expletive at his cohort.

They had coolers full of food on the bus, so they would not need to stop except for gas on the way. There was even a bathroom situated in the back for their use. The driver had a panel separating him from the cargo in the back. The trip went without incident.

Chapter 46

Leah woke not knowing where she was. She looked at her surroundings. She was in her own bed! Peter was lying beside her, asleep. Had she been dreaming? What was going on? She felt the unmistakable symptoms of drugs. Her mouth was dry and felt like cotton. Her head was pounding.

She jumped up out of bed and ran to her daughter's room. There, fast asleep was Sarah, her little butt up in the air. Her teddy bear was right by her side as usual.

Leah ventured into the kitchen. There was her window above the sink. She opened the blinds. There it was; the view of the next building, so close that she might reach out and touch it. She opened the window itself. There was the noise of the city, cars honking, people shouting, the general feel of New York was there. The distinctive smells of the city permeated her nostrils. She still did not feel right.

She did not even make coffee. She called on Peter to get up. He would not budge. She had never had that problem before. She shook him again. He finally roused.

"Wh . . . what's going on, Leah?" he asked groggily.

"Peter, there's something terribly wrong. I can't put my finger on it, but I know someone drugged us. I can feel it!" Leah exclaimed.

Peter tasted his mouth. Immediately, he knew they had indeed, been drugged.

"Leah! Where is Sarah?" he asked, panicking, now wide-awake.

"She's just fine. She's asleep in her crib. Oh, God, Peter! They must have drugged her too!"

Peter and Leah both flew to Sarah's room to shake her awake. Sarah was groggy.

"Mommy, bad men gived me a shot!" she whined when they woke her. Then she began crying.

"Oh, Peter, what are we going to do? Where are we?"

Peter strode to the front door. Someone had locked it from the outside. He then went to the kitchen window. He ripped off the screen and put his hand outside. His hand went through a movie-type screen. This confirmed his fears. They were at Tanas.

Peter wondered how long it would be before someone showed up. He had no idea the wait would be so long.

Dr. Hanson was observing the couple and the child on closed circuit TV. It was interesting that Peter was so protective of his little family. It also surprised him that Peter had given in to his own libido and married the prize he had longed for all these years. It angered him to think of Peter violating her, impregnating her, when she should have been pure when she had her first child. He comforted himself with the knowledge that it had not hurt her reproductive organs.

They had no idea that they had been out long enough for Hanson to examine them all. He narrowed his eyes calculatingly. He recalled how Leah had moaned when they did her pelvic exam. He was well aware that he had hurt her, but then, it was a minor irritation she should have been glad to suffer for the cause.

He remembered how he had approached Sir to ask his permission to dispose of his enemy, Peter. What surprised Dr. Hanson most was Sir's response.

"Hanson, think about what you are asking. We do not yet know what kind of power that little girl holds. She could very well destroy this facility. We just have no way of knowing. I read her right after you brought them here. She has a very strong connection with Peter, as well as her mother. If anything were to happen to either one of them, there is no telling what she might do. So, no. I am going to have to say no; we need Peter alive. Once she is a little older, then we can try to reason with her.

"There is only one thing that bothers me about her; she is very convinced of the existence of God. That, I do not like at all. We both know He was a myth. See what your people can do with that. She was more protective with that, than she was with her parents. See to it soon, Hanson."

With that, Sir dismissed him.

~

Peter was pacing in the living room. Leah needed to feed Sarah, so she prepared breakfast. She felt a little insane, doing a normal task in the face of their situation, but it gave her some comfort.

They all sat down to eat. Sarah was unusually quiet since she made that first declaration of getting the shot. Leah knew what it was. She could read her daughter. They had been communicating since they woke up.

Leah marveled over the difference between Sarah's verbal communication and her mental ability. Mentally, she sounded like an adult.

Leah warned her not to say too much that way. "Sarah, sweetie, they might be listening."

"I know they are, Mama. I can hear him talking to me, but I'm ignoring him. He's mad."

"I can't hear him. How come you do?"

"Because I'm the only one he's talking to right now. He's only listening to you."

They ceased communication for the moment.

~

They had been in the room for over two days when Dr. Hanson entered their quarters. Peter, Leah, and Sarah were all sitting in the living area, not saying a word.

"Good morning, Leah. Peter. Hi there, Sarah. Do you know who I am?"

Sarah just stared at him. She knew she could not pretend to be any normal infant, for she could read him, and he was hoping to glean some useful information from her. She would not give him either the satisfaction to show her true intelligence, nor would she insult him with an attempt at fooling him. He was very intelligent himself. She had to give him that. She also knew that attempting this could make him very angry. She saw his anger and it frightened her. It was a hideous creature that lurked in his mind. It would drive him insane one day soon. He was already a little mad, anyway. It would not take much "pushing" to drive him over the edge.

Sarah also knew he wanted her to do something else. He wanted her to become a mommy. She knew she could not do that, but he was planning to make a way for her to provide something to make it happen. This frightened her even more. She communicated to her mother all that she had read from Dr. Hanson.

"Mommy, he wants me to provide something to make a baby. I'm frightened."

"I know, Sweetie. I won't let them hurt you. I'll take care of it."

Aloud, Leah said, "Dr. Hanson, I know what you want. I will not mince words with you. I will do as you ask, not because I believe in what you and your henchmen are doing, but to protect my daughter. If I sense that any of you are going to lay a hand on her, I will and can, fix it so that you will not have access to either of us. We will kill ourselves first. Do I make myself clear about this?"

"Thank you, Mrs. Wiler. You make yourself very clear. I know I cannot fool you. You are able to read me, I see. That will come in handy, indeed." He narrowed his eyes as he finished speaking. He would have to be very careful from now on, he mused. He had a lot of mind control himself. He would attempt to block her from now on. He would go talk to Sir to ensure that ability.

Leah read that thought. She did not know who this Sir was, but there was a terrible sense of foreboding with the mention of his name.

~

In the recesses of Tanas, Sir was pacing. His persona was still humanoid. He was beginning to think his use of Dr. Hanson was a mistake. He had known for some time that Dr. Hanson had become mentally unstable to a certain degree. It happened with all the humans he had used over the centuries since he had landed on this god-forsaken world.

He remembered back when the fall had just occurred. He remembered that many of the great warriors had been products of angels and human women. Goliath had been one of his most prized warriors ever. Unfortunately, young David had proven to be much more than he had bargained for.

However, he laughed with glee when he had placed Bathsheba in his path. The instinct for lust had served him well during that time. What he had not realized was that even with all that he tempted David with, David was still a man after God's own heart. This was frustrating for Sir. Even after all that David had done, God used him.

Solomon was still a sore spot with him to this day. Solomon, David's son, had prayed to God for wisdom and knowledge. He soon realized that all was vanity. Not only that, but God had blessed him beyond anything that anyone had ever had, or ever would have.

He paced some more, waiting now for Dr. Hanson to arrive. He was taking too long to get there and wondered if he should just shock him with his real form, or let him keep thinking that he was still the benevolent creature, come to assist mankind. Narrowing his startling blue eyes, he knew he would reveal himself soon, but not in the form anyone would ever think. Once he imbedded himself in the man-child, the plan would go off without a hitch. He knew he was going to have many, great and small, bond and free, worship him. They would think he was the Christ--his nemesis. He was going to steal all of the ones He had died for. Sir could sense victory was near completion.

~

Peter, Leah, and Sarah did not speak for fear of being overheard. They decided to communicate another way. Leah assisted Peter with being able to read both Leah and Sarah. She did not even realize that she had that capability until now. She was still learning so much about her abilities.

This got her to wondering if there was some way that she could get them out of there. She knew she had to be careful, for fear of the one who had communicated to Sarah previously. Even though she was now a Christian, she reverted to some of the teaching that Dr. Poskinski had instilled in her.

She told Peter what she was going to do. She went into the bedroom, closed the door, and began to concentrate. In her mind, she saw the file cabinet. She took thoughts and memories, filed them away, and then she saw herself closing the cabinet, locking the drawers, and placing the key on a chain and putting the chain around her neck. She came out of the room feeling at peace inside.

"Peter, we need to talk, Honey," she said as she entered the living room. "I know this is going to sound off the wall, but I'm now willing to go through with their request."

She held her hand up when she perceived that he was about to protest.

"Before you say anything, let me finish. If I do not do as they ask, they'll find a way to use Sarah. I don't want that at all. I'm going to bargain with them. If they let you and our daughter go, then I'll do as they ask. I'm not willing that you or Sarah be subjected to anything they might decide to do to you. I couldn't bear the thought of that. I also know that no matter where you two go, I'll always be in touch through Sarah. Distance is not an issue with us. As long as I know you're both safe, I can endure whatever it is they want from me. Peter, you know they're going to impregnate me, right?"

Peter could only nod in answer to her question. He was too angry to say anything for fear of what might come out of his mouth.

~

Leah summoned Sir telepathically. He sent for her the next day. He was looking forward to his meeting with the mother of the next world leader. She was wise to comply. He knew he would have to honor her demands about her family, but he could never allow their release into society. They would forever remain at the compound, to live out their lives in seclusion. He would make sure she understood that when they spoke.

~

An orderly led Leah away from her family the next morning. Her stomach, tied up in knots, kept her from eating. She even thought she might be ill as she followed Dr. Hanson down long corridors, and eventually came to a plain looking wall. Dr. Hanson waved his hand at a seemingly non-existent location, and the wall began to transform. It slid back to reveal an elevator behind it.

They took the elevator down. There were no floors, just a long moment of descending into the earth. The elevator finally stopped, and what confronted Leah's eyes was a mass of hallways, maze-like in their construction. Massive doors, which looked like huge vaults, flanked the main corridor. A jeep driven by what appeared to be a soldier pulled up right after they exited the elevator. They got into the back seat and took off.

She saw much the same thing as her grandfather had seen, as he had described to her during their many long talks. He had wanted her to know everything he had gone through. She could almost see everything he had experienced as she rode along in the jeep. Dr. Hanson at first attempted conversation with her, but when she stubbornly remained quiet, he lapsed into an angry silence.

She noticed how her grandfather's description of this area had been so accurate, that she knew if she had ever stumbled across this place on her own, she would have had no doubt about where she was.

The giant doors still contained the codes with various colors. She remembered well, the description of the one door that had the highest security level posted over it. They now stopped at this door. The difference now with the doors was that each one was equipped with a Retina-scan, and Identi-pad. The soldier remained in the jeep while Dr. Hanson went through the procedure to gain access to what was on the other side of the door.

This area was cavernous. It was dark enough that the soldier had to turn on the headlights of the jeep in order to navigate his way down the main path. She could glimpse smaller doors from time to time. She was curious about what sorts of things might be going on inside those doors. She shuddered to think of the possibilities, and would have fled if she did know. Behind those doors, different subjects were going through testing, in vitro fertilization, and other procedures, some of which were excruciatingly painful. The nurses administered nominal pain medication to the subject. Due to the insulation, no one ever heard their screams.

Sir did not care if Dr. Hanson's penchant for sadism bled over into his experiments, but he had made it clear to the good doctor that under no circumstances was he to inflict pain upon Leah again, after finding out about the initial exam and how she had moaned in pain.

"Hanson," he had begun, "you and I both know I could have you terminated from this project. You also know that the method of termination would not be pleasant, not at all. I suggest you keep that in the front of your mind when dealing with Leah again. She is to receive the best care that our advanced technology can afford her. Do I make myself very clear on this matter?"

Dr. Hanson visibly shrank at the warning from Sir. He knew firsthand what could happen to those who did not comply with the rules. He had rather enjoyed seeing the writhing bodies begging for mercy, before they died. However, he would not want to be the one receiving the punishment.

~

Leah found herself concentrating on calming her nerves, using the same methods taught to her by Dr. Poskinski, again. She thought she would never have to resort to it, but right now, it came in handy. She was feeling nauseated once again, suspecting something, but did not even want to venture to that place. She blocked it out the minute the faint suspicions began to form, knowing Sir must have been reading her. What she did not understand was that she and Peter had used every precaution to prevent another pregnancy. She was hoping against hope that this was simply nerves.

What she did not know, was that they had already impregnated her before she had arrived. Once they examined her, they discovered that she was ovulating. They took advantage of the moment.

Now that she had agreed to cooperate, Sir could give her the good news himself--his own seed, implanted in her--how wonderful that was going to be.

If he calculated it correctly, the birth of his son would be the same as that of his nemesis.

He thought about how the humans had so adapted to the perverse way he had set things up, celebrating the birth of Him on a pagan holiday. What really got him was the fact that they celebrated for the wrong things on the very day of His birth. Chuckling to himself, he wondered how many humans would be shocked to know that October 31 was the actual day of the birth of Christ.

Oh, there were a few humans who had discovered that winter was not when He had been born. They had been smart enough to know that the shepherds would not have been tending their flock by night had it been.

Sir stopped his musings, for he could feel her nearing. He could sense even now, the communication of the creature within her. She closed her mind. She'd learned to control her abilities well, he thought.

She would open herself up to him soon, however. He would make sure of that. She would not hide anything from him when he was finished.

Something was wrong. He sensed the child within her was not a male, but a female.

He seethed with anger. He had instructed them explicitly to ensure that the impregnation yielded a male child. In the world, the surety of choosing gender was not as accurate as here. The technologies housed within this compound held far more advances than anything did on the outside. Someone had made a grave mistake. He would have no use for a female child. It would have to be terminated and soon.

He almost cancelled the interview with Leah, but immediately decided against it. She did not need to know that she was with child again. He would arrange termination as soon as the interview was over.

He realized that he was not in human form yet. He took care of that quickly and then waited for her to enter.

Chapter 47

They escorted Leah into the inner sanctum of Sir's office. She had no idea what to expect, but she never thought he would be human; at least he appeared to be human. She suspected that he was capable of changing his appearance at will. He was a chameleon. She could not see into his true form, but she would not have wanted to see him that way, anyhow.

He greeted her cordially, offering her a comfortable chair placed in front of his massive desk.

His human appearance was striking; she had to give him that.

As the first words came out of his mouth, she knew he possessed a power stronger than she ever thought possible. She had a hard time praying now. She had been doing that from the time she left her quarters. Now, it seemed impossible.

She inwardly quaked.

"My dear Mrs. Wiler," he spoke. "We finally meet at last."

She sat mute, unable to speak. He knew he was intimidating her. He had purposely instilled it in her. He wanted her undivided attention, and he was getting it now.

"You do not have to speak to me if you do not wish. I can understand how you might be overwhelmed right now. The good doctor here," he said, indicating Dr. Hanson who stood behind her chair, "was kind enough to inform me of the conditions you required in order for us to have your full cooperation. I do not have any problem with your requests, except for one thing; I cannot and will not allow your husband or your daughter to leave this compound. You must realize that it would be impossible for them to be set free on the outside."

He waited for her response.

She suddenly found her voice and a calm, which she never knew she could possess. "Sir, I will not compromise on this. You may choose the place, if it will make you feel that they could not pose any threat to your project, but I will not cooperate if they cannot leave."

She folded her arms across her chest to enforce her resolve.

Sir's jaws flexed. He was angry--she could feel it. He seemed to be contemplating her demands. He unclenched his teeth and his jaw relaxed.

"I will do as you wish on this matter. I will choose the location. I will allow you to speak with them once each month. If the project is a success, then you will be free to join them once the child is born."

At his last sentence, she blanched. He saw maternal instinct rising violently within her; she had given him the desired response.

"I will not leave my child in the hands of strangers, Sir."

"I thought not, Leah. I just wanted to find out how committed you would be to the child after it was born. He will need the nurturing of a mother, at least for a while. I will make sure you are as comfortable as possible. You will have the best quarters, the finest food, and the best medical care you will ever receive. If you wish, you may attend the church located on the compound."

"Thank you."

He liked her answers curt and brief. He admired her convictions, even if they were misplaced.

He was so self-deceiving, he had no idea that the Creator was allowing this in order to fulfill the prophecy foretold in the Book of Revelation. It was not that God was manipulating things, but that He would not fail to fulfill His purpose.

Leah still cringed inside. She knew her strength was not her own, but One who loved her beyond reason--beyond human understanding. She thought about her destiny for a number of years now. She knew she would birth him. Somehow, even in the deepest regions of her subconscious, she had always known something huge was going to happen in her life. She had never dreamed it would be something this profound; that she was going to birth the Antichrist. She inwardly shuddered again.

What would her child be like? Would he be evil from birth? Would he eventually become evil? She could not, would not, allow herself to venture any further than those two questions, nor would she allow herself to answer. Her mind just would not let her.

The meeting went as well as expected. Leah returned to her quarters. Leah did not say much when she got back to Peter and Sarah. What she did say made Peter's blood run cold.

"Peter, I agreed to the impregnation, but I need to tell you something."

He waited for the bad news.

"Peter, I think they've already impregnated me. I also think that Sir, which is what he said to call him, knows about it. I feel that this child is a girl, somehow. She's in danger, too. He does not want this child to be born."

Peter stared at her, his face pale and his jaws flexing through gritted teeth.

"Leah, I will not allow this child to be aborted!" he exploded.

"Calm down, Peter. They can hear and see everything in here. Do you want to jeopardize our daughter and your own life? They will see to it that you do not interfere with anything. I feel so responsible for all of this," she lamented through tears.

"Honey, you're not to blame for all of this. I promise."

Peter held her as she cried things out. Then they prayed together for strength.

EPILOGUE

Leah watched her second child, Ivah, play with her toys. Leah had managed to save her from termination by sheer stubbornness. She turned out so beautiful. Sir had not been too pleased with the name that she chose for her, but he indulged Leah.

Sir and Leah had developed a tense, spiritual dance of sorts; him wanting to own her soul; her fighting to keep it.

Leah was currently huge with the man-child Sir had been longing for. This child was already communicating with Leah from the womb. He did not project emotions like Sarah and Ivah had. He verbally communicated with her. This unnerved her at first, but after a while, she became used to it.

One of the things that made her uncomfortable was that he seemed not to have any emotions at first. After a few months of her pregnancy, she began to feel his love for her. She never thought that the Antichrist would ever be capable of any emotion, much less the strong essence of love.

Theirs was a wonderful communication. He taught her a lot during the pregnancy. What he communicated to her, she could not utter. The love that was emanating from her womb astonished her.

~

Leah had been sleeping, but awakened with labor pains. She knew it was time. She pushed the buzzer installed in the quarters that she had shared with Peter and Sarah. Tanas had installed it during her pregnancy with Ivah.

She knew it was time.

Eliel (pronounced E'lee'ul) Ahshatan was born on October 31, one minute after midnight. He was a beautiful baby. His hair was jet black and his skin was a deep olive tone. What struck Leah the most were his eyes. They were a startling pale, ice blue. This was one of the most unusual babies ever born.

Sir allowed her to contact Peter and Sarah to tell them the news of his birth.

She had thrilled at the sound of her husband's voice. She had longed for this--longed for a reunion with her husband and daughter. She had no idea that this was just what she was going to have within a year. Sir would not keep his word to her that she could raise the baby.

~

They whisked Peter and Sarah away after her encounter with Sir for the first time. Among many tears and hugs, they left Tanas. She had no idea where they took them, for they forbid them to disclose where they were. All of them had been afraid to violate that order.

Peter and Sarah awaited Leah's arrival. Sir permitted Leah to take Ivah with her when she left.

~

Mt. Ayers, Iowa was a very small town, but it held a big secret. Most of the residents there were oblivious to the history of Peter and Sarah. Leah's arrival brought a lot of curiosity to the little town, yet something instinctive told them not to become overly curious and they let it go.

Peter had gotten a job as a ranch hand. Leah settled in to raising her two daughters. They were doing the best they could to provide some semblance of normalcy for the two girls.

In the spring of the first year that they were reunited, the boiler in the basement of their home exploded. Ivah was the only survivor.

Peter, Leah, and Sarah were all lost. The fire was so intense, that there was virtually nothing left of the structure. It was as if someone had dropped an atom bomb on the house.

An agent took Ivah to the only place she knew--Tanas.

Eliel, at the age of two, began his initiation into what the purpose of his life was to be. Sir doted on him. Ivah was a mother hen--often she spoke to Eliel about his future. She pushed him to learn. Ivah instilled in Eliel a passion for politics.

Ivah was cunning, intelligent. She knew what her father wanted and took great pains to help him accomplish it.

During the next twelve years, Eliel completed school and his indoctrination by Sir and Ivah. He was ready to be unleashed upon the world, by now devastated by many events.

First, there was the tragedy of another major attack worse than that of September 11. The next devastation rocked the entire world. A great tsunami hit the Indian Ocean and devastated many of the coastal countries. The earth's poles actually shifted during the tsunami. Then a number of years later, another more intense quake very nearly split the world in two.

~

Eliel and Ivah moved to a middle-eastern country to launch Eliel's career in politics just prior to the huge quake. His level-headedness and supernatural abilities made him the man-of-the-hour afterward.

He pressed for meetings with the European Economics Union, EEU--the UN had been destroyed during the quake. The world seemed impressed by his ideas, his powers; and Eliel had definite ideas on how to help the poor victims. He eloquently expressed how he hated to see all the suffering.

With the power Eliel wielded, he solved most of the problems of starvation. Deserts became plush and green. His powers were indeed, supernatural. He was able to heal people.

Eliel set up and created the Global Union, which housed politicians, dignitaries, and other key people from every nation. He declined an offer to be the Global Union chair.

The Global Union, built in Jerusalem, rivaled other monumental sites. Soon, it became known as the eighth wonder of the world.

By now, the entire world knew the name Eliel. It became synonymous with Gandhi, Mother Teresa, and even Jesus Christ. Many religious news articles speculated on whether he was the Messiah returned.

However, Christian news articles had become underground tabloids, accused of spreading propaganda against Eliel. Persecuted, Christians forced underground as well, suffered torture, exile, and death.

~

Ivah was right by Eliel's side all the way. She was the driving force.

"Eliel," Ivah said one day. "I know you are destined to rule the world. Your powers, along with your compassion for people, will put you there. Mark my words, Brother. Just remember all that I've taught you."

He looked at his beloved sister and smiled.

A few days after that, Sir passed away. It was a shock to them both, for they had grown to admire and respect him greatly. At the moment, they too, had been convinced that Sir was a benevolent alien, come to save the world from its own destruction; everything Sir taught them, they remembered.

They traveled back to Tanas without anyone knowing. Their strong, inherited powers gave them this ability.

Eliel spent some final moments with his father. "Sir, I know you will never leave me. Somehow, we will be together again, to rule side by side!"

Sir was in the spirit realm, once again. He knew he would not remain there for long, however. From his dark throne, he watched his son and daughter coming rapidly into power.

Eliel and Ivah traveled back to the mid-east, resuming their political ambitions.

Two weeks after their return, the GU called for a special meeting, inviting Eliel to attend.

~

"Eliel," the vice chairman of the GU began. "We are at a loss. You seem to be the only one who can sort out all the chaos and calamity. We have never seen anyone with your popularity, power, and charisma. What we are proposing is that you step up to the plate and take over as Commander in Chief for the GU."

He became quiet to give Eliel time to absorb it all.

Finally, Eliel spoke.

"Ladies and Gentlemen, I am most honored by your invitation. I do not wish to lord it over anyone. I do wish, however, to create a better world. I can and am able to eliminate the suffering of the people. I accept your offer with all humility. I am but your servant."

Ivah was bursting at the seams with pride. She knew he would accomplish what their father had set out to do.

The applause from the GU council was thunderous. Every journalist, reporter and other media possible attended this meeting. They were all scrambling to phone their papers, news stations, and magazines. Teletypes were buzzing with the announcement. Films were rolling, cameras were flashing to capture the historic handshake between Eliel and the chairman of the GU.

One month after that meeting, a coronation was to commence officially bringing Eliel into office.

Ivah was at his side. Eliel appointed her second in command. The GU was pleased.

Eliel and Ivah were in his bedroom, deciding what Eliel would wear.

"Oh, Eliel!" she exclaimed. "Now, we shall honor our father's death. His efforts will not be in vain. I am so proud of you!"

"Thank you, dear sister. Now let us pick out the perfect suit for me to wear."

The coronation aired worldwide. Security was unparalleled for this event. Metal detectors were everywhere. Eliel's men placed security personnel in many locations; bomb squads, complete with bomb sniffing dogs walked constantly.

Factions of what the world considered 'radical' Christians protested this event. There was talk of a rebellion, possible threats on Eliel's life and the GU took no chances.

The commencement took place on May 14, the anniversary of Israel's statehood. The coronation commenced in historic Jerusalem, on the hallowed ground where the Dome of the Rock once stood. Several years before, factions had destroyed it during a fierce war.

Everyone who was anyone was there. Nothing in the history of the world came even close to this event.

Crowds clamored to get close to the Savior of the world. All that he had accomplished beforehand they touted via huge screens, positioned strategically to afford all a glimpse into the miracles he wrought.

"Ladies and gentlemen of the world," Eliel began. "As the new Commander in Chief of the Global Union, and to honor the nation of Israel, I present to them a drawing of the new Temple to be erected right where I stand. It will be exactly as the original temple before it was destroyed centuries ago."

He held his hand up to quiet the frenzied applause and cheers so he could continue.

As he finished his speech, sudden shots rang out. Terror ensued, creating havoc among the huge crowd. Men, women, and children ran for safety.

A powerful slug hit Eliel. Bits of skull and brain tissue hit Andrew, Eliel's Secret Service captain. The bone struck him on the cheek, creating a deep laceration. Other Secret Service officers felt the sting of brain tissue, blood, and slivers of bone.

By the time the chaos finally ended, Eliel lay in a pool of blood. It was obvious to those who were near him that he was dead.

When paramedics arrived, they checked his vital signs, surprised to find a pulse.

"Is he dead?" Ivah asked.

"Ma'am, he's got a pulse, but it doesn't look good. You can ride in the front with my partner."

For the next few days, the world hung in silence, waiting to hear the final word on Eliel's demise.

In a secluded wing of the Beth-Judah hospital, Eliel still lay in his hospital bed; breathing machines, IV's and other vital tubes attached, were all that kept him alive. His sister, by his side, was loath to let him go. She chased everyone out of the room except his personal physician, who had just come back from announcing to the world that Eliel's condition was grave, and that he was essentially brain-dead.

In the tomb-like silence, they stood, trying to say goodbye to the man they believed would have been the world's savior.

"Dr. Rosenstein, isn't there anything you can do?"

"Ivah, I'm sorry. I did everything possible to save him. He's gone. It's time to remove the life support."

"Fine, Doctor. I, along with Eliel's staff, will make the funeral arrangements." Then she walked out, leaving the current task to Dr. Rosenstein.

~

Eliel Tanas's funeral had more in attendance and was viewed by more people than anyone in history had ever been.

A global day of mourning, issued by Global Union council members, was strictly enforced. No one worked, went to school, or did any business that day.

People watched from their cell phones, computers, and televisions, to mourn the death of the man who had solved so many problems, and brought the world together. News coverage came from every TV station, cable news channels, radio, Internet, newspapers, magazines; every media source attended.

Eliel's casket, pearl with white satin interior, remained open for viewing as he lay in state in the Global Union's headquarters rotunda. Eliel wore a deep blue Armani suit and stark white shirt, which sported a royal blue silk tie.

Everyone clamored for close up shots of him, wanting to capture the dramatic moments when family and close friends came near.

Ivah, assisted by two aides, refused to leave Eliel's side. Tears streamed down her grief-stricken face, as one by one, invited mourners held the privilege of saying a final goodbye to the savior of the world.

Everyone, both small and great, rich and poor, free or bond, mourned his death.

~

Christians neither celebrated his death nor mourned him. They knew even before the TV cameras and mini-cams, what was about to happen.

They prepared for the horror to come--and for battle.

~

The global viewing went on for three days. On the third day, Ivah, in a dramatic display of pulling herself together after whispering to one of the aides by her side, left her brother's casket. Mourners gasped from every corner of the globe, wondering why she would suddenly leave.

Everyone fell silent as Ivah walked out to the podium that had just been set up for those who wished to speak about Eliel. Eulogies were not scheduled to start for another three hours--noon. She stepped to the microphone and began.

As television cameras zoomed in and photographers flashed, creating strobes of light around Ivah, she said, "Citizens of the world, I know what you're going through. Losing Eliel . . . " she paused, trying to compose herself, "is the hardest thing I have ever gone through. As you know, we were orphans and he was the only family I had, but I tell you this; Eliel is the Christ. I have always believed this. I believe he will rise again!"

Whispers of, 'He's been embalmed,' and 'How could this be, he's been dead three days now?' echoed all over the rotunda.

News microphones picked up every comment.

Chaos broke out then, and camera crews, photographers--everyone wanted to watch to see what would happen now.

As Ivah spoke, branches of electricity flowed from the microphone, encasing the immediate area in an energy web. Wind whipped all around Ivah as she stood there. Claps of thunder rumbled, shaking the Global Union building. People scrambled, trying to get out of the rotunda, several trampled to death by the panicked mob.

Almost as quickly as the chaos began, it died. Those left in the rotunda were media. As they kept the cameras rolling, Ivah still had not moved. She seemed to be in a trance, or in shock. Dr. Rosenstein had backed away when the fireworks began. He now approached Ivah, albeit cautiously.

The world still watched.

"Ivah," Rosenstein said. "Ivah, can you speak?"

The cameras were picking up every word, even though Rosenstein spoke barely above a whisper.

"Dr. Rosenstein, look over there," Ivah began in a monotone, pointing toward the middle of the rotunda, "See the Messiah."

He turned his head in the direction she pointed; at the same time, cameramen scrambled to aim the monolithic lenses in the same direction.

~

Eliel's body felt like it was on fire. He could not breathe and his insides twisted in pain.

Even as he struggled to breathe, he could hear Sirius's voice inside his head. "I am here with you, Eliel; inside you. I will guide you from here on."

~

As everyone watched, Eliel's body began to jerk and twist. He sat up in the casket. He choked, gagged, and breathed in deep gulps of air. The wound now appeared as it had when he was first shot. The bullet, which they had been unable to remove, shot out of his temple, landing on the tiled floor. It echoed through the cavernous room, and the world saw and heard the miracle.

As everyone watched--some of the cameras had zoomed in on the wound by now, others chose wide angles--his temple began to heal. Auras of light spilled all around him, colors more vivid than the aurora borealis. The room still bathed in darkness, added to the drama unfolding.

As Eliel began stepping out of the casket, Ivah ran to him, wrapping her arms around her brother.

"Eliel, I knew you were the Messiah!"

And the world celebrated.